Not just for Christmas

HANNAH ELLIS

Published by Hannah Ellis
www.authorhannahellis.com
Postfach 900309, 81503 München
Germany

Cover design by dmeacham design

For Sue and Kathy,
with love

Chapter One

According to Erin's mother, a romantic couple's retreat over Christmas was the height of indulgence.

"What better time to indulge in a dirty weekend away and spice up a relationship?"

Those were her mum's exact words when she suggested it to Erin over coffee at the end of September.

"In the Cotswolds, of all places," her mum crooned while clicking onto the online advert.

Without a lot of thought, Erin agreed that the boutique hotel in the quaint village looked stunning. And that the programme of festive events did indeed sound lovely.

Stupidly, she'd gone on to echo her mother's sentiment that it *did* sound like the perfect Christmas present.

If she'd realised her mother had *her* in mind as the recipient of the extravagant Christmas gift, she wouldn't have nodded along so readily. She'd have made her reservations clear.

The first one being that she was single so a couple's retreat was an inappropriate gift. Weirdly enough, she hadn't felt it necessary to point that out.

Secondly, she'd have argued that she didn't need guilt gifts just because her parents were choosing to spend the festive season in Australia while her newlywed sister spent Christmas with her in-laws.

Erin didn't have a problem with a quiet Christmas this year. She absolutely didn't need a five-day romantic retreat in a picturesque village in one of the UK's areas of utmost beauty.

And yet, here she was on the 22nd of December, following a two-hour train ride from London, standing in the market square in Chipping Campden and feeling as though she'd stepped out of the taxi and into a scene from a greetings card.

The historic curved terrace street was made up of exquisite buildings in the famous Cotswold stone. Warm light radiated from the windows and twinkling lights dripped from the slate roofs. More lights adorned the Christmas tree in the patch of green beside the old open market hall, which made up the centrepiece of the square.

They really didn't scrimp on fairy lights here. They weren't the gaudy every-colour variety either, but gentle golden lights which complemented the caramel-coloured stonework of the buildings.

Her accommodation for the next five nights stood snugly in the row of buildings. From the photos, Erin had the impression that the hotel would be bigger and more imposing, but found it much more charming in real life. Deep red curtains framed the large bay window, and the stone columns which formed the portico entranceway were stylishly adorned with twinkling lights tucked into crawling ivy. The door had been trussed up with a festive wreath and the overall effect was gorgeous.

With her case by her feet, Erin was about to set off for the door when her phone distracted her.

Automatically, she did a quick calculation of the time difference before she answered.

"Isn't it the middle of the night there?" she asked her mother.

"It is, but the jet lag has me all messed up. Besides, your aunt was being a bad influence and kept topping up the wine. I had no choice but to go along with it. She's my big sister, after all."

A joyful whoop in the background made Erin smile. "So the pair of you decided to drunk dial me? Should I be flattered?"

"I called your sister, but she just gave us a lecture about how we should act our age."

Her aunt's voice came shrill down the line. "I said we should call my fun niece instead!"

"Thanks." Erin rolled her eyes.

"How's your romantic break?" Aunt Laura asked, then howled with laughter. "I'm sorry," she said, catching her breath. "I can't believe your mum did that."

"It's a great present," her mum chimed in.

"A great present for *a couple,*" Erin said, smiling lightly at the absurdity of the situation.

"September!" her mum screeched, while her aunt laughed loudly in the background. "I told you about it in September."

"You never said it was my Christmas present," Erin said adamantly, even though they'd already had this discussion.

"My exact words were, *would you like this as a Christmas present?* I don't know how I could have been any clearer."

"I assumed it was a hypothetical question."

"Why would I ask it hypothetically?"

Erin turned her face from the freezing wind as she smiled into the phone. "Because I'm single. Why would I think you were offering to treat me to a couple's holiday for Christmas?"

"*September!*" her mum said again. "I gave you plenty of time to find yourself a man."

"I didn't know I was supposed to be looking for someone to share my Christmas present with." It was only a few days ago, before her parents set off for Australia, that the booking voucher had been handed over and September's miscommunication unveiled. "Also, you knew last week that I didn't have a boyfriend. You could have mentioned this then. Or last month... sometime before it was too late to cancel."

"I knew you didn't have a boyfriend, but I assumed you'd got someone lined up to go with you."

"Like who?"

"Someone from the internet. A casual fling."

Erin felt as though her head might explode at any moment. "You thought I'd find a random guy to share my hotel room for five nights?"

"Christmas treat," her mum said cheekily, setting her aunt off into another fit of the giggles. "Or you could have hired someone."

Erin's eyes widened dramatically. "Excuse me?"

"A male escort," her mum said. "Women do it all the time."

"Which women?" Erin demanded. "Who do you know that hires male escorts? I think you may be in with a bad crowd, Mum."

"Not people I know," she giggled. "But people in films."

Erin sighed. "Of course."

"I feel bad now," Aunt Laura said. "If I'd known, I'd have bought you an escort instead of the bath set I sent."

"It's not Christmas yet, Aunt Laura, so I haven't opened the present. Thanks for the spoiler!"

The pair of them cackled down the phone. With Laura living on the other side of the globe, it wasn't often the sisters got to catch up in person. Whenever they did, it was pandemonium.

"Imagine if I'd sent you a man all nicely wrapped in a bow!" Laura sniggered.

"A bow and nothing else!" Erin's mum shrieked.

"Is Dad around?" Erin asked. "Or Uncle Jim. I feel as though you two need adult supervision."

"They're in bed," her mum said. "Pair of lightweights. They can't keep up with us."

"I think it's great that you've gone on this holiday alone," Aunt Laura said, suddenly serious. "You enjoy yourself, love."

"I didn't have much choice," Erin said. "It was too late to cancel."

That wasn't the only reason, though. When she'd read what was on offer during her stay, and seen the beautiful pictures of the hotel, her previous plans had paled in comparison. Not that she hadn't been looking forward to eating her Marks and Spencer's turkey dinner in her pyjamas, but five nights in a fancy boutique hotel, with meals prepared by a gourmet chef, was slightly more enticing. On top of that, the package included entrance to a bunch of local Christmas-themed attractions and it all sounded magical in the description.

"There's no shame in being alone!" Aunt Laura called merrily down the phone.

"I know that, thanks."

She fully intended to enjoy the hotel experience. She would eat the multiple course meals and go ice skating and explore the light trails in the gardens of the local Manor House.

Why shouldn't she enjoy the romantic atmosphere, just because she didn't have a significant other? She wouldn't be discriminated against because she was single.

She'd have a fantastic time enjoying her own company.

With absolutely no shame at all.

Not one jot.

Chapter Two

Despite speaking quietly, the voice of the young receptionist seemed to reverberate around the cosy reception area and travel into the adjoining lounge too. The people there had turned to look.

"You're alone?" she asked, her thick eyebrows squishing together.

"Yes. Just me," Erin said, while bobbing her head in time to the jolly Christmas music.

The nervous-looking woman – Jenny, according to her name badge – leaned closer, a lock of her dark ringlets falling into her face as she did. "It's just that it's a couple's retreat," she said in her unaccountably far-reaching whisper. "Everything is set up for two. Didn't you realise when you booked?"

Erin smiled. "My mum booked it a while back and apparently hadn't thought I'd be single at Christmas."

"Oh, my goodness." With a look of horror, Jenny brought both hands to her face. "I'm so sorry. That's awful."

Before Erin could figure out what the awful thing was, an older grey-haired lady wandered over from the lounge. "Any chance of a couple more mince pies?" she asked Jenny. "We missed lunch and we're famished."

"Add them to the bill if you need to," a sturdy older gentleman called from the couch which was nestled in the bay window, close to the twinkling Christmas tree in the corner of the room.

Jenny's gaze skittered from Erin to the older lady. "I think that should be fine," she said, presumably about the mince pie situation. "Once again, I'm very sorry." Her eyes were back on Erin. "It's only that I need to check what to do, because the welcome mince pies and champagne are for two... was it your husband or just a boyfriend?"

"Sorry?" Erin gave a quick shake of her head. "What?"

"The one who dumped you?"

"Oh, no," Erin began but was distracted by the lady next to her placing a hand on her arm.

"You poor thing. You've come all on your own?"

"Well, yes, but..." Erin hesitated. While she wasn't at all ashamed of her situation, she didn't know anyone in Chipping Campden and could give them whatever story she wanted. "We were engaged," she said, then pressed her lips together in a show of overwhelming emotion. "He called it off last week."

"You poor love," the older woman crooned in her ear.

Quietly amused by the bizarre situation, Erin nodded and did her best to look like a jilted fiancée. "Too late to get a refund for the hotel," she told them with a sigh. "And, of course, with my Christmas plans ruined, I thought I'd just come alone."

"How brave." The grey-haired lady patted her arm. "Bless you."

Across the reception desk, Jenny had turned a festive shade of crimson. "I'm so sorry," she murmured.

"Everything okay?" The cheerful voice belonged to a young guy in a crisp white shirt which contrasted with his short, dark hair. As he sidled up beside Jenny, Erin's eyes went to his name tag – Lewis. He was probably around her age – in his mid-twenties – and had an air of professionalism that Jenny lacked.

"Mr and Mrs Ward would like more mince pies," Jenny said out of the corner of her mouth.

"I don't blame them. They're delicious." He offered the woman – Mrs Ward, apparently – a friendly smile. Then he looked back at Jenny. "There are plenty in the kitchen. It's not a problem."

Jenny turned her head slightly, lowering her voice a little more. "I don't know whether to add it to their bill."

"No," he said, with a slightly pained expression. "We like our guests to be well fed. I'll bring them over to you."

"Thank you," Mrs Ward said, and gave Erin another sympathetic look before returning to her husband.

"Have you just arrived?" Lewis asked Erin. "Has Jenny got you all checked in?" He clicked the computer mouse as his eyes flicked to the screen. "Erin Grant, I presume? Here for the five-night Christmas package."

"Yes," Erin said. "That's me."

"I haven't checked her in yet," Jenny said. "There's been a small problem. Also, I'm not supposed to be working on reception now, but Ivy hasn't turned up yet."

"I'm sure she'll be here soon." He looked at the computer. "What was the problem?"

Jenny placed her hand in front of her mouth. "She's on her own."

"Excuse me?" Lewis said.

"Her fiancé jilted her," Jenny explained into her palm. "So she's come on her own."

Inwardly, Erin cringed. This was exactly why you shouldn't tell lies. Because, while she had no problem with people like Jenny and Mrs Ward pitying her for the breakdown of a non-existent relationship, she'd really rather the cute guy with sparkling blue eyes didn't view her as some pathetic dumpee.

Why had she even thought it was funny to pretend to be broken-hearted? God, she was weird sometimes.

"I'm not sure what the problem is," Lewis said to his colleague.

"It's just that she's on her own…"

"Is she also deaf?" he asked quietly. "Because unless she has a hearing impairment, she can still hear you speaking behind your hand." He caught Erin's eye and smiled apologetically.

"Sorry," Jenny said, her voice going all squeaky. "It's just that the bedroom is set up for a couple. The entire stay is set up for a couple."

Lewis looked perplexed. "It'll be fine. Why don't you fetch Miss Grant her champagne and mince pies while I get her room key?"

Automatically, Erin gave a nod of agreement. She could definitely do with the champagne.

Jenny walked quickly away.

"Sorry about that." Lewis tapped on the computer keyboard. "Jenny's new."

"It's fine," Erin said at the same moment that Jenny returned, wringing her hands as she approached Lewis.

"Everything okay?" he asked her.

Her brow was furrowed so tightly that her eyebrows almost met in the middle. "I'm not sure whether I should bring enough for one or two?" She bit down on her lower lip. "She's paid for two, but--"

"Definitely enough champagne for two," Erin said, interrupting her. "Actually, sod it, it's Christmas – I'll take mince pies for two as well."

"If you can't manage them all," a voice boomed from the lounge, "I'll help you out!" The old man on the couch raised his champagne glass in her direction.

"No chance," Erin muttered under her breath. "I've been dumped at Christmas, I'm not sharing."

The low chuckle from Lewis told her she hadn't uttered the words as quietly as she'd thought. She caught his gaze and the warmth in his smile made her feel like the most amusing person on the planet.

Not a bad feeling at all.

Chapter Three

She was pretty. Lewis had noticed as soon as he set eyes on their latest arrival at the hotel. Her dark blonde hair hung to her shoulders in glossy waves and her cheeks had a rosy glow, which highlighted the green of her eyes.

The price of the rooms meant the hotel tended to attract a certain type of clientele, but Erin Grant appeared down-to-earth in her jeans and jumper. Her long green coat with faux fur trim looked as though it had probably seen several winters.

It wasn't her physical appearance that really grabbed his attention, though. It was the air of joyfulness about her. Positivity radiated from her as she eyed the Christmas tree and strings of tinsel with childlike wonder. Then there was the way she reacted to Jenny's lack of tact about her situation.

He'd always appreciated people who found the humour in a situation, and she definitely seemed to have a good sense of humour.

Once he'd checked her in, he invited her to take a seat in the lounge and wait for her welcome drink while he took her bag up to her room.

It was a service they offered to all guests over Christmas and one that was always well received.

Erin looked especially delighted by the prospect and thanked him with a radiant smile before moving to the lounge.

Her case wasn't heavy – unlike some of their guests, who seemed to arrive with everything they owned.

At the top of the stairs, he glanced back to see Erin chatting happily with a young Scottish couple who'd arrived the previous day.

She didn't seem particularly upset about her breakup, he thought as he walked along the hall. Maybe she was putting on a brave face, or maybe the breakup had come as a relief.

Perhaps she was one of those people with such a cheerful disposition that nothing could touch it. He'd read something a while back about people having set levels of happiness that they would always come back to, no matter what happened in life. There'd been a study following people who'd either won the lottery, or suffered a debilitating accident. A year after either event, people returned to their previous level of happiness.

From Lewis's experience, it sounded about right. His mind flicked to two years ago, when his girlfriend had split up with him on Christmas Day. He distinctly remembered thinking he'd never get over it.

He'd been wrong, of course. With hindsight, the breakup was for the best, and he hadn't remained perpetually unhappy because of it.

Perhaps Erin had just bounced back from her breakup incredibly quickly.

Holding the key card against the lock mechanism, he waited for the green light, then pushed at the door. His intention was to set the suitcase inside the door and retreat, but his gaze travelled over the room and he stopped to take it in.

It was the best room in the hotel – larger than the others and with an imposing four-poster bed that immediately drew the eye. Beside the bay window was a set of armchairs with a mahogany table between them. The perfect spot to sit and watch the main street below.

The room might not be quite as striking to people who hadn't seen it prior to the renovations a few years earlier. When the ownership had changed hands, the entire hotel had undergone a revamp. Lewis had worked there since he was sixteen – ten years now – and could say for definite it was a more cheerful place to work since the renovations. He also dealt with far fewer complaints from guests. Hardly any in fact, these days.

He was about to close the door again when something caught his eye. Flower petals were strewn all over the bed. So that was what Jenny had been concerned about when she said the room was set up for a couple.

Would petals upset someone who'd just been dumped? If Erin was merely putting on a brave face, the rose petals might send her into a downward spiral. He could remove them quickly. But were the petals on the marketing materials for her stay? He couldn't remember, but suspected they were. Would it be more awkward if she knew he'd removed them?

He moved back into the hallway, leaving the flower petals in place. On the way back downstairs, he gave himself a mental shake for overthinking things.

He was all set to go and give Erin the key when he caught Ivy waving at him from the reception desk and veered in her direction instead.

"You're late," he told her, aiming for a stern expression and knowing she'd only laugh at him. They'd been friends since primary school and working with her was one of his favourite things about the job.

"Are you going to tell the boss and get me sacked?" She beamed and shook her head. "I doubt it, since you'd have to deal with the rest of the staff alone." She pulled her fiery red curls back into a loose ponytail. "I don't know what it is, but every time I look at Jenny she seems as though she might burst into tears."

"I'm glad it's not just me who has that effect on her." He glanced around. "Where is she?"

"In the restaurant, helping Kate set up for dinner." She switched her focus to the computer screen. "All the guests have arrived now. No more check-ins until after Christmas."

"Yep," Lewis confirmed. The small hotel only had twenty rooms but they were all booked out for the festive season. A little extra attention to detail would be needed to ensure the guests all had a perfect Christmas, meaning the staff would be working hard over the next few days. "The last guest only just arrived," he told Ivy, glancing over at Erin, who was smiling politely at whatever Mrs Ward was saying to her.

The Wards were regular guests of the hotel and Lewis would describe their personalities as an acquired taste. They were actually pretty nice, but neither of them minced their words and Lewis had found them hard to take until he'd got to know them.

"Where's her partner?" Ivy asked, following his gaze.

"She's on her own."

"Really?" Ivy frowned at the computer screen. "I thought she was booked in for the couple's package."

"She is, but her fiancé ended things last week and she came alone."

"Oh, wow. I don't know if that's depressing or inspiring."

"Jenny was pretty shocked by it."

"And not great at hiding that, I presume?"

He shook his head. "She wasn't exactly tactful, not that Miss Grant seemed to care. I need to give her the key." He tapped it against his palm. "I'll see if I can smooth things over while I'm at it."

"I'm sure you'll have her charmed in no time." There didn't seem to be any subtext to the words, so Lewis wasn't sure why he felt slightly hot under the collar as he resisted the urge to argue that he wasn't intending to charm her.

"Did you see the note I left in the office yesterday?" Ivy asked when he took a step away. "About Mr Garrett?"

"Yes," he grumbled. "Couldn't you have put him off until after Christmas? I don't have time, not with all the events over the next few days."

"The problem is you fobbed him off last week and now he's insistent. He's coming tomorrow to go through the books and you're going to have to deal with it."

"But I hate it," he complained. "Also, it's weird how excited he gets about numbers in an excel spreadsheet."

"He's an accountant," Ivy pointed out. "That's what turns him on."

Lewis snorted a laugh. "Could you do it?"

"No." She looked thoroughly amused. "It's your job."

"What if I put a good word in with the boss and try to get you a pay rise?"

"There isn't enough money in the world for me to sit in that stuffy office with Mr Garrett for hours on end."

"Great." Lewis sighed. "Some friend you are."

"You love me really," she said, but he was already walking over to the latest guest.

There was something about the broad smile on Erin Grant's face as she took pictures of the lounge that had him transfixed.

Chapter Four

The hotel lounge was beautiful with its selection of elegant armchairs and couches. If it weren't for the sympathetic looks Erin was getting from the other hotel guests, she'd have been absolutely in her element.

Admittedly, she was the only guest sitting alone, but she really didn't see why that caused such a spectacle. She supposed it was because the mousy foghorn on reception had announced to everyone that she'd been unceremoniously dumped just before Christmas. Apparently, that made her quite the object of pity.

It also meant she got double the mince pies, which made the pitying looks easier to bear. A young couple even admitted that they'd overheard and offered their condolences. They were actually quite sweet.

After a few minutes chatting with the older couple – Mr and Mrs Ward – she pulled out her phone and waved it at them while mouthing an apology. It hadn't been ringing, but she switched her attention to the screen and shot off a message in the group chat with her three closest friends.

She told them she'd arrived and was stuffing herself with

champagne and mince pies, before snapping a few photos of the hotel lounge. Sending pictures was easier than describing the elegant hotel.

She'd just hit send again when she spotted the guy from reception heading in her direction. He was one of those people with a lovely, friendly face. Not in-your-face good looking, but easy on the eyes. His vibe was so warm and inviting that Erin felt instantly at ease.

"Your case is up in your room," he said, handing her the key card. "It's room number four."

"Thank you." It felt like the height of luxury having someone carry her bag to her room while she sat around drinking champagne.

He rested his forearms on the back of the armchair next to hers. "Also, I wanted to apologise for earlier. The front desk is usually a little more professional."

"It's fine," she said, plucking the second mince pie from the plate and giving Mr Ward a gleeful smile. He'd had his eye on her mince pies since she sat down -- like a sad little puppy begging for a treat.

To be fair, they were possibly the best mince pies she'd ever tasted, with insanely buttery pastry. Nothing store bought. These were clearly made from scratch. In all honesty, she wouldn't readily give up a mince pie even if it was the supermarket variety, but homemade ones would have to be pried from her cold, dead hands.

"These are amazing," she told Lewis after taking a large bite. "I'm something of a mince pie connoisseur, so you can compliment the chef for me."

"I will." Dimples appeared on both cheeks when he smiled, making him look even more youthful than she'd previously thought. "Anyway, I hope we haven't given a bad first impression. Jenny on reception is brand new. Apparently, she's not the most tactful."

Erin smiled politely, not sure what to say on the matter.

"I just wanted to check something with you, though," he said, lowering his voice and leaning in a little. "I figured out why Jenny was concerned about your room..."

"Oh?" Erin said, wondering how a hotel room could be unsuitable for someone travelling alone.

"As it's sold as a romantic package, there are a few extra details," Lewis explained. "Like rose petals on the bed."

"Seriously?" Erin resisted the urge to clap her hands together in delight. "I've never stayed in a place with petals on the bed."

"So it's not a problem?"

"No. Definitely not. I'm excited to see the room now. I'll go and roll around in flower petals before dinner."

"Great." Lewis looked visibly relieved, and also faintly amused. "Do you know where the dining room is?"

"Yes. Jenny showed me when she brought my mince pies." The whole of the ground floor was very stylish, with panelled walls throughout and a formal but relaxed restaurant and bar at the back of the building.

"Dinner is between seven and nine," Lewis told her. "Just head to the dining room whenever you're hungry. I can also show you up to your room if you'd like?"

"That's all right," she said, already feeling spoiled by the service. "I'm sure I'll find it." She stood and picked up the remaining glass of champagne. "Is it okay if I take this up with me?"

"Of course. I hope you like the room. If you have any problems, just let us know."

She thanked him and took another swig of champagne before setting off towards the staircase. Tinsel wound around the banister and she trailed her hand above it so it tickled her palm as she ascended. The sound of Christmas music faded the further she got from the lounge.

The champagne was probably partly to blame, but she was

almost giddy when she let herself into the most luxurious hotel room she'd ever stayed in. The carved dark wood of the four-poster bed was like something from a film, and the rose petals made her feel like a princess.

Hastily, she snapped a few more pictures and added it to the group message where her friends had been asking questions and exclaiming about how lucky she was.

It gets better, she told them, typing with speed. *There's a member of staff who is total eye candy.*

While a flurry of replies came through, she flopped back onto the bed and grinned at the ceiling. Her first Christmas spent without her family was looking pretty good so far.

Chapter Five

Each of the four courses at dinner was divine. The roasted duck was especially delicious and the apple crumble with custard that followed it tasted like heaven. Between the food and the old gentleman tinkling away at a piano in the corner, Erin could easily ignore the whispers among the other diners.

Maybe being a part of a couple wasn't all it was cracked up to be, considering most of them appeared to find her the most interesting thing in the room.

When she'd sat down, it occurred to her that she should have brought a book, but she quickly dismissed the idea. She didn't need a distraction, and refused to feel uncomfortable for eating alone.

It was actually something she was used to. She just wasn't used to people being so shocked by it. But then she was used to London and the 'live and let live' mentality of a big city. Apparently, things were different out in the sticks.

She'd just scraped the last of the custard from her bowl when the older couple from earlier arrived beside her table.

"I just wanted to say I think you're very brave," Mrs Ward

said. "Breakups can be difficult, but you seem to be making the most of things. It's very admirable."

Oh, right. After the champagne and excitement about her room, Erin had forgotten about that. It explained the glances she'd been getting. It wasn't just that she was alone, but that people were waiting to see if she was going to break down in tears at any moment.

"Better that things ended now," Mr Ward said in his deep baritone. "And not after you were married."

"That's true," Erin agreed. "A wedding would have been nice, though. I always love a wedding."

They stared at her like she was mad.

"Enjoy your evening," Mrs Ward said, patting her arm before striding away with her husband at her heels.

Tempting as it was to head straight up to the four-poster bed and a subsequent food coma, it was a little too early to sleep, so she went up for her coat and headed out for a stroll around the village.

She didn't venture far, sticking to the main street. Despite the frigid breeze, she felt a warm glow inside her from the sight of all the twinkling lights. A bit of snow would be a lovely addition to the scene, but in true English style drizzle dampened the air. On the plus side, the wet ground reflected the Christmas lights, making the quaint street even more delightful.

The church at the end of the road advertised a midnight mass on Christmas Eve and she made a mental note of the time. Belting out some carols would get her in the mood for the big day.

It was going to be a weird Christmas Day this year – not spending it with her family – but she was feeling positive about it. There'd be food and a four-poster bed, and she wouldn't be alone like she would be if she'd stayed at home. Not that she had an issue with spending time in her own company, but she suspected it would be a pleasant atmosphere in the hotel with the staff and other guests.

There were also a bunch of activities to look forward to before then, she remembered as she strolled back to the hotel while smiling at everyone she passed. She couldn't recall exactly what was included in the hotel package, but was certain ice-skating was on the list. Not that she could skate, but the idea of it was fairly idyllic, even if she just drank hot chocolate on the side-lines and watched other people slide around the ice.

Warmth enveloped her as she stepped back inside the hotel. There was something wonderfully charming about staying in such a small hotel. It had the personal touch that you didn't get in the big chains, and the faces of the hotel staff were already familiar to her.

"Hi!" she said to Lewis, drawing his attention from the computer screen on the front desk.

His smile was as warm and welcoming as the temperature in the room. "You look like you need a hot chocolate to warm you up."

"That sounds amazing." She shoved her mittens into her coat pocket and rubbed her hands together.

"Whipped cream?" he asked.

"Yes, please!" She took a step towards the desk and lowered her voice. "One question, though; when I need a crane to get me out of the hotel at the end of my stay, who pays for that?"

Lewis beamed so widely that his lovely dimples puckered his cheeks. "You've been out for a walk, so you've definitely earned a hot chocolate."

Erin raised a sceptical eyebrow. "I strolled to the end of the road and back."

"It's cold out," Lewis told her. "You burn more calories in the cold."

"Is that really true?"

"I've no idea but it sounds right."

"In that case, I'll feel no guilt while I drink my hot chocolate."

"Make yourself comfy," he said, tipping his head to the lounge area where a few other guests were enjoying after-dinner drinks. "I'll bring it over."

First, she hung her coat on the old-fashioned hat stand at the side of the room, then she headed for the green velvet couch by the window, which was just as comfy as it looked. A young couple who she'd seen at dinner smiled at her and she returned the greeting happily.

"Do you know what's really lovely about being in a village?" she said to Lewis when he set the hot chocolate in front of her. With whipped cream and grated chocolate on top, she suspected it was about a million calories in a mug, but she refused to care.

"What?" he asked, the amused sparkle in his eyes making his face light up.

"Everyone is so friendly. I walked up the street and about five people wished me a good evening. Everyone I passed smiled at me *and* made eye contact. It's not like that in London. Don't get me wrong, I love London. A bit of eye contact goes a long way, though, doesn't it? It makes me feel all warm and fuzzy." She grimaced. "I suppose that could also have been the wine with dinner. Or the champagne before dinner!"

"People are pretty friendly around here," Lewis told her. "Especially at this time of year."

Erin spooned whipped cream from her drink and popped it in her mouth.

"Enjoy," Lewis said, as he walked away.

"Hang on," she said, waving him back. "I have a quick question."

"What can I help with?" he asked, sinking to perch on the couch beside her.

"I might have got it wrong," she said, "but I thought the stay included entrance to some local attractions. I can't quite remember, and there's a chance I just imagined it."

"No, you're right," Lewis said. "It's a whole package."

"Great. I didn't see any information in my room. I was expecting there'd be vouchers or something."

Lewis scratched at his jaw, which had a hint of stubble along it. "You should have received an itinerary via email."

"An itinerary," she repeated.

"Yes. Hang on. I can grab one." He went to the front desk and was back before Erin had time to figure out what he meant by an itinerary. "Sorry," he said. "You should have got one by email. I'm not sure why you didn't."

"I didn't make the booking," she said while her eyes roamed the piece of paper in her hands.

"Of course." He winced. "I hope you don't mind me saying, but I think it's great that you came alone. I don't think most people would do that."

"Ah." Erin moved her attention from the paper and winced. She really hated lies, and this was why. They snowballed and before you knew it, you were completely caught up in them and living an entirely fake life. Maybe not entirely fake, but she didn't like the lie.

"I hope I don't sound condescending or anything," he went on. "It's just that I've been there myself and I know how it feels."

"I'm not sure you do," Erin whispered.

"No, really. It wasn't recent, but I was dumped at Christmas, so I know how hard it is."

She leaned closer to him, continuing to whisper. "I wasn't actually dumped." She wasn't sure why, but there was something about Lewis that had her feeling as though they were friends. She didn't want to lie to him.

She also didn't want him thinking she was some heartbroken mess. Nothing to do with him being cute, obviously. She just didn't want his pity.

"Oh." His smile was still of the sympathetic variety. "Breakups are difficult, no matter whose decision it is."

"No, you don't understand. I wasn't engaged. There was never a fiancé or even a boyfriend." She shook her head as she heard how she sounded. "Well, there was a boyfriend, but that was ages ago."

"I'm not sure I understand."

"My mum booked the hotel as a Christmas gift," she explained. "Apparently, she optimistically thought I might have a boyfriend by Christmas."

"Oh, I see." Except his puzzled expression would suggest he didn't actually see at all.

"The woman on the front desk was completely confused when I turned up alone. I may have said something misleading, but she assumed I'd been dumped and it felt easier to go along with it than explain that I was intentionally here alone. I feel as though that scenario would have been much more shocking for her, but I also didn't realise she'd announce to the entire hotel that I'd been dumped. Now I feel like a bit of a fraud."

"That's kind of funny," Lewis said. "Sorry about Jenny."

"It's fine. Except that I've been getting funny looks from some of the other guests, as though people think I might start crying about my cheating fiancé."

"Did you say he cheated on you?" Lewis asked, amused.

"No, but I assume they're all making up their own little stories."

"Let them talk," Lewis said. "Who cares?"

"Not me," Erin said, picking up her hot chocolate. Her gaze dropped to the paper in her other hand. "I'm confused," she said. "We meet in the lounge tomorrow afternoon for the Christmas markets? Which lounge?"

"Here," Lewis said.

"Oh." Erin drew the syllable out as things became clear. "So we all go together?"

"Yes. It's the first year we've done it this way. In the past, guests have commented about issues with parking. Plus, a lot of these events involve mulled wine, but since they all involve a drive to get there, only one person can have a drink. Or they have to get taxis." He smiled bashfully. "So this year we're putting on a minibus to ferry people around. The guests also seem to enjoy the idea of not having to make decisions. They're told where to be and when, and we take care of the rest."

"That makes sense," Erin mused. "Somehow I had it in my head that the hotel was just providing vouchers for local attractions."

"No. There's an entire plan." He tipped his head at the paper. "I guess if you wanted to go it alone, I could figure something out..."

"No. It's fine. Like you say, it's nice not having to make decisions. And I don't have a car so I'd have to get taxis. This is perfect." Her eyes continued to scan the paper. "Wreath-making," she said, as her eyes snagged on the activity for the following morning. "I like a bit of crafting, but I've never made a Christmas wreath."

"It should be fun," Lewis said. "That's just in the hotel restaurant so we don't need to go anywhere."

"I'm excited," she said.

"Hopefully you'll manage to enjoy it," Lewis said mockingly. "I'm sure it will be a difficult time for you, what with your breakup."

Erin laughed freely, then forced her features into a serious expression. "I think with enough mulled wine and mince pies, I'll manage not to dwell on my heartache too much."

Chapter Six

The wreath-making workshop took place the following morning. Erin had noticed the staff setting things up for it while she ate breakfast. An hour later, she returned to the dining room to find it transformed. Now, the tables created a square with a space in the middle. Materials were laid out at intervals along the tables and the scent of pine from the fir twigs was intoxicating.

A few people sat along the bar and more wandered beside the tables, surveying the materials.

Inside the ring of tables, a young woman wove wire around a circle of straw, presumably the base for a festive wreath. With her head bent, she didn't notice Erin approach and jumped a little when she said hello.

Finally, she lifted her face, revealing the most flawless skin Erin had ever seen. Her naturally rose-pink lips matched the blush on her high cheekbones. With her dark hair cut in a perfect bob, Erin couldn't help but think she should be on the cover of a glossy magazine, or an actress or something in the public eye.

"Are you joining the wreath-making class?" she asked Erin with a nervous smile.

"Yes." Erin thrust her hand out and introduced herself.

"I'm Anna," she said. "Will your husband be coming along too?" She winced. "Or boyfriend?" Again, she winced and her neck flushed bright crimson. "Or girlfriend... *partner*! That's what I meant to say. Will your *partner* join us today?"

"No, it's just me." Erin smiled warmly. "In general, men are my preference, but I'm currently single."

"And you're staying in the hotel alone? Over Christmas?" She slapped a hand over her mouth. "I'm sorry. That sounded judgemental."

"Don't worry." Erin shrugged. "It's a bit odd, I know, but my family all had different plans this Christmas, so my mum booked this little getaway for me. I'm really enjoying it so far. The hotel is gorgeous."

"It is lovely," Anna agreed quietly. She pulled the sleeve of her cream shirt back to reveal more porcelain-like skin and a dainty analogue watch with a black, leather strap. "We're just waiting for a few more guests. Then we'll get started. There's complimentary tea, coffee, and soft drinks at the bar if you want to get something."

"Thanks," Erin said, then drifted away to grab a coffee.

Lingering by the bar, she watched more guests arrive, then noticed Lewis appear from a door at the other side of the room, which was marked 'staff only'. He seemed to draw everyone's attention. A young couple moved straight over to speak to him, and then the blonde-haired barmaid approached to ask him something. It took him a few minutes to cross the room while fielding questions, but finally he reached the tables and ducked underneath to join Anna in the middle.

From her spot at the bar Erin couldn't hear what was being said, but she caught the look of annoyance Anna shot Lewis and the way he laughed in response to whatever she'd said. Then he wrapped an arm around her shoulders and kissed the side of her head.

Erin's stomach squeezed at the obvious closeness between them. Which was ridiculous. It wasn't as though she was going to have a Christmas fling with a member of the hotel staff.

If she'd indulged in such a scenario while lying in bed the previous evening, it was only a harmless fantasy. She wasn't delusional enough to imagine it might happen.

While she continued to stare at them, Lewis and Anna suddenly looked in her direction. Right at her. Instinctively, she dropped her gaze to the coffee in her hands and then took a sip. Had Anna noticed Erin staring at Lewis from the moment he walked into the room? The thought was fairly mortifying.

Risking a glance, she found they'd turned away and were head-to-head as they continued to chat quietly. Erin wandered back over to the tables and casually sidled along until she was close enough to hear their conversation.

"I'm telling you, it'll be fine," Lewis said, his hand resting lightly at Anna's elbow.

"I don't know how I let you talk me into this," she hissed quietly.

Lewis's eyes sparkled with affection. "Because you love me so much."

"I don't think I love you very much at all at this moment." Anna glared at him again, but still looked beautiful even when she was scowling.

"Of course you do," he replied, giving her another side hug. "Anyway, there's nothing to worry about. I'll introduce you and you'll do your thing. I promise it'll be easy once you get going."

"You owe me for this," she muttered.

Turning back to the room, Lewis caught Erin's eye. His smile was far too flirty for a guy standing beside his girlfriend, but maybe Erin was mistaking flirty with friendly professionalism.

She only vaguely listened as Lewis greeted the guests and instructed anyone who was joining the workshop to find a spot at a table. Mostly it was women who took the seats, but a few of their partners joined too.

Anna, when she spoke, was shy but engaging. She had everyone's complete attention as she talked briefly about the history of Christmas wreaths, then discussed various styles of wreaths and showed examples. Some were more modern, with glitzy baubles and ribbons, and others more natural and rustic.

Erin's favourite was the traditional one with holly and berries and pine cones tucked into the pine twigs. Maybe she'd add a couple of cinnamon sticks, too.

By the time she'd watched Anna demonstrate a few techniques, she was eager to get going and immediately began to cover her straw base with fir twigs, securing them in place with fine wire. Anna had made it look easy, but Erin soon found the demonstration had been deceptive. It wasn't as easy as it looked and she found herself entirely concentrated on the task.

She lost all track of time and hummed along to the Christmas music while she worked. Once the wreath was completely covered in fir twigs, she made a start on the creative part. She'd clumped a few sprigs of holly together and was arranging them on the wreath when she pricked her thumb. Sticking it into her mouth, she tasted the metallic tang of blood and swore gently when she pulled it out to look.

"You okay?" Lewis asked, appearing beside her.

"Fine. Just losing a battle with a holly leaf."

"Let me see." He bent beside her.

"It's fine," she told him.

"It's bleeding." His brow creased. "I'll get you a plaster."

"No need. It's honestly fine..." She trailed off since he was already halfway across the room.

He grabbed a first aid kit from behind the bar and was back in a moment and pulling up a chair beside Erin.

"It's really not bad," she insisted.

"Even so, better to clean it up and cover it. Can I?" He held his hand out and she gave him hers, then got annoyed with herself for the way her heart rate sped up at his touch. She hardly breathed when he ran an antiseptic wipe over her thumb and wrapped a plaster around it.

"Thank you," she whispered.

"You're welcome." He didn't immediately let her hand go, but kept a hold of it as he looked her right in the eyes.

Finally, she pulled her hand away and busied herself with choosing a pine cone for her next embellishment. "I'd never have thought making a Christmas wreath would be so absorbing."

Lewis smiled lightly. "That's what Anna always says. That she gets lost in it and forgets about everything else."

"She's really great," Erin murmured, looking over at Anna, who was helping Mrs Ward with some sparkly baubles.

"Yeah, she is."

"She's so beautiful," Erin blurted out, then felt her cheeks flush as Lewis looked at her in amusement, as though he could read her mind and see all of Erin's jealousy laid out.

"Everyone says that," he said flatly. "Our younger sister, Carla, always says that Anna got all the looks while she got all the confidence." His lips twitched upwards. "Carla isn't ugly or anything, so I don't think she got it right about the looks, but she was right about the confidence. She got more than her fair share and Anna has none."

Erin turned the pine cone in her hand, wondering if she'd understood correctly. "Anna is your sister?" she asked, needing clarification.

"Yeah. She's only a year younger than me, so we've always been close."

"That's nice." It was crazy how relieved Erin felt to find out they were siblings. Not that it meant he was single, but she could go back to assuming he was and that she wasn't imagining the vibes between the two of them.

"You don't look alike," she said when her brain clicked back into gear. "When you were chatting I sort of assumed she was your girlfriend." There, she'd set the conversation up for him to make his relationship status clear. If he wanted her to know his relationship status.

"Nope. She's my sister," he said, amusement clinging to his words. "And I don't have a girlfriend," he added quietly.

"Oh," Erin said, then felt like a bumbling idiot. Once again, she turned her attention to her wreath while she struggled to think of something else to say. "Do you offer the wreath-making class every year?" she asked eventually.

"No. First time. And if Anna has anything to do with it, I'm not sure it will happen again."

"Really? She's great at it."

"She hates speaking in front of people. I wasn't exaggerating about her lack of confidence. I had to beg her to do this. Part of me thought it might be good for her, but now I mostly feel bad for dragging her out of her comfort zone."

"Sometimes it's good to get out of your comfort zone," Erin mused.

"Speaking from experience?"

"No. I tend to stay in my comfort zone. I only meant that in theory it sounds like a good thing to do."

"I wasn't sure if you were feeling out of your comfort zone now," he said.

It took her a moment to figure out what he meant. "Taking a trip on my own?" She shook her head. "I don't have an issue doing stuff on my own." In recent years, anyway. It hadn't always been the case. "I have amazing friends and I spend a lot of time with them but they all have boyfriends, so if they're busy I'm quite happy to go to the cinema alone or a museum. I don't have a problem eating out alone either."

"That's cool," Lewis said. He sounded as though he meant it too, not like the people who smiled awkwardly while secretly thinking she was nuts. Or not-so-secretly, in the case of her sister.

While Erin braved another attempt at adding holly to her wreath, Lewis leaned a little closer. The scent of his aftershave tickled Erin's nostrils and made her heart beat faster again.

"Can I ask you a question?" he said quietly.

She gave him an encouraging nod.

"Do you think it's weird to make a wreath so close to Christmas?"

She frowned, wondering when you would make it if not at Christmas. "How do you mean?"

"The other reason Anna wasn't keen to do the workshop was because she says it's too late in the season. You should make them earlier so you can hang it on your door and make use of it for longer. But I wanted to include it in our Christmas package. I thought it would be a fun thing to offer."

"I didn't even think about that," Erin told him. "I just thought it sounded fun. Plus, it will make my hotel room smell gorgeous."

"Good. She made me self-conscious about it."

"Did you plan the programme of events?"

He tapped on the table. "Not just me. It's a joint effort. The staff all pitch their ideas and then we pick the best."

The conversation trailed off as Anna walked over to them. "How are you doing?" she asked Erin.

"Good. I had no idea I'd enjoy this so much."

"I'm glad you're enjoying it," she said, then inspected Erin's wreath. "Maybe some berries will look good. And possibly a red bow. It'll add a bit of colour, but still look rustic and traditional."

Erin was voicing her agreement when mousy Jenny came over to speak to Lewis.

"There's someone to see you," she told him. "Mr Garrett.

He said he has an appointment, and he'd wait in the office. I told him I didn't know if it was okay for him to go into the office alone, but he just shook his head and went anyway."

Lewis let out a growl of frustration. "I forgot about that."

"You forgot about what?" Anna hissed at him.

"I have a meeting with Mr Garrett, but I'm sure it won't take long."

"You said you'd be here the whole time," Anna whispered. "Please don't leave me."

"It shouldn't take long," Lewis said, already out of his chair. "Also, you're doing brilliantly. You don't need me around." His gaze fell to Erin. "I'll see you later."

"Bye," she said before he strode away across the room.

"Brothers are awful and never to be trusted," Anna mumbled, then caught Erin's eye. "Sorry. That sounded mean. He's a good brother, really."

Erin attached another small pine cone to her wreath. "Lewis was saying he dragged you into this. Was it a workshop in the hotel you weren't keen on, or do you not like running classes in general?"

"In general. I make wreaths to sell, but this is the first time I've done a class."

"Really?" Erin was genuinely surprised. "I'd never have known. You're great at it."

Her neck flared red again. "Thank you. I get nervous talking in front of people."

"I couldn't tell."

"That's good." She shook her head. "Lewis promised me he'd be here the whole time."

"Was it his boss he had to meet with?" Erin asked idly.

"No. Mr Garrett is the accountant and Lewis hates him." She reached for a red ribbon and held it at the bottom of Erin's wreath.

"That looks great," Erin said, taking it from her to attach it.

"I don't think he actually hates him," Anna went on. "I think it's more of a love to hate situation. He enjoys complaining about him."

"He seems to have a lot of responsibility around here," Erin remarked. "It seems as though he runs the place, but he also looks too young to run a hotel."

When Anna didn't respond, Erin looked up from her wreath to find her staring at her with an unreadable expression.

"Sorry," Erin said. "Did I sound really nosey?"

"No, it's not that." Her eyebrows drew together and she lowered her voice. "He does run the place. He's got a baby face, but he's twenty-six. He's worked here since he was sixteen. Just during school holidays and at weekends to start with. He worked his way up, and he got a degree in hotel management too." Pausing, she glanced around as though worried she might be overheard. "He's done well for himself and he loves his job, but sometimes I worry that he's kind of obsessed with it. We're always nagging him to take more time off."

Erin was listening so intently that it took her a moment to register when Anna stopped talking.

"That was probably too much information," she said bashfully. "I feel as though I always say too much or too little and there's no in between."

"I did ask," Erin pointed out. And she did sit there hanging off her every word.

Anna gave a small smile and wandered away to help someone else.

Maybe it was a trait that every member of their family had, but Erin felt an immediate connection to Anna, just as she did to Lewis. Well, not quite the same – she wouldn't be having fantasies about a fling with Anna – but the sense of knowing her for longer than she had was definitely there.

Chapter Seven

There was only so long that Lewis could feign interest in the accounts. He'd passed that point about half an hour ago and had been nodding along since then. They'd been over all the important stuff. Now it was a case of Mr Garrett loving the sound of his own voice.

"I really don't know if this Christmas package you're offering this year is a good idea," he grumbled, staring at his laptop on the desk. "Was this really the cheapest minibus hire you could find? It seems excessive."

"I shopped around," he said, hating how Mr Garrett always made him feel about twelve.

"I just don't see why the hotel needs to offer all these frivolities."

"It's Christmas and the guests love it. That's what matters, isn't it?"

"That and profits," he said, pushing his glasses further up his nose. "I think you could easily have charged more."

"It's too late to change the price now," Lewis told him. "And I spoke to you about it beforehand. You knew how much we were going to charge. Also, it's not cheap."

"But people will pay way over the odds at Christmas."

Lewis leaned back in his chair, telling himself to grin and bear it and Mr Garrett would be gone soon. "Do we really want to be known as the hotel who rips people off at Christmas?"

Before Mr Garrett could reply, a knock at the door had Lewis sitting up straighter and looking hopefully across the office as the door opened.

"Sorry," Anna said. "I just needed to speak to you before I leave." Her head flicked to the accountant in the chair opposite Lewis. "Hello, Mr Garrett," she said in that sickly sweet tone that Lewis knew was entirely fake.

"Anna!" Mr Garrett said, a sudden jolliness in his tone. "How are you?"

"Fine, thank you. I was doing a workshop – teaching the guests how to make Christmas wreaths. It's been lovely. I think they all really enjoyed it."

"I'm sure they did. It sounds fantastic. If my Judith had known about it, she'd have signed straight up."

"Maybe I'll run some more next year," she said. "I was sceptical about doing it, but it turns out that Lewis was right after all. He always knows exactly what the hotel guests will enjoy."

"Of course," Mr Garrett said eagerly, apparently having wiped from his memory the last two hours where he'd been picking holes in everything Lewis said.

"Anyway..." Anna looked meekly at Lewis. "I wondered if you have time for a quick word before I leave? I've been ever-so worried about Mum recently and..." She gave a quick shake of the head. "Sorry, you're in the middle of a meeting. I can wait, but I will need to leave before too long."

"We're all finished here," Mr Garrett said, all but leaping from his chair to offer it to Anna. "Family comes first, especially at this time of year. I was about to leave anyway," he added, as he collected up his things and shoved them into his briefcase.

"Thank you," Anna said, slipping into his vacated seat. "I didn't mean to rush you out."

Lewis was sure that was exactly her intention, and he absolutely loved her for it.

"Not a problem," Mr Garrett told her, a warmth to his words which was never present when he spoke to Lewis.

"Why don't you nip into the dining room before you leave," Anna suggested. "There are a few of my example wreaths on the back table. Take one for Mrs Garrett."

"She'll love that," he said, his features all affection as he smiled at Anna. "Thank you. Have a wonderful Christmas." His attention flicked to Lewis. "I'll see *you* next week."

"Surely not next week," Anna said smoothly. "I don't think anyone actually needs to hold business meetings between Christmas and New Year. Lewis will be taking a bit of time off, and I'm sure you will be, too. Mrs Garrett will want you at home."

Lewis watched with interest to see how the stuffy accountant would react to that suggestion. Surely he wouldn't go along with it. He'd shake his head and tell Anna that business doesn't stop because of Christmas.

"You're right," he said, causing Lewis to put a hand on the desk to ensure he didn't fall all the way out of his chair. "Of course, you're right. I'll see you in the New Year." He raised his hand to wave and left absolute silence in his wake.

Lewis waited a moment, making sure he was out of earshot before he spoke.

"I love you," he said flatly. "You are brilliant."

"The man's a prat. I heard what he was saying about the Christmas events before I walked in. Why do you let him speak to you like that?"

Lewis shrugged. "Sometimes it's easier to nod and smile."

"I don't like him, and I feel very sorry for Mrs Garrett. Do you remember her from school? She was always so lovely."

He nodded. Geography lessons with Mrs Garrett had been his favourite class. "Thank you for saving me. I presume there isn't a problem with Mum?"

"No, she's fine."

Lewis let out a long sigh. "For someone lacking confidence, you're very good at getting what you want."

"Mr Garrett is easy to manipulate. But he's been here for ages, so it must have been time for him to leave, anyway. Was the two-hour meeting necessary?"

"No. I don't think so. The man just enjoys torturing me."

"Then I have no qualms about getting rid of him for you."

"Was it at least true what you said about the workshop today? Did you enjoy it?"

"*Enjoy* is probably the wrong word." She looked thoughtful. "It wasn't as bad as I imagined."

"That's good. I was expecting to be in trouble for leaving you alone."

"You would have been," she said. "But your friend Erin started telling me how great I was, and it was a nice little confidence boost."

"Why did you refer to her as *my friend?*" He echoed her tone. "She's a hotel guest."

"She's lovely," Anna said. "And I saw the way you were looking at her. You totally fancy her, don't you?"

He laughed loudly, but couldn't bring himself to deny it.

"It's all right," Anna said. "She was looking at you in the same way."

He wouldn't rise to the bait. He absolutely wouldn't.

"Really?" he asked, cursing himself for how needy he sounded.

"Absolutely," Anna said. "She was asking about you, too. When you left."

"Asking *what?*" Panic crept up his spine and his palms felt suddenly sweaty.

"About your role at the hotel." Anna tapped her fingers on the arm of her chair. "She doesn't know about you, does she?"

"I met her yesterday," he said with a shrug.

"Yes, but lots of people know about you who have never met you."

"What's your point?" he said, the conversation becoming increasingly tedious.

"I think she seems great. And you deserve someone great. I worry about you since all that stuff with Gemma."

"No need to worry about me. I'm over it."

"Yes, but I think it stops you from getting involved with anyone else. It'd be good if you met someone."

"I've nothing against a relationship if the right person comes along. But Erin is a hotel guest."

"So? There's no rule about that, is there?"

"Not a *rule,*" he said. "But it seems a bit..."

"A bit what?"

"I don't know." He threw his hands up. "I met Erin yesterday. I don't even know her. And she lives in London and will go back to London in a few days."

"Yes, but who knows what might happen in that time," Anna said. "If you have the chance, you should spend more time with her. Even if it's only a bit of fun over Christmas. You should let yourself have fun now and again."

"I have fun," he insisted. "Besides, I'm not sure you're the right person to give this lecture. Isn't it a case of the pot calling the kettle black?"

"Maybe. But that doesn't mean I'm wrong." She stood up and gave him an indecipherable look. "Thank you for bullying me into doing the workshop. I actually think I was quite good at it."

"You were brilliant." He stood and wrapped her in a hug. "But I never had any doubt about that."

She kissed his cheek. "I have to go. Why don't you think of a reason to go and hang out with Erin?"

"Because I have work to do," he told her, screwing his nose up. Then he softened his features. "But there's a trip to Stratford-upon-Avon this afternoon to look around the Christmas markets. Maybe I'll have time to speak to her then."

"Ooh! That sounds romantic."

Lewis rolled his eyes, but deep down, he thought his sister was probably right. He should lighten up a bit.

And he liked the idea of spending more time with Erin, even if it couldn't realistically come to anything.

Chapter Eight

A finger food lunch was served in the lounge directly after the wreath-making. Stupidly, Erin spent most of the time scanning the room for Lewis, then cursed herself for acting like a lovesick teenager. It wasn't like her to get hung up on a guy. Especially one who she'd known less than twenty-four hours. She blamed her friends for encouraging her to have a Christmas fling in their messages.

Thinking of her friends made her check her phone, but their group chat was unusually quiet. Then again, it was the 23rd of December and they all had plans with their families and significant others over the Christmas period.

Full from lunch, she took her wreath up to her room and gave it pride of place on the table by the window. Then she sat and watched the world go by outside while contemplating going for a walk before the afternoon activity. In the end, she didn't move from the comfort of her room until the middle of the afternoon when she went and joined the assembled group in the lounge. Four couples were waiting, including the Wards, who waved at her as though they were old friends.

"We're all here," Lewis said, flashing her a quick smile. The rest of the group looked at her too and she felt uncomfortable at being the last – as though she'd kept them waiting, despite being exactly on time. "Who's ready for some Christmas shopping?" he asked jovially, then directed them to the minibus which was parked around the side of the hotel.

Erin had wrapped up well for the trip to the Christmas markets. Her green winter coat was an old favourite and her hat and scarf added extra protection from the cold, but she peeled them off as soon as she took her seat in the middle of the minibus.

A heavily made-up middle-aged woman in the seat in front of her held a hushed conversation with the man beside her before she turned and looked between the seats at Erin.

"What's happened to your man, then?" she asked in a thick Cockney accent. "Is he ill? I hope it isn't food poisoning. My Phil had a dicky tummy after dinner yesterday, but he often has a dicky tummy. IBS, you know. Also, he drank six pints of beer and had a few shots of vodka, so I told him it was probably that."

"Oh," Erin said, wondering if she was managing to hide her surprise – and horror – at the conversation.

"He hasn't got food poisoning, has he, your fella?"

"We *hope* he has," a low voice grumbled from the seat behind Erin.

Oh, god. Erin felt her cheeks heating. "No." She shook her head, hoping Mr Ward wouldn't involve himself in the conversation any further. "No food poisoning. I'm just on my own, that's all."

The woman's unnaturally plump lips moved into a confused pout.

"Terrible thing..." The female voice came from behind Erin. She didn't bother looking, but from the shift of the Cockney woman's focus, Erin gathered that Mrs Ward was probably now peering between the seat from the row behind. "Her fiancé split up with her last week. So she had to come here alone." Mrs

Ward's hand arrived on Erin's shoulder. "The poor thing. She's being very brave."

"Oh, my word!" the other woman reached through the seats and took Erin's hand. "That's awful. And here I am going on about blooming food poisoning and IBS." She squeezed Erin's hand. "Would you like to talk about it?"

Erin caught Lewis's eye in the rear-view mirror and had to stifle a laugh.

"I'm trying not to think about it," Erin said, removing her hand from the stranger's and shifting in her seat to dislodge Mrs Ward's hand from her shoulder. "I think it's better not to dwell on these things. Focus on the present, that's what I always think."

"Yeah," pouty lips said, while looking slightly put out that she wasn't getting a story out of Erin.

"That's the spirit!" Mr Ward called.

Erin smiled tightly at the woman in front, then pulled her phone from her coat pocket. "I just have to send a few messages."

She kept her head bent over her phone for the entire drive. At least she kept her friends entertained by regaling them with descriptions of the other hotel guests and the misunderstanding about the fiancé. That's how she was thinking of it – a misunderstanding. It felt better than thinking of herself as a liar.

Once Lewis had given everyone instructions for what time to meet back at the minibus, the group dispersed, heading in the direction of the Christmas markets, which Lewis had pointed out.

Erin hung back, glancing up and down the street and trying to come up with a plan. Preferably one that wouldn't involve bumping into the other guests, so she could avoid her web of lies growing wider.

"If you're not in the mood for the markets," Lewis said. "Stratford is lovely just to wander around. Have you been before?"

"No." She pulled her mittens from her pockets. "I was only thinking that I don't want to keep running into the other guests in the market and have to deal with questions about my imaginary fiancé. I'm usually a very honest person, you know?"

"I believe you," he said, zipping his coat all the way up.

"What else is there to do in Stratford?" she asked, stamping her feet to ward off the cold.

"If you've never been before, I'd just have a walk around and take in the atmosphere. There are a lot of historical landmarks, mostly to do with Shakespeare. You can see his birthplace and his grave and there's the theatre."

"That sounds like a plan. I'll wander around the sights and maybe stop off at the markets later. Hopefully, the other hotel guests will do it the other way around." She shifted her weight. "What do you do while you wait? Will you go back to the hotel, or hang around here?"

"Hang around. It's not worth driving back. I was planning on finding a nice warm pub where I can sit and people-watch."

"That sounds good, too." She cringed, because it definitely sounded as though she was angling for an invitation. Which she kind of was.

"You're welcome to join me," he said. "Or if you'd like a tour guide, I can give you a quick tour of the town and then we can find a pub once we're thoroughly frozen."

"That sounds great," Erin said, feeling a tingle of anticipation ripple from her stomach up to her chest. "Are you sure you don't mind?"

"Not at all," he said. "The company would be great."

And the company *was* great. Erin felt completely at ease as they wandered through the historic town with Lewis pointing out the sights along the way.

After an hour, they walked into a traditional pub tucked away in a narrow, cobbled street. The warmth felt glorious after so long out in the cold.

"Do you think we'll get snow?" Erin asked as they sat with their drinks beside a log fire at the side of the room.

"Maybe." Lewis removed his coat and took a sip of his coke. "The weather forecast says not, but who knows? My mum will claim it's too cold for snow, but I've never really understood that."

"Me neither. I'd love to see Chipping Campden covered in snow. I'll bet it's gorgeous."

"There's definitely something magical about it when it snows."

The fire crackled beside them, and they fell into a comfortable silence. Erin's glass of mulled wine was wonderfully warm and spicy and she smiled, thinking of all the little indulgences she was enjoying on her trip. Spending time with Lewis was definitely one of those indulgences.

"I wanted to say..." Lewis broke her thoughts. "Thank you for whatever you said to Anna. She said you gave her a confidence boost."

"She seemed as though she needed it. But I didn't say anything that wasn't the truth. I thought she was a natural at running the class."

"The other guests were enthusiastic about it too," Lewis said, then turned and held his hands in front of the fire to warm them. "Do you have siblings?"

"Yes. A sister, but she's not as nice as yours."

Lewis grinned before his eyes widened. "Oh, you're serious?"

"Unfortunately. It always makes me a bit sad when I hear about people who are close to their siblings, but I just don't get on with Zara. We see the world very differently."

"How so?"

Erin considered the question. "Zara is kind of old-fashioned,

I suppose. She only ever wanted to get married and have a family. Not that I think that's a bad thing, but I'm sure she thinks that any woman who wants anything else is kidding themselves because they can't find a man."

"So what do you want?" he asked, eyeing her intently.

"I love my job," she told him slowly. "And I have great friends and a lovely cosy flat. I genuinely like my life and I suppose it's not that I'm against having a relationship if I found the right person, but they would have to be pretty perfect for me to risk them messing up my life." That was something she didn't generally admit, even to herself – but she was happy and she'd worked hard to build a life that she wanted.

Her eyes flicked to Lewis, whose mouth twitched into a smile.

"Oh! That sounded bad, didn't it?" She twirled her glass on the coaster. "What I meant was, I think it's important to be happy first and then find someone to share that with. My sister needs a relationship to make her happy. I think that can backfire."

"Is that the voice of experience?"

It absolutely was, but that wasn't something she wanted to discuss with Lewis in this beautiful rustic pub. The atmosphere was too lovely to ruin it with such a depressing conversation.

"We seem to have ventured into some deep conversation. Since I've only known you for a short time – and because it's Christmas – let's stick to lighter topics."

"Fair enough," he agreed with a twinkle in his eyes. "What do you do for a living?"

That was a much safer topic of conversation and she relaxed back in the chair as she told him about her job in content marketing, and about the two friends – Alicia and Irina – who she'd made when she started the job. That led to telling him about her wonderful friend, Jessie, who lived next door to her and who she'd met when Erin had moved into the flat four years ago.

Once she started talking about her friends, who were now all friends with each other, she came up with one anecdote after another. Since Lewis seemed thoroughly entertained, she kept on chatting until she checked her watch and found that almost another hour had passed.

They had to make a mad dash back to the minibus, but they made it approximately on time and Erin was feeling exhilarated from the wine and the jog through town when they reached the bus.

"Wish me luck for the drive home," she said out of the side of her mouth as they waited for the Wards to arrive back at the minibus. "Although, now I have some alcohol in me, the questioning might at least feel a bit more amusing."

Lewis slid the side door of the van open and gestured for the guests to get in. Then he put a hand on Erin's arm to stop her from following them. "You can always sit in the front with me if you want."

"Really?"

"Yeah. I promise not to ask you awkward questions about your non-existent ex-fiancé."

"In that case, I don't see how I can say no."

He opened the passenger door, and she climbed up onto the bench seat. As he closed the door, she heard him greeting Mr and Mrs Ward and ushering them into the back.

Erin had a mental battle over which seat to take. There were two passenger seats, and she was currently occupying the one nearest the door. She could slide over and sit close to Lewis, but maybe he'd feel crowded.

At the sight of him walking around the front of the van, she made a quick decision and slid across the bench.

She wanted to be close to Lewis and didn't particularly care if she seemed too keen.

It was Christmas, after all.

Chapter Nine

Following another delicious dinner, Erin moved into the lounge and made herself comfortable in an armchair between the Christmas tree and the fireplace. Whenever any of the guests tried to catch her eye, she looked away and avoided getting sucked into conversations she'd rather not engage in.

Discreetly, she kept an eye on Lewis. Her afternoon in Stratford with him had felt decidedly like a date, and the drive home had been far more pleasant than the drive there. They hadn't spoken much, apart from Lewis telling her tidbits about the local area. Even so, she enjoyed his company immensely.

Now, she found herself eager to speak to him again and was following his moves as he came and went from the kitchen and reception desk. There was also a door behind the reception desk which Erin assumed went to the office and possibly cut through to the kitchen, too. Whenever Lewis passed the reception desk, he chatted with the red-headed woman there. They seemed to get on well and Erin ignored the twinge of jealousy every time the redhead made him laugh. Which was quite often.

She reminded herself that he'd told her he didn't have a girlfriend, and also that she'd only met the guy two days ago and had no right to be jealous of anyone.

An hour passed with her exchanging a few messages with her mum and with her friends, catching up on what they were all doing. Her mum was apparently helping the Australian economy by drinking a lot of their wine.

Lewis never seemed to stop, and it occurred to Erin that he seemed to have been working consistently since she'd arrived. Presumably he went home to sleep, but as far as she could tell, was otherwise working non-stop. Maybe he didn't even go home to sleep. For all she knew, he could sleep at the hotel.

It annoyed her suddenly, that she didn't know, and that he worked so hard. Anna had also commented that his family was always nagging him to take time off.

Without a lot of thought, she waved to him and he moved out from behind the reception desk immediately.

"Anything *I* can help you with?" the red head asked while she deposited a tray of tea in front of an elderly lady by the window.

"No." Erin felt suddenly self-conscious. "Thank you."

The woman looked slightly bemused but continued serving the grey-haired lady.

"Hey," Lewis said. "What can I get for you?"

"I just wondered if you could sit down for a minute?" She nodded to the chair at the other side of the little antique table beside hers.

He sat down and looked at her expectantly. "Do you need more information about the area?"

"No." A smile tugged at her lips. "It's just tiring to sit here and watch you constantly on the go."

"That's my job," he said, amused.

"I know, but you never seem to take breaks. Do you ever go home? Because you seem to have been here all the time since I checked in."

"I..." Nervously, he glanced at the redhead who was now standing in front of them and glaring at him.

"She's right." The woman – Ivy, according to her name tag – propped her hands on her hips. "And if even the guests think you work too hard, maybe that should tell you something."

"Why do I feel as though I'm being ganged up on?" Lewis asked.

"Just sit for a while." Ivy looked at Erin and gave a small shake of the head. "He works as though he has something to prove to the world." She squeezed his shoulder. "You have nothing to prove," she murmured before walking away.

Erin watched her go, trying to fathom what she'd meant, but failing to make sense of it.

"These chairs are actually really comfortable," Lewis said, sinking back into it.

"So, do you have a home?" Erin asked, tilting her head. "Or do you sleep here?"

"I have a home," he said, resting his head on the wing of the armchair. "About a five-minute walk from here. And, yes, I sleep there every night."

"Is it a flat or a house?" she asked, not caring that it sounded like an inquisition.

"A house," he said. "A little cottage. Three bedrooms and a cute little garden."

"That sounds lovely."

"It is." There was a touch of pride in his voice. "Ivy grows around the door."

"Talking about me?" his colleague asked, reappearing with a tray of drinks.

"No." Lewis smiled softly. "I was talking about the plant ivy. At my house."

"It's lovely," Ivy said as she slid the tray onto the table between them. "I believe someone ordered tea and shortbread for two?"

Lewis shook his head. "You know, I actually have work to do."

"I know *you think* you have work to do," Ivy said. "I also know there's nothing I can't manage or that can't wait a little while. Chill out for a bit, will you?"

He thanked her and she walked away.

"That was nice of her," Erin remarked, then swatted at Lewis's hand when he went to pour the tea.

He withdrew and raised an eyebrow. "What was that for?"

"Sorry." She grimaced. "I didn't mean to physically attack you."

"Do you often just randomly slap people?" He held his hand to his chest in a show of being wounded, despite her barely having touched him.

"I don't," she said, chuckling. "I just didn't want you to wait on me. You're supposed to be taking a break."

"Who said I was going to pour yours?" he asked, with a wonderful glint of mischief in his eyes. "Maybe I was going to pour my own and ignore you."

"Somehow, I don't think so. Also, when using a tea set, you should put the milk in the cup first and then the tea." She lifted the dainty milk jug and poured into both cups.

"You wouldn't do that if you were making tea with a kettle, though, would you?"

"No. But there are different rules. My gran taught me, so it's just the way it is."

"I'm not disagreeing," he said. "I'm just never sure of the reasoning behind these traditions."

"Who are we to question tradition?" She lifted the teapot. "Although I do actually know the reason behind this tradition, if you'd really like to know."

"Go on then," he said with a sly smile.

"In the olden days," she said, as she poured. "Most people could only afford cheap china, which was prone to cracking with the heat of the tea. Adding milk first made sure it was cool enough that the cups didn't break."

"I never knew that." His fingers brushed hers as he took the cup and saucer from her.

"I'm not sure if it's the most useful piece of knowledge. Honestly, I'm not even sure if it's true. My gran told me, so I assume it must be true. I might look it up at some point."

"Are you close to your gran?" he asked, the dainty cup and saucer looking extra delicate in his large hands.

"I *was.*" She dunked a piece of shortbread in her tea and bit off the soggy part before it could fall apart. "She died."

"Sorry," he whispered.

"Thanks, but it was ages ago. Five years." It didn't actually feel like ages. It felt like no time at all, and she felt a pang of regret that her gran didn't get to see her life now. Her gran, who had tactfully suggested Erin's relationship with her ex wasn't right for her, but which Erin hadn't been able to see.

"I don't think time really does heal all wounds," Lewis said softly. "Some stick with you."

"Tea and biscuits help, though," Erin said to lighten the atmosphere. She took another piece of shortbread and nudged the plate to Lewis. "Help me out here, please."

He gobbled an entire piece in one go, making Erin laugh and breaking the sombre atmosphere in an instant.

He sat with her for twenty minutes, asking about her Christmas traditions and her favourite things about Christmas. When he insisted he should get back to work, she wished him goodnight and headed up to her room. She was at the top of the stairs when she passed Ivy, going the other way.

"Thanks," she said with a conspiratorial smile. "I can never get him to take a break."

Erin faltered over her response. It was hard to know how to respond when someone thanked you for spending time with a cute guy who you were attracted to. *You're welcome* felt like an inappropriate response. "Yes," she said, and swallowed hard. "He's... I mean... I... It was nice."

"He's lovely," Ivy said, again with the smile which seemed to convey more than Erin could decipher. "Also, I heard about the thing with your fiancé. Sorry about that. It sounds rubbish."

Erin winced. "Yeah."

"I hope you're enjoying your stay so far."

"I'm having a lovely time," she said.

And that was one heck of an understatement.

Chapter Ten

On the agenda for the afternoon of Christmas Eve was a trip to a local palace, but Erin hadn't bothered to look it up, deciding she enjoyed the element of surprise. Lewis had been right about people enjoying not having to plan. Just turning up at the minibus at the appointed time really took all the stress away.

Today, Erin had automatically taken the passenger seat in the minibus and felt a bit special that she got to sit up at the front.

"What's the name of this palace again?" she asked.

"Blenheim." Lewis didn't take his eyes off the road. "Birthplace and home of Sir Winston Churchill."

"Ooh, you sound as though you're in tour guide mode. What year was it built?"

"Really? You're going to test my knowledge?"

"Yeah. I suspect you said that thing about Churchill to sound knowledgeable but that's the sum of all your knowledge about the place."

He cast her a quick glance before putting his attention back on the road. "It was built between 1705 and 1722."

"That took them a while," she mused, making Lewis chuckle. "Who owns it now?"

"The twelfth Duke of Marlborough."

"And his name is?" She crinkled her nose, sure she'd catch him out soon.

He hesitated for a moment. "Charles James Spencer-Churchill. But he doesn't own the land, just the palace. So he has to pay rent on the land."

"Who owns the land?" Now she was genuinely curious.

"The king."

"Which king?"

"King Charles. How many kings do we have?"

"So the most recent Mr Churchill has to pay rent to the king?"

"Yep."

She stared ahead, watching the brake lights from the traffic. "It's impressive if all that is true, but you could easily have made it up, knowing I'd have no way to verify."

"No way to verify?" He gave her another sidelong glance. "I don't know if you've ever heard of it, but there's this thing called the internet."

His teasing warmed her insides and she reached out to give his leg a friendly tap. "How do you know all those facts?"

He gave a one-shouldered shrug. "I'm taking a group there, so I thought I should swat up."

"Are you actually going to give a proper tour?"

"No. But just in case someone asks questions. Thanks for asking and making my research worthwhile."

"You're very welcome."

He slowed with the traffic at the turnoff to Blenheim Palace. "To be honest, I already knew it."

"How come?"

"It just interests me. We did a project about it at school and it was one of those things which grabbed my attention. The queen owned the land back then."

Erin smiled at him, then got distracted when he pointed through the windscreen.

"Wow! It's huge." Huge, and beautifully lit, giving the honey-coloured stonework an enchanting glow.

"Bigger than Buckingham Palace," Lewis told her.

"Does someone actually live there?"

"Yes." He joined the queue of cars crawling into the car park. "It's hard to imagine, isn't it?"

She nodded. "I'll bet it's draughty."

"I'd say so," he agreed. "Awful place to live. We should probably feel sorry for them."

"We should. Poor people in their massive, draughty palace."

Five minutes later, Lewis handed out tickets in the car park and gave his usual spiel about what time to meet for the drive home.

"Three hours sounds like a long time," he told them. "But there's lots to see. I recommend looking around the palace first and *then* the light trail around the gardens when it's darker. Save the markets for last in case you run out of time. Enjoy!" As the group dispersed, he reached for Erin's arm. "Let's give them a head start so we don't keep bumping into them in the palace." A flash of panic hit his eyes. "Sorry. That was presumptuous. Of course, you can also get a head start on me if you'd like."

"No." Butterflies erupted in her stomach at his assumption that they'd go around together. "I'd really like to go around with you."

"Yeah?" His shoulders drooped. "Are you sure? Because you don't need to be polite. If you'd rather go alone, just say so. You did say you're quite happy doing things alone."

"Yes. But I also like company when I have someone fun to hang out with."

"Well, I'm definitely fun," he said, then bounced on the balls of his feet as he looked across the car park.

"What's wrong?" Erin asked.

"Nothing. I'm just excited."

"I take it you've been before?"

"Yes, but they transform the palace every Christmas with a different theme. This year is Peter Pan."

Okay, now she was excited too. "We could just set off slowly," she suggested.

They needn't have worried about the whereabouts of the rest of their group. Inside the palace doors it was difficult to register anything other than the scene before them. The sound of Christmas carols interwoven with melodies of Peter Pan instantly brought a smile to Erin's face.

Instead of a star on top of the enormous Christmas tree in the entranceway, a figure of Peter Pan stood proudly – one hand on his hip and the other holding his sword aloft as though inviting them inside. Nearby, a Tinker Bell ornament was suspended in mid-air, her dainty hand outstretched as she blew pixie dust over the tree ornaments.

"Oh, my goodness," Erin whispered, not sure where to look as her eyes feasted on the combination of the majestic palace architecture and the dazzling Christmas decorations.

"It's amazing, isn't it?" Lewis said, close beside her.

Amazing, didn't quite do it justice and Erin's mouth hung agape as they wandered from one room to the next. Everywhere she looked were evergreen garlands and shimmering fairy lights, and woven into them, iconic scenes from Peter Pan. In one room, Peter Pan's shadow was projected onto the walls of the children's bedroom. Visitors stood and watched in wonder as it fluttered around the room.

Each room they entered offered a new scene, from Wendy reading a Christmas story to the Lost Boys around a crackling fire, to a moonlit Mermaid Lagoon.

In a long hallway, floating lanterns hung from the high ceiling, mimicking the stars of Neverland with Peter Pan and Wendy flying between them.

"It's just incredible," Erin murmured feeling the back of Lewis's hand brush against hers as they stood gazing up at the scene. "I can see why you were so excited."

"Every year I think they can't possibly come up with a better theme than the last, but they always do."

Erin checked her watch to find more than an hour had passed with her barely noticing.

"We should go outside and check out the light trail," Lewis said. "We don't want to miss that."

"I don't see how it can be better than this," Erin said, but followed him anyway, catching the amused twitch of his lips.

The gardens, as it turned out, were just as breath-taking as the interior of the palace. Multitudes of lights led them through the immaculate grounds. Trees and lawns glowed brightly and hedges were draped in twinkling lights. They wandered through a tunnel of lights, and craned their necks to view colour-changing stars hanging from tree branches.

Larger than life illuminations continually drew the eye, and all the while, festive music floated on the air. Erin felt the magic of Christmas seep into her every pore.

Once again, her time was enhanced by Lewis's company. They pointed things out to each other and every now and again, she caught his eyes on her and had the feeling he was enjoying her reaction as much as the experience itself.

"This is the best bit," he told her eagerly as they rounded a corner and the lake came into view. Wandering closer they found a spot among the spectators and stood shoulder to shoulder to watch the glow of lights reflecting on the surface of the water. A moment later water shot up from a hidden jet, illuminated in mid-air by light from below. More jets erupted and sleek arcs of water danced above the lake, the bursts of light synchronised to a soundtrack of classic Christmas carols.

The sequence must have lasted five minutes and when it began again, Erin remained rooted to the spot. After watching the show three times, she shifted her weight and wiggled her toes in the hopes of increasing blood flow and warding off the cold.

"It's incredible, isn't it?" Lewis asked, cheeks rosy from the cold. "If it wasn't absolutely freezing, I could stand here all night."

"Me too." Shivering, Erin automatically turned towards him. All her instincts pushed her closer, his body heat like a magnet.

She only realised just how close she was when she looked into his eyes to find their faces inches apart. He made no signs of moving, but traced his gaze over her face, lingering on her lips in a way that made her mouth inexplicably dry.

She'd only have to move a matter of centimetres to kiss him. The thought made her breath catch and her stomach flip.

"I guess we should move," Lewis said, putting enough space between them that thoughts of kissing him were put aside.

"Do we need to get back to the bus?" she asked, having lost all sense of time.

"We've got a little while left," he said, as they fell into step again. "Let's see what else we can find."

Erin nodded, feeling slightly foolish that she'd almost kissed him. But also, desperately wishing she'd seized the moment.

Chapter Eleven

"We've got about twenty minutes until we need to be back at the bus." Lewis pointed at the collection of wooden huts. "We could have a look around the market." His eyes narrowed. "Or..."

"*Or?*" Erin asked, but he was already leading her in the other direction with a huge grin on his face. "Where are we going?" He seemed to be moving in the direction of the impressive Santa's grotto in a small log cabin. Outside was a long line of excited children with their parents.

"We have time for a quick visit to the big man," Lewis said.

"I don't mean to dampen your enthusiasm, but there's a huge queue. Also, we're grown adults."

"It's okay," Lewis told her. "I know the elf. We can jump the queue."

"Jump the queue?" she asked, pulling on his arm to slow him down, but being rather ineffective. "You mean make all these children wait even longer?"

"We'll be in and out in a couple of minutes," he said confidently. "Just enough time to sit on his lap and tell him what we want for Christmas."

"I'm not sure that's allowed these days," Erin said.

He laughed, then waved to get the elf's attention.

She walked quickly over to them. More of a waddle really due to her fancy green boots, which curled at the toes and emitted a dainty jingle from the shiny bells on the end. Her tights were green and white striped below her green tunic. The buckle on her belt was shiny and gold, and maybe it was the effect of the circles of red blusher on her cheeks, but the elf looked positively ecstatic at the sight of Lewis.

She launched herself at him so hard that she ended up off the ground when she landed in his arms.

"You're here!" she squealed. "I didn't know you were coming. Why didn't you say?"

"I was bringing hotel guests and didn't know if I'd have time to stop by. Besides, I always enjoy the element of surprise."

"It's good to see you," she said when he set her back on the ground. Confusion flashed in her eyes as she looked at Erin.

"This is my other sister," Lewis told Erin. "Carla, this is Erin. She's staying at the hotel over Christmas."

"You were at Anna's workshop!" Carla said excitedly.

"Yes," Erin said, feeling oddly nervous at the thought that they'd been talking about her.

Her nerves dissipated when Carla flung her arms around her. "It's great to meet you," she said and squeezed Erin hard before she released her. It was clear what Lewis had meant about his sisters being very different on a confidence level.

"Any chance we can sneak in and see the big fella?" Lewis asked.

"I reckon I'd be in trouble with him if I didn't let you in," Carla said, then looked at the family who were next in line. "I'm really sorry," she said. "There's going to be just a few minutes longer to wait."

Erin felt decidedly uncomfortable at pushing in front of all the small children. She looked at the mother beside her to offer an apologetic smile, but the woman's eyes were on Lewis.

"Oh, hello!" she said brightly. It seemed they were in luck and he knew her, too.

"Hi," Lewis said, the uncertainty in his feature suggesting he couldn't remember her name. A situation Erin always dreaded.

"Billy!" the woman said, pushing the tallest of her two boys in front of her. "This is the lovely man who sponsors your football team. Can you say thank you to him?"

The poor boy looked confused as he dutifully muttered his insincere gratitude.

"It's actually the hotel," Lewis said. "But you're very welcome."

"You're very generous," the woman went on, gazing at him with what Erin could only describe as a look of awe. "They were absolutely thrilled last season to get the shirts with their names on the back. And their Christmas party was all paid for by your sponsorship."

"The hotel," Lewis said again. "But like I said, you're very welcome, and they had a brilliant season, so they earned their party. Anyway, would you mind very much if we nipped in front of you? I promise we won't be long."

"Of course," the mother said. "You go in."

Another elf was leading a couple and their baby out of the cabin when Lewis and Erin slipped inside.

The entire room was magical, with the scent of pine and cinnamon permeating the air. A large, cosy rug covered the floorboards in front of the fake fireplace where stockings hung from the mantel. In the corner, a Christmas tree twinkled with glittering ornaments and gentle fairy lights. Wooden toys adorned the shelves which lined the walls, and Erin's eyes darted all around, captivated by every detail.

Santa's costume had the same exquisite quality and attention to detail that the elf costumes had. Even from across the room, the deep red velvet coat with bright white fur trim looked so soft that Erin was sure she wouldn't be able to resist stroking it. Hopefully she wasn't about to get kicked out for inappropriately pawing Santa.

"Ho ho ho!" he said, in a wonderfully rich baritone. His beard was real, and he was without a doubt the most authentic-looking Santa that Erin had ever seen. His eyes twinkled as he rose from his plush throne-like chair. In a matter of seconds, he had Lewis in a bear hug so tight that Lewis croakily told him he couldn't breathe.

"What a brilliant surprise," Santa said, holding Lewis by the shoulders as he looked him up and down.

"Why are you looking at me as though you haven't seen me in a year? You saw me last week."

"Only briefly. And this is such a lovely surprise." His eyes flicked to Erin, and he said a cheerful hello.

"This is Erin," Lewis said quickly. "She's staying at the hotel."

He strode over, extending his hand.

"This is my dad," Lewis added.

"What?" Erin widened her eyes. "Your dad is Santa? You must have had such an amazing childhood!"

Santa laughed loudly as he enveloped her hand in both of his. "You're funny. Anna said you were lovely, but she didn't mention you being funny, too."

"Anna talked about me?" Erin asked, while glancing around Santa to catch Lewis grimacing with obvious embarrassment.

"Yes. Telling us how much she'd enjoyed meeting you at her wreath-making session."

"I had a great time." Erin squeezed his hand. "It's really nice to meet you."

"I'm Nicholas," he told her, his tone suddenly serious.

"No way!" Erin's eyes flicked to Lewis and then back to Santa. "Like jolly old St. Nick?"

"That's the one." He grinned. "My parents must have known I'd end up looking like Father Christmas."

"Is he winding me up?" Erin asked Lewis.

He shook his head. "That's his actual name."

"Brilliant," Erin said.

"We're going to have to go, Dad. You have a massive line of kids waiting to see you."

"You can't go yet. *You* already told me what you want for Christmas, but I need to know what Erin would like."

When his gaze landed on Erin, she stared back at him until she realised he was genuinely waiting for an answer. "Um... I don't know. I already know I'm getting a bath set, and the stay at the hotel is my main present. I don't really need anything else."

"I'll let you in on a little secret," he said, tapping the side of his nose. "Christmas isn't really about what you need. It's about what you want."

"I don't think there is anything I want," she murmured, but her eyes darted quickly to Lewis and then bounced away again. Her mouth went dry and the room felt suddenly sweltering.

Santa shook his head and walked back to his chair. "Always a conundrum when people don't know what they want. I have to figure it out for them." He rummaged in his sack and Erin exchanged an amused glance with Lewis. "Am I about to get a doll or a toy car or something?"

"Quite possibly," Lewis replied.

"Here we are. Just the ticket!" Santa's hand was outstretched when he came back to them, and Erin automatically reached out to take the small pieces of paper.

"Tickets to ride on the carousel," she said, staring down at them.

"It's just around the corner by the market stalls. Beautiful old thing. You'll love it."

"Thank you," Erin said, while Lewis shook his dad's hand.

"See you tonight," Santa said. "Don't be late!"

"I won't." Lewis stopped at the door and turned back. "When did I tell you what I wanted for Christmas?"

Santa tapped his nose. "I'm always listening."

"That could be worrying," Lewis said to Erin, on the way out. "Except my mum buys the presents. I'm not sure my dad has ever chosen a Christmas present for any of his kids."

"Same with my family," Erin said. "It's always mum that chooses."

Carla interrupted them, coming over to hug them both at once. "I'll see you tonight," she said as she released them, then skipped away to rouse the people in the queue into a chorus of jingle bells.

Erin bopped her head to the melody as they walked away. "What's happening tonight?" she asked.

"Midnight mass at the church down the road. Family tradition. I imagine a lot of the hotel guests will go too." He frowned. "I might have tried to cram too much into the schedule. There's also ice-skating after dinner this evening."

"That is a busy day," Erin remarked.

"I thought I'd try to fit a lot into the first two days because Christmas Day and Boxing Day will be very lazy."

"I think it's fine," Erin said. "People can always skip ice-skating if they're tired. It's a nice way to kill time between dinner and midnight mass, though."

"That's what I thought." He veered to the left. "The carousel is this way."

"Do we have time? If we need to get back to the bus--"

"It's Christmas!" Lewis cut her off. "It's not about what we *need* to do."

"Tell that to the people freezing by the minibus."

"They'll be fine. Besides, we still have a few minutes."

Erin's insides flooded with warmth at the sight of the vintage carousel, illuminated by strings of orange lights.

"Just in time!" a wiry young man called out as they

approached. "There's one spot left here." He patted the rump of the large horse.

"Um..." Erin glanced at Lewis.

"Don't worry," the man called out. "They easily fit two people. Up you get!"

"Okay," she told him, handing over the tickets and hauling herself up onto the horse to clutch the cool metal pole. The polished golden surface reflected the fairy lights overhead. "Come on," she said to Lewis, and he swung his leg up and over just before the ride shuddered to a start.

"I'm not sure where to hold on," he said beside her ear as the horse began to rise upwards.

"The pole." She pulled his arms around her waist and guided his hands to the pole. "That better?" she asked merrily.

"Perfect." The warmth of his voice against her ear sent a delicious shiver all the way up her spine.

The carousel horse whirred up and down as the ride moved around at a lazy pace. Christmas music floated in the air and Erin couldn't keep the smile from her face as she basked in the feel of Lewis's chest pressed against her back and his arms encircling her tightly.

It shouldn't have been surprising that Santa was exceptional at choosing gifts.

But he really had got it spot on.

Chapter Twelve

Maybe Lewis should be concerned about letting standards slip, given he was probably going to be late to meet the guests at the minibus. It would only be a couple of minutes though, and riding the carousel with Erin felt like a good reason to let standards slip a little.

There was a moment when he'd worried it might be awkward to share the horse, but then Erin pulled his arms around her waist and all the awkwardness vanished.

Her hair tickled his cheek, and he caught the citrusy scent of her shampoo. The feel of her pressed against him stirred something primal in him which he hadn't felt for a long time.

When she turned back to him with her radiant, unbridled smile all he could think of was how it would feel to catch her lips in a kiss.

"I feel like a kid again," she said, eyes dancing with joy.

The ride slowed and he suppressed the urge to kiss her. Before he knew it, they were alighting the horse and her body was no longer pressed against his. He missed it immediately.

"We better hurry," she said, leading the way through the crowd towards the car park.

"It's okay." He felt more relaxed than he'd felt in a long time. "It's not as though they can go anywhere without us."

"I suppose that's true." She pushed her hair off her face as she turned to him. "You're always so conscientious that I assumed you wouldn't want to be late."

"They've probably all been on the mulled wine and won't even notice. But I don't think being a few minutes late is the end of the world, anyway."

When the crowd became denser, he took the opportunity to reach for her hand, keeping tight hold of it as he shouldered his way through the knot of people mingling around the Christmas market.

When the crowd thinned he relaxed his fingers slightly, then waited to see if she'd pull away. His heart fluttered when she kept her fingers firmly entwined with his.

The walk to the car park wasn't long enough and there were only a few minutes before they broke apart to approach the bus. The other guests were all in high spirits and chatting amongst themselves. As he'd suspected, no one was put out at having to wait, and they filed onto the bus without comment.

"I loved the palace," Erin said, craning her neck to look back at it as Lewis manoeuvred the minibus out of the car park.

"It certainly has the wow factor," he said idly. Really, it had been watching her face as she'd taken it all in that had delighted him the most.

"I'm so impressed by the itinerary so far. The activities you picked are perfect."

"It was a group effort," he said. "But thanks. It seems the other guests are happy with it, too." He glanced in the rear-view mirror to see them all leaning over their seats as they engaged in a group discussion about the light show over the lake.

"I'm looking forward to ice skating," Erin said, drawing his attention again. "Although, I suppose when I end up with a bruised bum, I might not be so enthusiastic about the itinerary."

"Can't you skate?"

"No." She eyed him suspiciously. "You said that with the tone of someone who *can* skate."

"I do okay," he said. "Well enough that I don't tend to worry about bruising my bum."

She chuckled and pressed her head back into the seat, looking as though she might have a nap on the drive back. At intervals, his gaze flicked to her peaceful features and her golden lashes resting against pale skin.

It was funny to think that he'd only known her a matter of days. He felt as though he'd known her far longer, and spending time with her was fast becoming his favourite thing to do.

Once he'd delivered the guests back to the hotel for dinner, Lewis had a list of things to do before the ice-skating trip. It felt like a race against the clock as he went to fill the bus with diesel and then nipped into the office to make sure everything was in order for the upcoming hotel bookings. After that, he went to the kitchen to check in with the chef and make sure there were no issues back there. As usual, Warren had everything in hand and even insisted on feeding Lewis, despite still being in the middle of the dinner rush for the guests.

By the time he was heading to the lounge, where the group was waiting to go ice skating, Ivy had just arrived for her shift.

"I was on time," she told him proudly.

"Well done!" She often arrived a few minutes late, but she was otherwise so efficient that the staff were happy to cover for her until she arrived. "I'm off out again," he said, pointing a thumb at the waiting group.

"Have a good time," she said. He was turning away from her when he caught the flash of nerves in her features.

"What's wrong?" he asked.

"Nothing." Her voice was excessively cheery. "Why would anything be wrong?"

"You seem nervous."

"Nope. Everything is fine here. Off you go."

He stared at her, trying to figure out what was going on, when he caught a shuffling noise from somewhere around her feet.

After holding her gaze for a moment, he stepped towards the desk and peered over it.

"Sorry," Ivy whispered, her voice strained.

Lewis leaned further over the desk to catch the eye of the little girl sitting by Ivy's legs. "Hi, Poppy."

"Hi, Lewis." She lifted her gaze. "Do I have to keep hiding, Mummy?"

"No," Ivy replied. "You can come out."

"Were you intending to hide her down there for your entire shift?" Lewis asked.

"No." Ivy grimaced. "Just until you left."

That stung. "Why?" he asked accusingly.

"Because you'll try to fix this, like you always need to fix everything. But I will figure this out. It's fine."

"What happened?" he asked quietly.

"I had a minor problem with childcare, but I'll call around and find someone to pick her up."

"I have to go to bed early tonight," Poppy said, walking around the desk and looking up at Lewis with her adorable big brown eyes. "If I'm not in bed, Santa won't come."

He smiled and rested a reassuring hand on her messy brown hair.

"I thought you were staying at your mum's tonight," he said to Ivy. He'd specifically asked if she needed the night off and she'd said it was fine because they were staying with her mum and Poppy would be more than happy with grandma putting her to bed.

"Dad's not doing great," she said quietly. "Mum had to go over to the care home."

"Is he okay?"

Her nod had a manic edge to it. "He'll be fine."

Lewis sighed, thinking of how hard it was for Ivy and her mum to watch her dad's slow deterioration with dementia.

"Can you call around the staff and find someone to cover for you here?" he said eventually.

"I tried, but it's Christmas Eve. Everyone has plans. Don't worry, I'll figure something out."

Lewis looked down at little Poppy and felt his chest constrict at the innocence in her eyes. He ran his hand over her hair, trying to come up with a plan that would keep the magic of Christmas alive for her and wouldn't involve her sleeping in the hotel lounge, surrounded by slightly boozed up guests, until Ivy's shift ended. The problem was there weren't enough staff working for Ivy to go home.

"Mum might pick her up once Dad is settled again," Ivy said. "I just didn't want her to feel that pressure on top of everything."

"Of course not," Lewis mused while his brain whirred.

"Don't look like that," Ivy said. "You look as though you're trying to figure out how to solve this, but I don't need you to. All I need you to do is go and have fun."

"Where are you going?" Poppy asked him.

He hesitated for a moment. "I'm going ice skating. Would you like to come?"

"Lewis!" Ivy growled, but he only shrugged. He didn't see why it was a problem. In fact, it seemed like the perfect solution.

Poppy bounced on her toes. "Can I, Mummy? Can I? Please!"

"No." Ivy glared at Lewis. "You're working. You can't look after Poppy as well. She'll be fine here. I'll give her a colouring book and some crayons."

"I don't want to do drawing again, Mummy," Poppy whined.

"It's Christmas Eve," Lewis said. "I'll take her with me and when we get back you can take her home."

"I'm down to work until eleven."

"I know. I'll cover for you."

Ivy massaged the creases on her forehead. "I don't need you to rescue me, you know?"

"I realise that. Now can we skip to the part where you give me your car key so I can get Poppy's booster seat?"

"Can I really come ice skating?" Poppy asked.

"Yes." He scooped her into his arms and gave her a quick squeeze. "Where's her coat?" he asked when Ivy handed over the car key.

Ivy reached under the desk and retrieved a purple puffer jacket. "Her hat and scarf are in the arm and the gloves are in the pockets."

"Perfect." Lewis wiggled his eyebrows at Poppy. "Let's go skating!"

She giggled and waved goodbye to her mummy.

"Lewis?" Ivy called as he turned to move away.

"Yeah?"

"Thank you," she said, eyes brimming with emotion.

"Bye, Mummy!" Poppy called as Lewis turned to the guests, who were happily chatting away in the lounge.

All except Erin, who was standing alone and had her eyes fixed on him. Her expression was unreadable, but he had the impression she'd been following his conversation with Ivy and couldn't help but feel a little self-conscious.

He cleared his throat to get everyone's attention. "Your chariot awaits," he told them with a wide smile.

Chapter Thirteen

Following the crowd out to the minibus, Erin kept her eyes on Lewis, who was making the little girl on his arm giggle the entire time.

While the rest of the guests filed into the back of the bus, she lingered by the passenger door. "Can I still sit in the front?" she asked when Lewis reappeared, carrying the girl's car seat and her coat. She looked to be about five or six and spent most of the time looking adoringly at Lewis. Erin couldn't fault her on that score.

"You can if you won't be intimidated by sitting next to a princess." After positioning the booster seat on the bench, he turned to lift the giggling little girl in.

"I'm not a princess," she said, eyes shining with joy.

Lewis screwed his features into a frown. "I was sure you were a princess. Princess Poppy, isn't it?" He winked at Erin as she hopped up beside Poppy.

"You're telling me you're really not a princess?" he said when he slid into the driver's seat a moment later.

"No." Poppy let out a dainty shriek of laughter. "I'm not a

princess. Mummy calls me Princess sometimes, but I'm not a real princess."

"Hmm." Lewis pulled her seatbelt around her and looked at her dubiously before turning in his seat to check that everyone was settled in the back.

"Are you certain you're not a princess?" he asked when he pulled onto the main road.

"I'm not!"

"Do you have proof of that? Some kind of identification which says you're not a princess?"

"No," Poppy said, gazing up at him.

"Then how do we know for sure?"

With a delighted smile, Poppy leaned her head towards him. "You're very funny, Lewis."

"Thank you. Maybe once you're a queen, you can hire me as your court jester."

"What's that?" she asked in awe, while Erin grinned at the adorable exchange.

"It's someone the queen hires to make jokes. That would be my job. To make you laugh."

"But you work in the hotel," she told him seriously.

"That's true. I didn't even think about that. You'll make a great queen because you think of everything." He paused. "Are you looking forward to ice skating?"

Erin had been so caught up in their playful conversation that it took her a moment to realise he was talking to her.

"I don't know," she told him, catching his eye over Poppy's head. "Kind of. I'm excited about watching other people skate, anyway."

"Have you ever skated before?"

"Yes. A few times when I was younger, but I could never get the hang of it."

"You'll give it a go though?" he asked.

"Yeah," she said hesitantly. "I'll probably shuffle around for a couple of laps and spectate for the rest of the time."

"I can't skate very well either," Poppy said. "I went with my mummy one time but I kept falling over. But there are penguins you can hold on to and they help you not fall over. Maybe you can get a penguin, too." She looked up at Erin with concern in her eyes.

"I think they're just for kids."

"I think so too." Poppy turned to look at Lewis. "Does it take a long time to get there?"

"No, not too long."

"We won't stay for very long, will we?" Poppy asked. "Because I need to be in bed early or Santa won't come."

"Don't worry, you'll be in bed in plenty of time."

"What did you ask Santa for?" Erin asked.

"Popcorn," she replied flatly.

Lewis caught Erin's eye, then looked at Poppy. "Popcorn?" he asked.

"Yes. I love popcorn."

"Me too." Lewis slowed at the junction and stayed quiet for a moment while he concentrated on the road. "Is that all you asked for?" he finally asked.

"No. I also asked for some sparkly hair things like I saw in a shop. And new paints. And most of all I want a bike, but Mummy said that's a big present and Santa can't always bring big presents. She said I shouldn't get excited about a bike in case Santa can't manage it this year."

A muscle in Lewis's jaw flexed but he kept his eyes on the road. "I hope he manages it," he said.

"Me too." Poppy banged her hands on her knees in her excitement. "I want one with a bell and a basket, but I don't care what colour it is. Just not black because that's the worst colour." Her eyes lit up and she pointed out of the window at an elaborately decorated house with a Santa figure climbing the wall. Her attention was on the festively decorated houses after that, and she seemed to forget all about the bike.

Judging by Lewis's frown, Erin suspected he was still thinking about it.

❄

The ice-skating rink was stunning. A large Christmas tree was all lit up in the centre with the icy track forming a ring around it.

In his usual easy manner, Lewis led the group through the admission gate and to the small hut where ice skates were doled out. The first pair that Erin tried were too small and then she seemed to take forever to get herself laced in. The rest of the group was already on the ice when she made her awkward waddle to the rink.

A jolt of nerves hit and Erin had the thought that maybe she should go straight for the mulled wine and enjoy spectating rather than risking her neck and her pride.

She gave herself a mental shake and a small pep talk about a sense of adventure, then she stepped onto the frozen arena and felt her legs wobble immediately. She grabbed the rail and avoided falling, but it was a close call which did nothing for her confidence.

Automatically, she looked for Lewis, relieved to find his focus was on Poppy and hadn't witnessed her Bambi impression. With one hand clutching the rail, she shuffled along while thinking that a sense of adventure was an over-rated quality.

"Hello!" Poppy called, passing her while clinging to her penguin and making an odd running motion.

"Hi!" Erin replied.

"You okay?" Lewis asked, turning in an impressive movement, and gliding backwards to speak to Erin.

"Fine." She aimed for a confident smile, but wasn't sure it would fool anyone. "Just finding my feet."

Smiling, he turned to face forward again and escorted Poppy around the track. Erin hadn't got very far when they came around again.

"Do you want some help?" Lewis asked. "I could give you a few pointers."

She opened her mouth to say she'd take all the pointers she could get when a guy called out to Lewis.

"Sorry," he said. "One sec." He sped up and then halted at the edge of the ice to reach across the barrier and shake the guy's hand. Then he turned to check on Poppy. "I'll catch you up in a minute," he told her, and she grinned at him before continuing her odd march on the ice. He stayed chatting to the guy, and Erin continued her undignified shuffle while clutching the rail.

With Lewis now blocking her path, if she continued, she'd have to use him for support at the point where he blocked the rail. And while she didn't dislike the idea of having her hands all over him, she suspected it would be more than a little embarrassing. Besides, everyone else was managing to make their way around the ice without too many problems.

Apart from the handful of people who were taking her approach of clinging to the rail – and the ones who kept landing on their bums. If she didn't focus on *them,* it definitely seemed like something she should be able to manage.

With a rush of courage, she pushed off from the edge and into the wilderness.

She didn't immediately fall on her bum or do the splits, and her wobbly legs seemed to grow in confidence. After half a lap, she even glanced around to take in the atmosphere.

It was odd really, that ice could create such a cosy vibe.

Her gaze snagged on Poppy, a little ahead of her, and she caught the flailing of her legs before she landed on her knees with the penguin stopping in front of her. Instincts had Erin moving in Poppy's direction, though she wasn't sure she'd be effective at helping her. She could at least provide moral support.

A bigger boy glided over to Poppy before Erin could get there. A young teenager. Sweet of him to help.

Erin's blood pulsed harder when she realised that wasn't his intention at all. He swiped the penguin and took off without a backwards glance.

If Erin could skate, she'd be having a word with him, but all she could manage was to slide awkwardly to Poppy.

"Are you okay?" she asked, leaning a little, but not sure she could bend down too far.

"I fell over and a boy took my penguin," Poppy cried.

"I saw. The big meany. I don't think Santa will bring him any toys." She frowned, knowing that wasn't the way the world worked. "Are you hurt?" She glanced around for Lewis, who was still deep in conversation.

"I just bumped my knees, but I can't skate without the penguin."

"A few minutes ago I thought I couldn't skate without holding the rail, but I gave it a go and it wasn't as bad as I thought."

"Can you help me?" Poppy asked.

"I can try." She held out her hand, then almost crashed to the ice when Poppy pulled on it.

After some wobbling, they were both upright. Poppy began with her stamping again.

"I don't think you should lift your feet up," Erin suggested. "Try pushing them forwards instead."

"I'm not good at that," Poppy said. "Lewis tried to teach me already."

"Just push one foot forwards," Erin said.

Poppy did as she was told and then grinned up at Erin.

"Hey!" Lewis sped around them, then turned to skate backwards just ahead of them. "Did you get too good for the penguin?"

"A big boy stole it," Poppy told him grumpily.

"What?" Lewis scanned the rink. "Which boy? Where is he?"

"There." Poppy pointed across the ice to the boy, who was laughing with his friend while they pushed the penguin around.

"I'll be back," Lewis told them before he took off with impressive speed. Erin couldn't help but smile at the way Poppy gasped when Lewis crunched to a stop in a way that threw up ice all over the shocked adolescent. She couldn't hear what Lewis said, but the boy quickly gave up the penguin and skated sheepishly away with his friend.

A moment later, Lewis was back and positioning the penguin in front of Poppy.

"Thank you," she said, staring up at him with pure adoration.

"You're welcome." He skated beside her and looked over her head at Erin. "Thanks for helping her."

"Of course. That big kid is lucky I can't skate, or he'd have more to worry about than a little spray of ice."

Lewis grimaced. "I probably shouldn't have done that."

"We enjoyed it," Erin said. "Someone needed to teach him a lesson."

"Speaking of lessons..." He looked at her shuffling feet and his lips twitched in amusement. "You need to relax your knees, don't keep them locked up."

"It's the fear that's keeping them locked up," she told him, while attempting to put a little bend in her knees. The front of her blade caught in the ice and she would have fallen if she hadn't grabbed hold of the penguin for support.

"Sorry," she said to Poppy.

"That's okay. I think it's easier to skate if you hold hands. You were better when you held my hand."

"That's true," Lewis said, suddenly right beside her and taking her hand. Even through their gloves, the feel of his touch was heavenly. "Stop trying to push off with the front of the blade," he told her. "Keep your weight over the middle of your blades and imagine you're a penguin."

"Excuse me?" She exchanged a silly look with Poppy.

"Waddle!" Lewis said. "Shift your weight from one leg to the other as you lift each foot."

"Weirdly, that makes sense."

"And don't look at your feet," he told her as she looked down.

"How am I doing?" she asked a moment later.

"Better," he said, then turned to Poppy. "I'm going to take Erin for a spin," he told her. "We'll be back in a minute. If anyone tries to take your penguin, scream as loud as you can. Okay?"

"I can scream very loudly," she told him.

"Good girl." He pushed off, dragging Erin along as he picked up speed.

"A spin?" she asked. "I really don't think I'm capable of a spin."

"A lap around the rink," he said. "Not a literal spin."

"Glad we got that cleared up." She clutched his arm with both hands as he sped up even more. "No," she said. "No, no. Too fast! Lewis! Slow down!"

"I have everything under control," he said, but slowed down all the same.

"They should make penguins for adults," she said. "I'd feel much more confident pushing one of those around."

"Let go of me for a second," he said, easing her hands from his arm.

She was sure she'd fall from panic alone, but Lewis did his fancy move again and ended up directly in front of her. "Here," he held out both of his hands. "I can be your penguin."

"I don't understand how you can skate backwards," she told him, feeling instantly more secure as she took his hands. "How did you learn to skate so well?"

He glanced behind him. "Anna was into figure skating for a while and she used to drag me along with her twice a week."

"Drag you?" Erin asked sceptically.

"I guess I enjoyed it too."

"So you really can spin around the ice?"

He squinted, looking wonderfully bashful. "When I was a kid I could. I had no fear and I think that's half the battle with ice skating. Anna used to get annoyed because I was better than her."

"I can imagine that would have been annoying. Whenever I was better at something than my sister it drove her crazy. She's still the same as an adult."

Lewis eased one hand from hers to turn back and skate beside her as they approached Poppy. "No offence, but your sister sounds horrible."

"None taken," she said with a smile. "You have described her perfectly! Anyway, I think I'm going to quit while I'm ahead. Can you escort me to the edge? I'll grab a drink and watch from the side-lines."

As much as she was enjoying holding hands with Lewis, it felt like a good time to stop. She hadn't embarrassed herself, so she was feeling pretty good about herself.

Watching Lewis glide around the ice would surely keep her well entertained, too.

Chapter Fourteen

Maybe he was showing off a little for Erin's benefit, but Lewis was also just enjoying being out on the ice. Having Poppy with him turned out to be beneficial too. Once Erin had gone to get herself a drink, he developed a tactic of switching his attention to Poppy whenever anyone tried to get his attention. He could pretend she was asking him something to avoid getting stuck in meaningless conversations.

It was the problem with living in a small town. Everyone knew him, and everyone always seemed to want something from him – whether it was merely to pass the time of day, or ask inane questions about the hotel, or coax him into supporting some fundraiser or other. There was always something. And while he didn't entirely begrudge it, sometimes he just wanted to saunter around an ice rink and not think about anything else.

Poppy was good company as well. She was undemanding and brimming with positive energy.

Her eyelids started to droop as Lewis fastened her seatbelt for the drive home. By the time they reached the hotel she was out for the count and he waved the other guests off the bus before going around to the passenger side.

"Can I help at all?" Erin asked, lingering by the open door.

"It's fine," he said automatically. "Go inside and get warm. I'm going to transfer her straight to Ivy's car." He'd already messaged Ivy to tell her to come outside.

Poppy didn't stir when he lifted her from the bus. Erin hadn't moved either.

"I can grab the booster seat," she said, reaching into the passenger seat.

His instinct was to usher her inside since she was a hotel guest and should be relaxing, not helping. But it wasn't particularly easy to balance Poppy's sleeping weight while also trying to fish Ivy's car key out of his pocket. "That's actually really helpful," he told her. "Thanks."

Erin opened the car door and set the booster on the seat, then murmured something about Poppy's hat and whipped back towards the minibus.

"Did she have a good time?" Ivy said, appearing while he was buckling Poppy in.

"Yes."

"Thank you for taking her. You're the best."

He tried to smile when he straightened up, but something had been bothering him all evening.

"Did you buy her a bike?" he asked softly.

"What?"

"Poppy wants a bike for Christmas. Did you get her one?"

Ivy arched an eyebrow. "What are you going to do otherwise, go and buy her one? Because I'm not sure where you'll legally acquire a kid's bike at ten o'clock on Christmas Eve. And, by the way, maybe you should look after yourself from time to time instead of trying to take care of everyone else."

"Did you buy her a bike?" he said again, this time through gritted teeth.

"Yes." She gave a frustrated shake of the head. "Of course I got her a bike. Why would you even ask me that?"

"Sorry," he muttered, feeling terrible for doubting her. "Poppy seemed to think she probably wouldn't get a bike."

"Yes." Ivy's face broke into a gentle smile. "I let her think she might not get it, so she'll be even happier when she does."

That made sense. He should have thought of that. "Can you take a video of her opening it?" he asked sheepishly.

"Yes." Ivy flung her arms around him and gave him a big kiss on the cheek. "Have a great Christmas!"

"You too." He squeezed her tightly, then turned at the sight of Erin hovering in his peripheral vision.

"Sorry," she said, then held Poppy's hat out to Ivy.

"Thanks," Ivy said. "And thanks again for taking her. Happy Christmas!" She walked around the car, but paused after opening the driver's door. "By the way, there's a little problem with the decorations in the entranceway. Can you sort it out?"

"What kind of problem?" Lewis asked wearily. There was always something.

"They're falling down a bit. Right inside the door."

"And you couldn't possibly have fixed it yourself?" He was sure she'd had plenty of time while they'd been out.

Ivy turned her nose up. "I thought it would be better if you did it." She beamed at him and hopped into the car.

As the car pulled away, he gave Erin a sidelong glance. "I've known Ivy since we were about eight," he said.

She nodded. "I take it Poppy's father isn't on the scene?"

"No. He ditched Ivy when she was pregnant. She doesn't have an easy time of it." They paused outside the hotel entrance. "I try to help when I can, but Ivy isn't great at accepting help."

"Sometimes it feels easier not to rely on other people."

He opened his mouth to ask if she was the same way, but she seemed to anticipate the question and diverted the conversation.

"I guess you should see about the decorations that need fixing," she said, pointing at the door.

"I suppose I should."

He held the door for her and looked for the damage as soon as they were inside.

There was absolutely nothing wrong with the decorations. There was, however, a huge sprig of mistletoe directly above their heads.

Chapter Fifteen

Lewis wasn't entirely sure how long it was appropriate to stare at a bunch of mistletoe for, but he'd definitely moved past a mild interest in horticulture and was now bordering on oddball behaviour. The trouble was, as soon as he shifted his gaze, he had a decision to make.

Should he kiss her? Or should he roll his eyes and mutter something about Ivy being an idiot, then get back to work? Because Erin was a hotel guest so he shouldn't really be kissing her. Plus, there was work he should be doing. There always was.

"That's mistletoe," he said dumbly when the silence became unbearable.

"Yes," Erin agreed, so close that he'd only have to lean a little until they were touching. He really wanted them to be touching.

Except it would be sleazy of him to kiss a hotel guest in the foyer. Wouldn't it?

Part of him didn't even care. A quick glance told him there was no one around.

As uncertainty gripped him, he moved so his fingers brushed hers. Ever since they'd left the ice rink, he'd been missing the feeling of her hand in his.

"I think it's bad luck," she said, the tips of her fingers caressing his.

"What is?" His whispered voice came out with a weird rasp.

"If you don't kiss under the mistletoe. It's bad luck. Isn't that what they say?"

He nodded slowly. "It sounds right to me." Mostly, it sounded as though she wanted him to kiss her, which was all the encouragement he needed.

He took half a step, then bent his head. Her green eyes locked with his and he swore he could get lost in them for weeks.

Inching closer, her breath swept over his lips in a soft caress that felt as though it might drive him wild.

And then she shifted and kissed him so softly that it made his heart stop dead and then race so fast it made his head spin.

He closed his eyes, savouring the softness of her lips and hating that he could already feel her pulling away.

Desperately, he wanted to take her face in his hands and keep kissing her until they ran out of breath. But this flirtation between them wasn't destined to be anything more.

She'd be gone in a few days.

When she pulled back from the kiss, he kept his fingers entwined with hers, but resisted the urge to kiss her the way he really wanted to.

For a moment, Erin had thought he wouldn't kiss her at all. She'd contemplated continuing on her way and brushing the moment aside. But she'd had a glass of mulled wine and was feeling daring. She'd wanted to kiss him and when she did, it felt like the world stopped, just for a moment.

Her heart was beating furiously as she drew away, hoping that he'd pull her back and demand more.

He didn't, but he also didn't run away. His fingers tightened around hers and his eyes trailed over her face as though he were drinking in every detail.

"Thank you," she whispered.

His Adam's apple bobbed as he swallowed hard. "Thank you?"

"I didn't want bad luck on Christmas Eve."

He moved closer and slipped his free hand over her hip. "No one wants that," he said. "I'm feeling pretty lucky at this moment."

His hungry eyes landed on her lips and her breath caught in her throat as she anticipated another kiss.

"Lewis!" a high-pitched voice called, making him take a small step back and whip around.

"Yeah?" he replied, his voice just a little frosty.

Jenny looked terrified as she stood completely still on the other side of the room. "A man asked if he can take his whiskey up to his room and I don't know if that's okay?"

"Of course it's okay." Lewis gave a small shake of the head. "Why wouldn't it be okay?"

"Ivy mentioned that sometimes guests steal stuff, so I wasn't sure."

"It's fine." He still had his fingers curled around Erin's and she felt an odd sense of pride that he hadn't dropped it when they'd been disturbed.

He'd just turned back to her when another voice called out to him.

"Your mum called," the guy in his chef's whites announced across the room. "I'm supposed to tell you to make sure you go to midnight mass."

"Why did she call you and not me?" Lewis asked.

"She said you weren't answering."

Lewis pulled his phone from his pocket and grimaced.

"I'm going home," the chef said. "The kitchen is closed until tomorrow. I'll see you bright and early."

"I need to talk to you before you leave," Lewis told him. "Just wait for two minutes."

He raised a hand in salute and sauntered back the way he'd come.

"Sorry," Lewis said to Erin.

"It's fine. Go and get on with your work."

"Are you going to midnight mass?" he asked as his fingers finally slipped from hers.

"Yes."

"Great. I have some stuff to do around here first, but I'll see you there. My mum will kill me if I don't make it."

"Is your family religious?" she asked.

"No. Mum is just big on traditions."

"I'll see you later," Erin said, then watched him leave with a cascade of butterflies fluttering in her stomach.

"I just kissed Erin," Lewis said, completely flustered as he walked into the kitchen.

Warren leaned casually against the counter on the back wall. "The woman staying here? The one you were just in the lounge with?"

"Yeah. That's when I kissed her."

"Wow." Warren folded his arms across his chest. "Nice work."

"I shouldn't have, should I?" He paced beside the shining, stainless-steel countertop. "She's a guest, and it's weird, but there was mistletoe and we'd kind of been flirting."

"When were you flirting with her?"

Lewis paused his pacing and shrugged. "Since I met her."

"That's cool," Warren said.

"Is it? She's a guest at the hotel."

"She's also a grown woman and I assume a willing participant?"

Lewis shot his friend a look. Warren had been the head chef for the past three years and had become one of Lewis's closest friends in that time.

"I don't think there's a rule that says you can't kiss a guest. It's not as though you're going to get fired, is it?" He didn't leave room for Lewis to speak. "If having liaisons with guests was a sackable offence, I'd be long gone. Though I am discreet, so I'd get away with it."

Lewis glared at him. "Which guests have you had liaisons with?"

"I don't kiss and tell, mate, but I'm telling you it's fine."

"It felt weird," Lewis said.

"In that case, you were doing it wrong."

"Not the kiss. That didn't feel weird. That felt great. The situation feels wrong. Is it an abuse of power or something?"

"No. That'd be if she were an employee and you were her boss. But that's not what this is."

"Then why do I feel as though I'm doing something wrong?"

"Because you don't usually do stuff like this. I'm telling you, it's not a problem. It's Christmas, have a fling!"

"I really like her," Lewis said.

"More than just a fling?"

"I think so, but I only met her two days ago."

Warren unfolded his arms and shifted his weight. "Does she know about...?"

Lewis shook his head. "Not unless she heard from someone else. I haven't told her."

"You probably should. If you're thinking it's more than a fling, anyway."

"I don't know if it is more than a fling. Or if she even wants a fling. It was literally a quick peck under the mistletoe."

“No tongue?”

“No.” He sank his teeth into his lower lip. “Still a good kiss, though.”

“How long is she staying in the hotel?”

“Three more nights.”

“Okay, then use that time to get to know her better.” Warren grabbed his backpack from the counter and slung it onto his shoulder. “And for god’s sake, next time you kiss her, get some tongue action.”

“I’ll bear that in mind,” Lewis said as his friend exited through the back door.

Chapter Sixteen

The inside of the church was considerably smaller than it appeared from the outside. Midnight mass on Christmas Eve was obviously a popular service, which Erin should really have expected. All the pews were occupied when she arrived, and there was already a crowd standing at the back.

Briefly, she contemplated ditching the idea and heading back to the hotel, then decided it didn't make much difference if she stood. It was a short service, and she was only there for the carols and festive cheer. Also, it was late and she was sleepy after an eventful day – if she sat down she might nod off.

Among the throng at the back of the church, the atmosphere was wonderfully cheery. Everyone she looked at had a smile for her, and she felt a warm buzz as she surveyed the carol sheet in her hands.

"Sorry," a low voice said, somewhere over her left shoulder. People around her shuffled out of the way as the familiar voice apologised repeatedly. "If I could just slip past," he said, squeezing between Erin and the man beside her.

"Lewis!" she said, drawing his attention.

His smile was quick and genuine. "You didn't find a seat?"

"No. It was already packed when I arrived."

"It always is. My mum arrives about two hours early and takes over a pew for the family. I need to go and sit with them or she won't believe I was here."

Erin smiled. "I'll catch up with you after."

"Come with me."

Before she could protest, he took her hand and pulled her along behind him as he shouldered his way through the crowd. The vicar had just started speaking when they hurried hand in hand down the aisle, then darted to the left to join what appeared to be a full pew.

Erin had the definite feeling they were doing something they shouldn't as they dashed into the row at the last minute. Laughter threatened as she squeezed past people's knees. The wooden pew groaned as its occupants shifted to let them pass. When Lewis hissed at people to make space for them, he sounded incredibly rude until Erin realised he was speaking to his sisters.

"Hi," Erin whispered to Anna and then Carla as she squished past them. "Sorry," she said, almost sitting on Carla's knee as she sat in the small space beside her. She aimed a finger in Lewis's direction. "It's all his fault."

"I believe you. I blame everything on him. Also, I saw him dragging you down the aisle." Her eyes sparkled with mirth. "Which is funny because I've always told him that's the only way he'll get a wife."

While Erin stifled a laugh, Lewis reached over and shoved his sister's leg. "Try not to embarrass me for once in your life."

"I would never embarrass you," she replied cheerfully. "Not when you can manage it so well by yourself."

A hand reached around Lewis to get Erin's attention. "Hello! Or should I say Ho Ho Ho!"

"Hi!" Erin beamed at Lewis's Dad who was quickly shoved back against the pew by the woman beside him.

"This is my mum," Lewis whispered.

"Fiona," the woman said, smiling warmly, but only for a moment. Then she gave Lewis's arm a quick, sharp slap. "You should have told me you were bringing someone. I wouldn't have let that old couple sit in our row." She tipped her head behind her. "You should have seen the looks the woman was giving me for saving seats. Silly mare!" She leaned so far towards Erin that she was no longer in her seat at all, but hovering over her husband and son. "It's so nice that you came. Nicholas was telling me about you this afternoon. I hope you're enjoying your stay at the hotel."

"I'm having a great time," Erin told her.

"Lewis will be looking after you well, I'm sure. He's always good at looking after people." She patted his cheek, then turned at the sound of the woman along the pew shushing her. "Not got a lot of Christmas spirit, that lady," she said, her voice no longer a whisper.

"Sit down and be quiet, Mum," Lewis instructed her. "Some people want to listen to the vicar."

"Not me," Carla said in Erin's ear. "I'm only here for the singing."

"Me too," Erin replied quietly.

"I can't hold a note." Carla gave her arm a friendly nudge. "But what I lack in vocal ability, I make up for in volume. I apologise in advance."

Erin stifled a laugh and switched her attention to the vicar, who was talking about the spirit of Christmas. His monotone voice would have been difficult to concentrate on even if Lewis's thigh wasn't wedged against hers and monopolising her attention.

It was a really solid thigh. Which perhaps wasn't the most appropriate thought to have in church, but she couldn't help it. It was the vicar's fault really for not speaking dynamically enough. Of course, her mind would wander.

And wander it did. From his thigh to the memory of their moment under the mistletoe. It had been a really lovely kiss and she couldn't help but wonder if there'd be a repeat. Maybe if they walked back to the hotel together after the service, they might get another chance.

The congregation stood for the first song, breaking her thoughts.

Carla hadn't been exaggerating about the volume of her singing, and after her initial amusement, Erin decided it was the perfect time for unselfconscious singing. She joined in heartily, then almost got the giggles when she caught Lewis's eye. Maybe she should be self-conscious with him beside her, but she felt far too at ease with him. Despite having only known him a short time, she knew he wasn't the type of person to judge her for singing her heart out on Christmas Eve, even if she wasn't quite on key.

Once or twice she caught him exchanging an eye roll with Anna, but his mouth was fixed in a grin for the duration of the carols. As the vicar brought the service to a close, Erin felt a jolt of disappointment. She'd happily have sung all night if it would keep the amused grin on Lewis's face. Though she could also think of other ways to put a smile on his face. The thought made her cheeks flush as the congregation moved slowly out of the church.

Erin stuck by Lewis and was soon stepping into the frigid air and pulling her gloves from her coat pocket.

"I have to get back to the hotel," he told his family, who were gathered around him. His gaze met Erin's while he hugged Carla tightly. "Do you want to walk back with me, or are you going to hang around for a while?"

"I'll walk with you." She bunched her shoulders up in a show of being cold – as though the weather was determining her decision and not the thought of spending more time with Lewis, or the possibility of getting caught under the mistletoe again.

She grinned as she was embraced by Lewis's parents and Carla. Anna was more demure but offered a warm smile as she wished Erin a happy Christmas.

As she fell into step beside Lewis for the short walk back to the hotel, Erin pressed her gloved fingers to her cheeks, giving her facial muscles a micro massage to relieve the ache from so much grinning.

"Usually, I feel the need to offer some kind of apology to anyone who spends time with my family." Lewis cast her a sidelong glance that was brimming with amusement. "But you were almost as bad as Carla back there."

Her cheek muscles tightened again as laughter bubbled out of her. "Nothing wrong with getting into the Christmas spirit, is there?"

"Not at all. Maybe you and my sister could start your own choir."

"We are extremely talented singers," she said gleefully.

"I was thinking of a choir for enthusiastic singers rather than talented ones."

She knocked her shoulder against his, then hooked her arm through his elbow when he offered it.

They continued in silence and were nearing the hotel entrance when she cast him a surreptitious look and caught the twitch of his nostrils as though he was about to sneeze. Instead, he raised his hand to his mouth to smother a yawn.

"Sorry," he said, chuckling as she mirrored his yawn with a dramatic one of her own. "It's catching."

"Do you still have work to do?" she asked, wondering again at the long hours he worked.

"Not really."

Erin frowned as they reached the hotel. "How come you're going back to work, then?" It had seemed as though he'd been in a rush to get back, but maybe he'd just been making an excuse to get time alone with her.

"There's mulled wine and mince pies for the guests who've been to church," he said, destroying her previous notion. "The other staff will have set it all out in the lounge before they left so theoretically the guests could help themselves, but I'll hang around for a bit and make sure everyone is happy."

"You're very dedicated," she said idly as he pulled open the door.

Stepping inside, the warmth and the gentle Christmas music enveloped her while the mistletoe overhead drew her gaze like a magnet. When her eyes dropped to Lewis, he was standing right in front of her, his attention fully on her lips.

Her brain coaxed her to make a joke about how they should stop meeting like this, but she intercepted the message between her thoughts and her mouth. She didn't need a lame joke to break the atmosphere or make it clear she wanted him to kiss her.

All she needed was for her heart to calm down a fraction, so she didn't get too lightheaded.

His warm breath swept over her lips, but was whipped away by an icy breeze as the door opened.

"It was a lovely atmosphere," Mrs Ward was saying as she bustled inside with her husband behind her. The Cockney couple were hot on their heels and Lewis and Erin stepped back to make room for them.

"The vicar wasn't exactly brimming with charisma," the woman said as she plucked her bobble hat from her perfectly smooth hair. "It didn't even matter though with everyone belting out the songs. It really puts you in the mood for Christmas." She joined in with the music filling the room, launching into a tuneful rendition of *I'm Dreaming of a White Christmas* as she sashayed over to the lounge.

Mr Ward appeared beside Lewis. "I heard there would be more mince pies on offer after the service. I'm not about to be disappointed, am I?"

"Definitely not." Lewis's smile was all professionalism as he gestured across the room. "The chef has them waiting for you."

"Good," Mr Ward grumbled. "I went into the kitchen to ask the chef for the recipe this afternoon, but his response wasn't exactly polite."

"You know what chefs are like," Lewis said amiably as he led Mr Ward away.

"Downright rude, he was," he said, casting an accusing glance at Lewis.

"Sorry to hear that," Lewis said patiently. "Let's get you a drink and a mince pie." He was halfway across the room when he glanced back at Erin and discreetly rolled his eyes.

It made her laugh, and she followed him to the table laden with a large metal drink urn and plates of mince pies.

"Do you want wine?" he asked as he poured steaming liquid from the urn.

She didn't want anything to eat or drink, but hesitated before shaking her head. "I should get to bed." That was what she *should* do, despite her overwhelming desire to hang around, hoping to get a moment alone with Lewis.

He handed the steaming mug to the curly-haired woman beside him before turning back to Erin. "Sleep well," he whispered.

"Thanks." She took a step back, fighting the urge to change her mind about the drink. "You too."

As she ascended the stairs, she told herself she was imagining the feeling of being watched. That wasn't even a real thing. How could you feel someone watching you?

Only when she reached the top step did she give in to the urge to look back at the lounge.

Lewis was still standing beside the table of refreshments.

And his gaze was most definitely fixed on her.

The smile he gave her kept butterflies dancing in her stomach all the way to her room.

Chapter Seventeen

Thoughts of Lewis were swirling in Erin's head when she woke, just as they had been when she fell asleep. It was a long time since she'd had such an all-consuming crush and, at the corner of her mind, she felt a little ridiculous over the intensity of her feelings, given she'd only known him for a few days. It was Christmas, though, and there was magic in the air. That's what she told herself – determined not to ruin her good mood by overthinking things.

Plucking her phone from the bedside table, she joined in the group chat with her friends, wishing them a merry Christmas and then filling them in on her kiss under the mistletoe. They were appropriately excited for her, which made her feel less self-conscious about her Christmas romance.

Her smile slipped when a call from her sister replaced the group's messages on her phone. She could hardly ignore her only sibling on Christmas Day, but she couldn't deny the temptation to do just that. At least she was getting it out of the way early in the day.

"Hi," Zara said curtly. "Happy Christmas."

Erin returned the greeting with the same amount of cheer. None.

"How is it in the Cotswolds?"

"Great," Erin said, her lips pulling into an involuntary smile as she lay back against the pillows.

"Not too depressing on your own?"

"No." There was no way she'd mention Lewis, not least because her sister would get all smug about her needing a man to be happy. "I'm having a great time. The area is beautiful and you wouldn't believe the hotel."

Zara sighed dramatically. "I think it's rude that Mum and Dad wasted that gift on you. Jake and I would have made much better use of a romantic break."

Erin rolled her eyes. "You'd already arranged to spend Christmas with his parents."

"I might not have done if I'd known there was the option of a hotel stay. Not that they'd have bought that for us, anyway. It was like a charity gift because you're single."

"Thanks," Erin said, her voice dripping with sarcasm.

"Whatever. I was just calling to wish you a happy Christmas and say thanks for my present."

"Was it exactly what you wished for?" Erin asked mockingly.

"Ha ha." Her sister's tone held absolutely no humour. "I don't know why you can't send me a link to what you want instead of making me choose something for you. If you don't like your gift, you've only got yourself to blame."

Zara sent out a link to her wish list in October, along with strict instructions not to buy anything that wasn't on the list. It was the same ritual every year, and every year she got annoyed with Erin for not doing the same.

"I just think it's more fun to choose presents for people," she said, though she wasn't sure why she was wasting her breath. They'd had the same discussions so many times. She and her sister would just never see eye to eye on some things. Most things, come to think of it.

"Have you spoken to Mum and Dad today?" Zara asked, changing the subject.

"No, have you?"

"No. I thought I'd speak to you first. Get it out of the way."

Erin would be offended if she weren't so shocked by Zara's bluntness. In fairness, she'd had the same thought, but the difference between them was that she wouldn't come out and say it.

"That's nice," she said, annoyed by the bitterness that crept into her voice.

"You know what I mean."

"I think you made it quite clear what you mean."

"Why do you always have to make things into an argument?" Zara snapped. "This is exactly why I wanted to get this out of the way. Have a nice Christmas."

"I will," Erin said, hating the way they always brought out the worst in each other. "You should look up the hotel online," she added. "It really is the height of luxury. It was very generous of Mum and Dad."

A noise that sounded distinctly like a growl reached her ear and she felt a jolt of satisfaction at it.

"Happy Christmas, sister dearest!" Erin said sweetly.

"Same to you," Zara managed before she hung up.

Erin spent a few minutes relaying the conversation to her friends on the group chat before showering and heading downstairs for breakfast. The few guests in the dining room offered her a smile and wished her a merry Christmas. She had a pleasant chat with the waitress who took her order, and tried not to let her gaze drift too often to the door behind the bar.

It was where she expected Lewis to appear from at any moment. The anticipation of seeing him almost made her lose her appetite. Not quite though – the eggs benedict was so delicious they didn't require much appetite, anyway.

Maybe he wasn't even at work yet, she told herself when he failed to materialise.

When the door to the kitchen swung open, her gaze darted to the tall, broad chef. Maybe it was his heavily inked forearms, or maybe his overall bulk, but he had a slightly menacing air as he wandered behind the bar. Then he smiled at the barmaid and his eyes crinkled, taking away all his hard edges.

Erin returned her focus to her breakfast, but her ears pricked up when the chef spoke.

"Where's Lewis?" he asked the barmaid. "Don't tell me he's come in late for once?"

Erin kept her head down to avoid being caught eavesdropping, but distinctly heard the barmaid mention the office.

He was at work then...

Erin shook her head, telling herself to get a grip. Setting her cutlery neatly on her plate, she pushed it aside. She'd finish her coffee, then go upstairs and call her parents and put her crush out of her mind.

Chapter Eighteen

The words on the computer screen had blurred in front of Lewis. A knock came at the door and broke him from his trance.

"How come you're hiding away in here?" Warren asked, wandering in without waiting for a response to his knock.

"Had a bit of work to do." Lewis pointed at the computer screen at the exact moment that it went into standby, the email inbox disappearing into darkness.

"Why are you doing office work on Christmas Day?"

Lewis shrugged, not wanting to admit that he *was* hiding. After Erin had made a comment about his long working hours, he felt self-conscious. Not that it should matter if he came across as a workaholic, but he found himself caring about her opinion of him far too much. Also, he didn't want her to feel as though he was constantly there every time she turned around.

"Your friend is having breakfast," Warren said as he dropped into the chair across from Lewis. Given the time of day, it was odd for him to sit.

"Which friend?"

"You know."

"I'm going to need a clue..."

Warren sank down on the chair, an amused glint in his eyes. "How long are you going to pretend you don't know who I'm referring to?"

"I could keep going for a while," Lewis said, stifling a smile. "But I assume you mean Erin?"

"Yep."

"And you felt the need to tell me that because...?"

"Just in case you were wondering." Warren gave a small shake of his head. "Happy Christmas, by the way."

"Happy Christmas!" Lewis replied, while ignoring the urge to go and find something to do in the dining room.

"I got you something." Warren shifted in the chair to get a hand in his pocket, then threw a small, wrapped package unceremoniously onto the desk.

"Did you wrap this yourself?" Lewis joked as he looked at the scrunched red paper with what appeared to be one long piece of tape holding it together.

Warren's mouth twitched to a lopsided grin. "My skills are endless."

"Should I open it now?" Lewis asked. Given the way Warren had encouraged him to pursue Erin and his tendency towards joke gifts, Lewis was hesitant. Especially since it was approximately the size of a condom wrapper.

"You can open it," Warren said, with an encouraging dip of his head.

He pulled at the tape until the gaudy red paper fell away, leaving a keyring in his hand. Underneath the plastic cover was a photo of Lewis and Warren from the previous New Year's party at the hotel. It had been the first time Lewis had seen Warren tipsy, and he'd been surprised to find his friend was sentimental when inebriated. In the photo, he was attempting to plant a sloppy kiss on Lewis's cheek, but had ended up with Lewis's hand smothering his face.

"Cute, aren't we?" Warren remarked. "Turn it over."

The picture on the other side was a hand drawn pink love heart with the words 'best friends forever' in the centre.

"Everything about this makes me want to vomit," Lewis said cheerfully.

Warren nodded approvingly. "Exactly the vibe I was going for." He held out his hand in a beckoning gesture. "What did you get me?"

Lewis grimaced. "We don't usually exchange gifts."

"I know, but I told you I was getting you something. That was a hint that you should get me something so this wouldn't be awkward. Now stop messing around and give me my present."

Tempting as it was to wind him up further, Lewis leaned down to open the bottom drawer of the desk and took out a square box, which was wrapped much more artfully than Warren's gift.

"It's not actually something good, is it?" Warren's eyes flashed with panic. "I assumed you knew I'd get you something daft."

"Yeah. It's just a silly thing, too." So he wasn't sure why he felt a stab of nerves when he handed it over. They hadn't ever exchanged Christmas gifts before and it felt a little intense to watch Warren unwrap his present. "Just a mug," he stated dumbly, while Warren turned it over in his hand. On the side were the words 'World's Best Chef' – like the wording you might find on a novelty item, except this mug was handmade by a local potter who'd charged him way over the odds since he hadn't given her much notice.

While Warren continued to scrutinise it, Lewis wished he'd just gone for the novelty variety.

"That's really nice, mate." Warren's Adam's apple bobbed and it took him a moment to peel his eyes from the mug. "Thanks."

"You're welcome," Lewis muttered. He definitely should have gone with a novelty gift.

"I should get back to work." Warren cleared his throat as he stood. Then he stopped and held up his index finger as though he'd just remembered something. "I meant to tell you... Hopefully it won't be a big deal, but some geezer came into the kitchen yesterday..."

"Asking for your mince pie recipe?"

He winced. "Yeah. Did he make a complaint?"

"He told me you were rude to him. Couldn't you just have politely declined?"

"I did, but the stupid old—–" He cut himself off and looked thoughtful. "He started saying all this stuff about giving the recipe to his wife and about how her place was in the kitchen. That's when I not-so-politely told him to get out of my kitchen."

"Right." Lewis sighed. "Maybe you could just nod and smile the next time a guest annoys you."

"I know. Sorry." He was almost at the door when he turned back. "He reminds me a bit of my dad. That's probably why he got my back up."

Lewis gave him a sympathetic smile. He didn't know much about Warren's family, but he knew he'd always rather work over Christmas than spend time with them.

"Don't worry about it," he told him. "I think I smoothed things over."

"Thanks."

"No worries." He spun his new keyring around his index finger. "Thanks for this. I'll treasure it."

His tone was jokey, but when Warren closed the door behind him, he stared at the gift and the words on the back. Warren had arrived at a weird time in Lewis's life, and he hadn't anticipated back then, how close they'd become. Possibly that was a sad reflection on how much time he spent at work, but Lewis also knew he was way better off with Warren as a friend than the group he'd spent his time with before he'd taken over the running of the hotel.

That felt like a different lifetime now.

He sucked in a deep breath and dragged his thoughts back to the present.

Erin.

That was where his mind went, and he couldn't bear to hide away in the office a moment longer.

Chapter Nineteen

Lewis only managed to say a quick hello to Erin before she headed upstairs to call her parents. It was another couple of hours before she returned and took a seat at the bar. He poured her a glass of wine, then lingered to chat with her and was still there an hour later when the first guests arrived for their Christmas dinner. Lewis left the other staff to wait on them.

"I'm still pretty full from breakfast," Erin told him. She gave a little wave to Mr and Mrs Ward as they walked in and went straight to their table. "I usually don't bother with breakfast on Christmas Day to make sure I'm really hungry for Christmas dinner, but it seemed rude not to today."

"Definitely." Lewis wiped down the bar with a damp cloth. "Besides, you'll still manage the roast. It's so delicious that you don't even need to be hungry."

"That's true." She swivelled on her stool and surveyed the room. Lewis couldn't be sure, but he thought her gaze snagged on her table – set for one. "Do you know what's cool about eating Christmas dinner alone?"

"What?" he asked with a gentle smile, anticipating a joke.

"I know for definite I'll win the gift in the cracker. If I'm pulling it with myself, it's a sure bet that I get the bigger half."

"And the smaller half too," Lewis pointed out. "You will both win and lose."

"Oh, I didn't think of that," she said, smiling as she turned back to him.

Not for the first time, he wondered if it would be appropriate to invite himself to join her for lunch. He didn't have to wonder too much, since he already knew the answer. He worked at the hotel and she was a guest, so it definitely wouldn't be appropriate.

"Are you working for the whole day?" she asked, breaking his thoughts.

"Most of it. I'll take a break and visit my family later."

"Will you eat with them?" she asked. "Or do you eat here?"

"Um..." Was that a hint? Did she want him to eat with her? There was no way he could ask in case he was reading the signals wrong. And it would be inappropriate, regardless. "I'll eat at my parents' place, I guess."

As though she could sense he was talking about her, Lewis's phone rang with a call from his mum.

He made an apologetic face for Erin, then moved down the bar to answer it.

"Happy Christmas!" his mum crooned as though she hadn't already spoken to him twice that day.

"Happy Christmas," he echoed, with significantly less cheer.

"What time will you arrive? Anna is here already and Carla shouldn't be long."

"I'll try to get away soon."

"Also, I was thinking, why don't you bring your new friend?"

"Excuse me?" His eyes went to Erin. "What are you talking about?"

"Erin. Bring Erin with you."

"To your place? For Christmas dinner?"

"Yes. She seems lovely, and it must be weird for her, spending Christmas Day in the hotel. Bring her over here and she can have some good old family time."

Lewis glanced along the bar. He assumed Erin couldn't hear the conversation – or his mum's side of it, at least – but he couldn't be certain. If she *could* hear, she wasn't reacting.

"I think that might be a bit weird," he whispered, turning away from Erin.

"I don't see why."

"Because I hardly know her."

"You came running into midnight mass holding hands with her! Also, Anna said Erin doesn't know about your situation..."

"I met her a few days ago," Lewis pointed out. "I'm sure there's a lot we don't know about each other."

"It's good though, isn't it? She'll get to know you without any prejudice or anything."

"Prejudice," he echoed. "How come you make me sound like some hardened criminal?"

His mum's laughter rang down the phone and brought a smile to his face. "You know what I mean! Are you going to invite her for Christmas dinner, or what?"

"No. I already told you it would be awkward."

A frustrated growl emanated down the phone. "Is she there now?"

"Yes. Why?"

"Put her on the phone and I'll ask her. If it's too weird for you to invite her, let me do it."

"No way. I have to go, Mum. I'm really busy here, but I'll see you soon."

"Don't hang up on me. This conversation isn't finishe––"

"Bye." He cut her off and hung up.

As he walked back along the bar, Erin shot him a smile that

made him contemplate doing as he was told and inviting her to eat Christmas dinner with his family.

"Was that your mum?" she asked.

"Yeah. Asking when I'll be over."

"It's good that you can take some time off and hang out with your family. This is the first Christmas that I haven't spent with my family."

"How's it going so far?"

"It's actually fine." She raised her glass. "I'm enjoying myself."

"Glad to hear it."

Five minutes later, Warren walked out of the kitchen, giving Lewis a look he couldn't read before pouring himself a Coke. "Could you do me a favour?" he said. "Let your mum know I'm going to be very busy in the kitchen for the next few hours and that she shouldn't call me again."

"Why was my mum calling you?"

"To ask me to send you home."

"She just called me," Lewis complained.

"Apparently, she doesn't trust you." His lips twitched upwards and his eyes brimmed with amusement. "Also she said that she forgot to mention it, but you should invite Erin."

Lewis could have sworn the entire restaurant fell silent. "What?" he muttered, shooting Erin a nervous glance.

Warren addressed Erin with a smile. "She said she really enjoyed meeting you last night and that she wanted to invite you to eat Christmas dinner with them."

"At their house?" Erin held her wine glass awkwardly in front of her.

"Yes." Warren turned squarely to face her. "She was worried about you eating alone in the hotel."

"That's kind of her," Erin said, pressing her lips together.

"Lewis's mum is lovely. The whole family is. You'll have a great time. The food might not be quite as good as mine, but it won't be far off." He shot Lewis a look and wandered back to the kitchen.

Lewis didn't know what to say to fill the ensuing silence. Especially since his mind was busy conjuring ways to exact revenge on his mum and Warren.

Erin beamed at him. "What did you say to your mum to make her think I'm a charity case?"

"She doesn't think that." He scratched at his jaw. "She'll just think..." He trailed off, no idea where he was going with the sentence.

"Don't worry, I wouldn't intrude. I'm sure she was just being polite. Tell her thanks, but I'm quite happy here and that I'm being well looked after."

"She'll have been genuine," he said. "It wouldn't be an imposition. Christmas Day is an informal affair with my family."

"But you're going for a break from work; you don't want to take work home with you."

"It's fine with me."

She gave a small shake of the head. "It'd be weird, wouldn't it?"

"Maybe," he said, unsure whether she was just being polite or whether she had no desire to spend Christmas with him and his family. "My family is a bit mad."

"All the best families are." She sipped her wine. "You'd better go so you don't get in trouble with your mum. Tell her I said thanks for the invite. I'll see you later." She shot him a smile that hit deep in his core. "If you find me slumped in a corner, unresponsive, it'll just be a food coma. Nothing to worry about."

Chuckling, he walked out from behind the bar. "Enjoy your lunch." He was almost at the door when he hesitated. Maybe he should be a bit more heartfelt in his invitation. He hadn't even sounded as though he wanted her to come, so of course she hadn't agreed.

Or she just didn't want to. He pushed the door and walked

out. She'd said it was weird – how much clearer could she have been? Did he really want to be the idiot who got turned down on Christmas Day?

He grabbed his stuff from the office and was all the way into his car with the engine running when he realised he didn't care if he looked like an idiot.

Chapter Twenty

Again, Erin glanced at the table set for one and felt a heaviness in her stomach. Until then, she'd been feeling fine about her first Christmas without her family. The lively morning video chat with her parents had made her feel that she wasn't alone at all. Hanging out at the bar with Lewis had helped, too.

The invitation from his mum was sweet, and as soon as Lewis left, she wished she'd accepted it. That would have been awkward though, given how uncomfortable Lewis had seemed by the idea. And it probably would have been strange. Just because she felt so at ease with him didn't mean she should gate-crash his family Christmas.

It didn't matter now anyway. She'd sit and drink her wine, then stuff herself with food and maybe have a stroll around the village before relaxing in the lounge and watching the other hotel guests come and go.

Perhaps she might get to spend time with Lewis again later. And maybe there'd be some conveniently placed mistletoe--

"Erin?"

She almost jumped out of her skin. Her cheeks flushed as she looked up at Lewis, standing beside her in his coat. She reminded herself that even though he'd interrupted her thoughts, he wasn't a mind reader, so there was no need for her embarrassment.

"I was just wondering," he said. "Even though it might be a bit weird and my family are kind of mad... would you like to come?"

"Yes," she said, her lips stretching into an uncontrollable grin. "I'd love to."

"Really?" His shoulders drooped.

"Yes." She almost laughed at his expression. "Why do you look so surprised?"

"I just didn't think you'd want to. You know, due to all the weirdness and madness..."

"That doesn't bother me at all. Keeps things entertaining, I find."

"Yes. There is that."

"I had the impression you didn't want me to before."

"I just didn't know if it was a completely weird invitation. I'd really like you to come."

"Good." She slid down from the stool and instinctively touched his arm as she did. "I'll grab my coat," she told him.

He nodded. "I'll wait at the front door."

The twenty-minute drive to Bourton-on-the-Water was a treat in itself. Passing through the quaint villages with the gorgeous stone cottages had Erin enthralled.

Bourton-on-the-Water was also ridiculously beautiful. Low limestone bridges arched gently over the river that ran through the town while cottages and shops lined the quiet street beside the river. All of it was lit by the glow of fairy lights which draped over tree branches and webbed across the street.

"We don't need to stay too long," Lewis said when they

pulled up in a quiet cul-de-sac on the outskirts of the village. "They know I need to get back to the hotel later, anyway, but if you want to leave at any time, just let me know."

"You're making me nervous," Erin told him, unbuckling her seatbelt.

"Sorry." He smiled across at her. "No need to be nervous. You saw what they're like last night, so it's not as though you're expecting anything remotely civilised, right?"

"God, no. I hope not, anyway. Civilised sounds incredibly boring."

He stepped out of the car and they were halfway up the drive when the front door burst open. Fiona flung her arms wide as she burst into a loud rendition of *I Wish It Could be Christmas Everyday* while wiggling her wide hips.

She hugged them both together while still singing.

"What time did you start on the wine?" Lewis asked her.

Pulling back, she gave his arm a playful slap. "I'm not drunk – just high on Christmas spirit." She gave Erin another hug. "I'm so glad you joined us. I didn't like to think of you in the hotel alone."

"It's lovely at the hotel, but it's also great to get out for a bit. Thanks so much for the invitation."

"You're welcome."

"Let them come in out of the cold!" a deep baritone boomed from inside, right before Santa stepped into view. Lewis's dad, that was. Dressed in his Santa suit.

"Why are you wearing that?" Lewis asked, his expression hovering somewhere between amusement and embarrassment.

"I heard we had a guest coming." He wrapped Erin in a tight embrace. "So I thought I'd get my best Christmas suit on!" He squeezed Erin's shoulders. "Ho ho ho!"

The laughter bubbled up from her stomach and she couldn't have stopped it if she'd tried.

"Let's just be thankful it's not his birthday suit," Fiona muttered, ushering them inside.

Within minutes, Erin had a glass of fizz in her hand and was sitting beside Lewis on the soft, pale blue couch. From across the coffee table, Anna asked Erin about her job, and then her family. Nicholas listened intently from the armchair, while Fiona kept coming and standing behind the couch and briefly joining the conversation in between trips to the kitchen to check on the food.

"Someone find out how long Carla is going to be," she said, during a gap in the conversation. "The food is ready and she was supposed to be here ages ago."

Anna brought her phone to her ear and had a brief conversation. "She's almost here," she said when she ended the call. "Apparently there was some issue with a gift and that's why she's late."

"Sounds about right," Fiona said. "She was probably still finishing making them this morning."

Lewis leaned in Erin's direction. "Carla has a tendency to make gifts instead of buying things."

"That's cute," Erin said.

"It might be if she had any creative talent," Anna said and shared a knowing look with Lewis.

"If she's on her way, we can move to the table." Fiona made some elaborate arm gestures to get them moving. "Everything will be cold if we don't eat soon."

Erin stuck beside Lewis as they went into the large kitchen with a solid farmhouse-style table all decked out in the centre of the room.

They'd only just sat down when the sound of the front door opening reached them. Carla called out a greeting.

"In the kitchen," Fiona called back. "You're late."

"Not my fault!" she shouted. To Erin's ears she sounded

angry, but she'd only met her briefly, so maybe it was her normal tone of voice.

"Is she talking to herself out there?" Anna asked, looking in the direction of the hallway where a muttered one-sided conversation was taking place.

"I told you my family is a bit mad, didn't I?" Lewis whispered in her ear. "There's usually some drama when Carla is around."

Erin only smiled and looked to the door which eased open.

"Happy Christmas," Carla said weakly as she shut the kitchen door firmly behind her. As everyone murmured greetings it was clear something wasn't quite right with Carla's entrance. The entire family stared at her quizzically.

"What's wrong?" Lewis asked, turning to face his sister.

Carla pressed her palm to her forehead. "I would just like to say that this was all Dad's idea. I was firmly against it--" She stopped speaking when her gaze landed on Erin. "Oh, no." She sucked in a breath and when she continued talking it was with the faraway quality of someone talking to themself. "Why is there someone else here? I didn't know there'd be someone else here. Why did no one mention this?"

"Carla!" Lewis hissed, glaring at her.

She seemed to come back to herself then and gave a gentle shake of her head as she moved to Erin. "That sounded rude. I didn't mean to be rude." She lay a hand on Erin's shoulder and gave a gentle pat. "It's great that you're here."

"Thank you," Erin mumbled, confused.

Carla eyed her sombrely. "I apologise in advance for the scene you're about to witness."

Chapter Twenty-One

While everyone stared at Carla, Lewis felt a flutter of nerves as he waited to see what drama she was about to invoke, and how much he would regret inviting Erin to join their family for Christmas.

"What on earth is wrong?" his mum asked. "And what has it got to do with your dad?"

"Nothing's wrong," Nicholas said. "Carla's being dramatic as usual."

"I'm actually not," Carla said. "And I'm really not sure how you talked me into helping you with your crazy scheme."

"What scheme?" Fiona asked, while Lewis's gaze darted between them.

Carla kept her eyes fixed on her dad. "I don't know why I let him talk me into helping with it, but he said he'd do it even without my help and somehow he convinced me it wasn't such a terrible idea."

"Carla!" their mum snapped. "Stop talking in riddles and explain properly."

She put a hand to her chest and inhaled deeply. "Dad wanted to get Lewis a present."

"Me?" Lewis said, head snapping to his dad. "You bought me a present?"

"I don't know why you look surprised. Is it so unusual for a man to buy his son a gift at Christmas?"

"It is for you," Anna said. "Mum always chooses the presents. Please don't say you chose mine as well?"

"What have you bought?" his mum asked, looking aghast at the idea. "And why didn't you mention it to me?"

"Because I knew you'd say no. Any time I suggest what to get the kids, you always say no, so this time I thought I'd go around you."

"What is it?" Lewis turned to Carla. "And why are you being so weird about it?"

"Because it goes against my principles, and it's a terrible Christmas gift."

"It's what he wants," Nicholas said.

"Oh, my goodness!" Carla tugged at the front of her sweater. "I should have just said no."

"I don't understand how it can be so bad," Lewis said. "Can I just open it so we can all stop wondering what the heck is going on?"

"It's not something you can open," Carla said, wincing. "And you can't return it. No matter what, you can't return it."

A flash of panic accompanied Lewis's suspicion of what the gift was. There was no way his dad would do that, though. His stomach rolled. "*Dad?*"

"Open the door," Nicholas said, waving a hand at Carla. "Let her in."

"*Her?*" Lewis echoed.

"Bloody hell," his mum said. "If you've bought him a wife, you've made a very grave error in judgement."

His dad's eyes sparkled as he chuckled. "Of course I didn't buy him a wife!"

Lewis put a hand over his face as Carla reached for the

handle. "Please tell me this isn't actually happening?" he muttered, then grimaced at the sound of a high-pitched bark and the clicking of a dog's nails on the kitchen tiles.

"Isn't she gorgeous?" his dad cooed.

The room fell silent.

"Is there actually a dog in the room?" Lewis asked Erin out of the side of his mouth while peeking at her through his fingers.

Erin nodded. "She really is gorgeous."

Taking a deep breath, Lewis removed his hand from his face and straightened up as he decided this couldn't be happening. "Anyway," he said. "What's my present?"

"*What's your present?*" his dad parroted mockingly. "The dog, of course. She's called Molly. Isn't that a lovely name?"

"You bought me a dog?" Lewis asked, rubbing at his forehead. "I hope this is a joke."

"It'd better be a joke," his mum said, her voice going as high-pitched as the dog's bark. "Because you can't actually buy someone a dog for Christmas."

"Why not?" Nicholas asked. "He wanted one when he was little. He begged for a dog for years and you always said no. I thought it was about time he got what he wanted." He looked at Lewis. "You said you wanted one a few months ago."

Lewis steepled his fingers in front of his face, elbows resting on the table while he continued to avoid looking at the dog. "What I said is that I'd love a dog, but I don't have time for one. Apparently, you switched off halfway through the conversation."

"What were you thinking?" Fiona glared at her husband. "Of course he doesn't have time for a dog. You know he works twelve-hour days in the hotel. When exactly do you think he has time to take care of a dog? And what is he going to do with the dog while he's at work?"

"He can take her with him," Nicholas said, then snapped his

gaze to Lewis. "You can take a dog with you to the hotel, can't you?"

Before Lewis could answer, his mum continued speaking. "You can't just buy someone a dog without discussing it with them." She shifted her chair back from the table and threw her hands up. "Sometimes it amazes me. How can I still be finding out how stupid you are after thirty years of marriage?" She turned her fiery gaze on Carla, who sat beside Anna with her head bent. "And what about you? How on earth did he talk you into going along with this?"

"I don't know," Carla said without looking up.

"You work in a dog shelter, for goodness' sake. You, of all people, should know a dog isn't an appropriate Christmas present. I didn't think they even let people take them right before Christmas."

"They usually don't, but I swore she was going to a good home, and I promised..." She glanced nervously at Lewis and then away again. "I promised a donation."

Lewis choked on a humourless laugh.

"You should have talked some sense into your dad," their mum said.

"I know that," Carla snapped. "But he was very convincing that it was a good idea. He fed me this story about how great it would be." Her eyes darted to their dad. "Tell them what you said about why it was a good idea."

"It's a good idea because he's always wanted a dog," Nicholas said matter-of-factly.

"That's not what you said," Carla complained. "You said because Lewis is always looking after everyone else and never does anything for himself. And a dog would be a nice thing for him. And you also said that if he had a dog, he'd have to walk it, so he'd have to take more time off work."

"Yeah," Nicholas said. "That was my argument. And I think

it's a good one. You think you don't have time for a dog, but I think if you have a dog, you'll have more time."

Lewis took another deep breath and slid his eyes to Erin. "I'm sorry. I was expecting them to be a quirky kind of weird, and not just plain insane."

"It is a really beautiful dog," she told him. Slowly, he turned his head and looked down at the eager face looking up at him. He'd always loved border collies and she really was beautiful with her sleek black and white coat and intense brown eyes.

"She's lovely," he said, managing to keep his voice level. He was sure that if it wasn't for Erin's presence he'd currently be in a shouting match with his dad. Which was a depressing thought since he never argued with his dad, and neither of them were prone to shouting. Plus, it would be weird to argue with a man dressed as Father Christmas.

"She's five years old," Carla said. "She was owned by an elderly lady who died a month ago."

Lewis reached down to Molly. She sniffed the back of his hand before nudging her face against it. "Hi," he said, stroking the silky fur on her head. In response, she nuzzled against his palm.

"I have her dog bed and bowls and everything," Carla said. "It's in the back of my car."

"What do you think of her?" his dad asked.

Lewis couldn't even bring himself to make eye contact, so he concentrated on Molly instead. "She's beautiful."

"I knew you'd love her. Having a dog will be good for you. You'll see."

Anger coursed through Lewis's veins and he struggled to keep his hand relaxed while he stroked Molly.

"I can't keep her," he said, his jaw so tight it was painful. "It's a huge commitment and a decision that people should make for themselves, not have thrust on them." Entwined with his anger, he felt a spark of guilt, because he knew his dad would have had the best of intentions. He'd have been excited to give Lewis what he obviously thought was a brilliant present. Presumably he'd been expecting Lewis to be enthusiastic.

"I told you," Carla said tearfully. "I knew this was a terrible idea."

The sight of Carla's tears made Lewis's guilt intensify even more. Maybe he should just slap on a smile and pretend to be overjoyed with his gift, as was the standard procedure at Christmas. Giving dogs as gifts definitely wasn't standard procedure, though.

"I thought you might react this way," his dad said.

"Then why the heck did you do it?" his mum shouted, asking the question Lewis had been about to ask.

"I'll make a deal with you," his dad said. "Keep Molly with you for a couple of weeks and if she's too much we'll take her. I'd be very happy to have her."

"Oh, I see!" Lewis's mum screeched. "Is this your elaborate scheme to get a dog for yourself?"

"No," Nicholas said. "Because I think after a couple of weeks, Lewis will want to keep Molly."

"It's not even about what I *want,*" Lewis said. "It's not fair to the dog. I work too much. She'll never get the attention she deserves. I just can't have a dog."

"We can do a dog share," his dad suggested happily. "Whenever I have time, I'll come over and take her for a walk."

"Let's do it the other way," Lewis suggested. "She lives with you and I walk her from time to time." He actually liked the sound of that. All the fun and none of the responsibility.

"No!" his mum shrieked. "Why is no one consulting me about this?"

"I'll take care of her," Nicholas said. "You'll hardly even notice her."

His mum waved a dismissive hand in front of her face. "Oh, I am sure!"

"You'll have to have her for the next week," his dad told him. "We're driving over to your Auntie Bernie's tomorrow, so she'll need to stay with you until we get back."

Lewis exhaled all his breath and was about to complain about how this seemed like a carefully contrived plot, but Erin reached down to stroke Molly and her hand met his in the soft fur. He wasn't sure it was intentional until she wrapped her fingers around his palm and gave a firm, reassuring squeeze.

He met her gaze, and his annoyance at his dad dissipated. "Fine," he said after a moment. "I'll take her for a week, but after that she's living with you."

"I've yet to agree to that," his mum said, her tone of voice sending a jolt of amusement rippling through him. He'd been fairly sure that at some point he'd regret bringing Erin to hang out with his family, but he'd been certain it would be Carla or his mum to embarrass him, not his dad making things awkward.

After the slightly intense atmosphere about the dog situation, Christmas with Lewis's family was pretty much how Erin had expected it to be. They pulled crackers and read the naff jokes aloud, then ate the delicious roast turkey dinner while wearing the brightly coloured paper hats. Following that, they moved to the living room and Erin watched as they exchanged gifts. She'd never really considered how revealing the giving of presents could be.

Carla gave little bags of homemade fudge, and slabs of chocolate bark that she'd iced people's names into, while Anna gave more practical gifts – a variety of winter hats and scarves. Lewis's parents gave each of their children a selection of gifts ranging from useful household items to indulgent spa vouchers. One of Lewis's gifts from them was a beautiful sketch of his cottage drawn by a local artist.

A few comical presents were thrown into the mix too, including a dish scourer in the shape of a sheep for Nicholas that everyone seemed to find hysterical. Apparently there was some story behind it which Erin didn't quite figure out.

When it came for Lewis's turn to distribute goodies, Erin watched eagerly to see what he'd chosen for his family.

For his dad, he gave a book – some autobiography from someone Erin had never heard of but which Nicholas seemed chuffed with. Then came his sisters who he gave beautiful handmade silver earrings, apparently from a local jewellery shop which they loved. His mum was equally thrilled to receive a necklace in a similar style.

"I think I'll put the kettle on," Nicholas said, pushing himself out of the armchair, then immediately straightening his red velvet jacket. "Time for Christmas cake, isn't it?"

"Yes," Fiona said. "But there's one more gift first." She pointed under the brightly lit tree in the corner. "Pass that to Erin."

"You got me something?" Erin's lips twisted in confusion. "You didn't know I was coming until this morning."

"It's nothing much," Fiona said, but looked fairly pleased with herself, nonetheless. She gave an encouraging flick of her wrist. "Open it up."

Erin glanced at Lewis beside her, who was stroking Molly – the dog looking completely at ease as she lay on the couch with her head resting on his thigh. Lewis raised an eyebrow at Erin's gift, seemingly as surprised as she was. Intrigued, she carefully tugged away the tape and peeled back the paper. The object in her hands was heavy so she wasn't overly surprised when she unveiled the large, scented candle.

"Thank you," she said, keeping her features in a smile as she raised it to her nose, noticing as she did, the blackened wick and the surrounding dip where the wax had already melted and hardened again.

"Mum!" Carla shrieked, slapping a hand against her forehead. "Could you honestly not have found something that wasn't blatantly already used?"

"I didn't have a lot of time," Fiona said.

Carla rolled her eyes. "So you just snatched the candle from the coffee table and wrapped it up?"

"It smells lovely," Fiona told Erin. "And there's plenty of burn time left. You get a lot of use out of these big, chunky candles."

"Thank you," Erin said, her entire body shaking as she chuckled.

"I'll get the Christmas cake," Nicholas said, standing once again.

"We'll get going," Lewis said. "I should get back and see what's going on at the hotel."

"I'm sure the place is falling apart without you." Anna's tone was mocking but her features were full of affection as she looked at her brother.

"We have to transfer Molly's stuff from my car," Carla said, standing while Lewis nudged the dog from his lap.

"I'm bringing her back here in a week," Lewis said to his dad in the hallway.

Nicholas insisted he'd be happy to have her, which sent Fiona into another unconvincing rant about how she didn't want a dog.

Erin had to stifle a grin at their bickering while she pulled her ankle boots and coat on. Spending Christmas with someone else's family was actually far easier and much more entertaining than spending it with her own family.

Chapter Twenty-Two

It took them a little while to transfer the dog's paraphernalia from Carla's car to Lewis's, and then secure Molly on the back seat. Then there was a second round of hugs before they were finally on their way.

"That was really lovely," Erin said, as they turned out of the cul-de-sac.

"Really?" Lewis asked. "You don't wish you'd stayed at the hotel and enjoyed the peace?"

"Not at all." She pressed her head back into the headrest. "Your family is great. I had a brilliant time."

"I'm glad."

Erin twisted to look at Molly, who was sitting upright and staring out of the window. "I still can't believe your dad gave you a dog. I'm assuming that was out of character for him?"

"Yep." He frowned and ran his tongue along his bottom lip. "Usually, he never does anything without running it by mum. Now I think that's probably a good thing. Dad really shouldn't make decisions by himself."

"Do you think he secretly wanted a dog for himself?"

"I don't think so." He tapped lightly on the steering wheel. "I think he genuinely thought I'd be happy about it."

"Are you *unhappy* about it?" Erin asked.

He glanced in the rear-view mirror and looked uncomfortable – like he didn't want to offend Molly.

"I thought I'd get a dog at some point in my life. But when I'm more settled. At the moment I'm focussed on the hotel, so it's just not the right time for me to have a dog." He paused for a moment, then spoke quickly. "It's also not just that which bothered me. I think what really made me angry was that my dad is usually the person who really gets me, but today it felt as though he doesn't understand my life and my choices."

Erin smiled sadly, resisting the urge to reach for his hand. "I think he had good intentions," she said gently.

"I know he did," Lewis agreed. "But that only means I end up feeling guilty and ungrateful on top of everything else."

After a beat of silence, Erin spoke again. "Do you think your mum will agree to them keeping Molly?"

"I guess so. If not, I could probably convince Carla to take her. Her life would easily accommodate a dog. I'm surprised she hasn't got one already."

Looking into the back again, Erin took in Molly's adorable face. "I can't imagine it will be easy to give her up after a week. She's a gorgeous dog."

"I know." Lewis glanced at her in the mirror. "I'll still get to walk her, though."

"It's not the same," Erin said automatically.

Lewis responded with a sigh and they fell silent for the rest of the drive. Darkness had already fallen and the villages they passed through glittered with twinkling lights, which lulled Erin into a state of utter contentment.

When Lewis pulled the car into his parking space beside the hotel, another car pulled up at the same time.

"That's Ivy," Lewis said, turning off the ignition. "She can't keep away from the place." His face lit up as he stepped out of the car and called out to her. "Isn't it you who's always telling me off for spending too much time here?"

Erin exited the car in time to see the affection in Ivy's eyes.

"The difference is I'm not here to work. We only came to see you." Ivy opened the back door and Poppy tumbled out.

"Santa brought me a bike!" she shouted, eyes wide with excitement. "It has a basket and a bell just like I wanted. Do you want to see it?"

"I'd love to," Lewis said, while Ivy went to open the boot of the car.

Poppy retrieved a pink helmet and set it on her head. "Maybe I can ride it here, Mummy."

"I think the pavement is slippery here too," Ivy said while lifting the bike from the car. She glanced at Lewis. "I didn't want to put stabilisers on because I think she'll be fine without them, but it's not exactly the ideal time of year to learn to ride a bike. So far, I just gave her a push around the house."

"It's not so slippery," Lewis said, rubbing his shoe back and forth over the pavement. "I think this is the perfect stretch to learn to ride a bike."

Ivy shook her head. "I'd rather not spend the evening in A&E, thanks."

"I'll hold on to her and give her a push down the road and back," Lewis said, then bent to hug Poppy. "Happy Christmas, by the way!"

"Happy Christmas!" she replied, pulling out of the embrace to move to her bike.

"Happy Christmas!" Ivy said as he hugged her too, then gave Erin a watery smile.

Lewis held the bike steady while Poppy clambered on.

"Don't let go of her," Ivy said sternly.

"I won't," he said. "Not until she's got her balance, anyway."

"Lewis," Ivy growled in that affectionate way she had, which gave Erin an irrational pang of jealousy.

"It's fine," he said, waving away her concerns. "Don't worry about a thing."

Ivy shut the boot of her car before coming to stand beside Erin and watch Lewis slowly push the bike – and Poppy –along the pavement.

"She must have been very excited this morning," Erin remarked.

Ivy smiled fondly. "Absolutely beside herself."

"I imagine Christmas is even more magical when you have a child."

"It is," Ivy agreed, then turned at the sound of Molly barking.

"Maybe I should get her out," Erin murmured, moving back to the car.

"Whose dog is that?"

"Lewis's."

Ivy stayed quiet while Erin unclipped Molly's car harness. She kept a firm hold of her lead as she jumped out of the car and then walked back to Ivy with her.

"Lewis doesn't have a dog," she said, a smidge of irritation in her voice.

"It was a Christmas present from his dad."

Ivy looked over at the car, confusion wrinkling her features. "Were you out with Lewis before?"

"Yes. I ended up having dinner at his parents' house."

Ivy screwed her features up even further. "I'm sorry... what?" She didn't even try to hide her displeasure and Erin was suddenly certain that she wasn't the only one feeling pangs of jealousy.

"I met his family at midnight mass and his mum felt sorry for me for being alone in the hotel. It was sweet of her to invite me."

"Yeah," Ivy said, her voice low and gravelly. "The Carrington family are lovely. And they're all very generous."

Erin reached to stroke Molly, sure there was some subtext to Ivy's words. Possibly that Erin was taking advantage of their generosity.

"Have you been enjoying your stay at the hotel?" Ivy asked after a moment of awkward silence. Since Lewis and Poppy were now out of sight, they were staring along the road at nothing.

"It's been really great," Erin said.

"It must be difficult, though?"

"How so?"

Ivy turned to face her square on. "You were supposed to be here with your fiancé, weren't you? I imagine you're dealing with a lot at the moment."

"Oh. That. It's kind of a stupid story, but--"

Poppy called out to her mum, interrupting them. "Look at me!" she shouted, pedalling madly and riding entirely by herself while Lewis ran beside her. She wobbled while getting her mum's attention, but righted herself immediately. The look on her face was pure joy.

Ivy dutifully cheered her on until Lewis took hold of the bike and brought her to a stop in front of them.

"I can ride a bike, Mummy!" Poppy declared proudly, before her eyes darted to Molly. "Is that your dog?" she asked Erin, bounding off the bike. "Can I stroke it?"

"You can stroke her," Lewis told her. "She's called Molly, and she's my dog. I got her for Christmas."

Poppy gasped and turned to stare up at Ivy. "I didn't know I could ask Santa for a pet!"

"You can't," Ivy said, her features softening for her daughter.

"It wasn't from Santa," Lewis said. "My dad gave it to me."

"Wow!" Poppy giggled when Molly licked her hand. "You're so lucky."

"You have a dog?" Ivy asked, the annoyance back in her eyes as she looked at Lewis.

"Yeah. Long story."

"Your parents just got you a dog without discussing it with you?" She shook her head, a look of utter disbelief on her features.

"Mum didn't know anything about it."

"What on earth was your dad thinking? He's supposed to be the sensible one in your family. You can't buy someone a dog as a surprise."

"It was slightly awkward," Lewis told her, catching Erin's eye and making her stomach flutter with his private smile. "But I'm not keeping her," he said, his attention shifting back to Ivy. "I told him it was ridiculous not to discuss it with me first and that I don't have time for a dog. She's staying with me for a week while Mum and Dad are away, and then she'll live with them."

"Did Fiona agree to that?" Ivy asked sceptically.

Lewis scrunched his nose up. "*Agree* might not be quite the right word. If she doesn't come around to the idea, I'll convince Carla to take her. It's partly her fault, anyway."

Ivy clicked her tongue. "We should go inside and say hello to Warren," she told Poppy.

"I want to ride my bike again first," she said eagerly.

"One more time up and down the road," Lewis told her as she straddled the bike. "Then we go inside and get warm."

Left alone, Erin and Ivy descended into another awkward silence.

"Don't feel you have to wait out here in the cold," Ivy said eventually. "Go in and get warm." It felt more like instructions than a suggestion.

Erin looked helplessly at Molly.

"I'll take her," Ivy said curtly as she took the lead out of Erin's hand.

Chapter Twenty-Three

The look that Ivy gave Lewis when he jogged beside Poppy and her bike was lacking in Christmas cheer.

"What's wrong?" he asked while Poppy reluctantly dismounted her bike.

"Nothing." The sweetness of her voice was obviously for Poppy's benefit. A scowl lingered in her eyes when she thrust the dog lead at Lewis and returned the bike to the car.

"Where did Erin go?" he asked.

"Inside." She closed the car door with excessive force.

"Are you hanging around?" Lewis asked, giving Molly a gentle pat and frowning again at the fact that his dad had given him a dog.

"We'll come in and say hello to Warren." She took Poppy's hand and gave Lewis another fierce look when they were inside. "Kitchen," she said.

He raised an eyebrow. "Excuse me?"

"Come into the kitchen. I need to speak to you."

"You can speak to me here. I can't take the dog in the kitchen."

She puffed out an irritated breath and her eyes swept over the lounge, where guests were scattered in the comfortable seats. Erin was in an armchair beside the window, chatting with a Scottish couple.

Ivy called over the young waitress, Kate, and passed her Molly's lead. Kate didn't have a chance to object to keeping an eye on the dog, since Ivy took Lewis's elbow and led him behind reception and into the staff corridor.

"What's going on with you?" he asked, but got no reply.

Poppy skipped ahead of them, then launched herself headlong at Warren when they entered the kitchen.

"Happy Christmas!" he said, swinging her into the air. "Did Santa come?"

She nodded enthusiastically as he set her on the countertop.

"What did he bring you?"

"Popcorn!" she told him, the delight in her eyes distracting Lewis from whatever was going on with Ivy.

"Popcorn?" Warren asked.

Poppy's cheeks were bright red from the cold as she beamed at him. "I ate it for breakfast."

"Did you pour milk on it like cereal?"

"No, silly." She giggled. "I just ate it."

"And did Santa bring anything else?"

"A bike and a helmet. And Lewis just showed me how to ride it." She looked at Lewis. "I'm a bit wobbly, aren't I?"

"Only a bit. You'll get the hang of it."

"So have you opened all of your presents already?" Warren asked her.

"Yes."

"Did you open the one from me?"

Poppy's eyes went to her mum, and Ivy shrugged in reply to her questioning gaze.

"Did you get me a present?" Poppy asked Warren.

"I did." He took a step away from her and reached for a tin

further along the counter. "I baked these especially for you," he told her, easing the lid off. "That means you don't have to share them with anyone unless you want to."

"Oh." Poppy looked at Warren and then down into the tin.

"You like ginger biscuits, don't you?"

"Yes." She looked entirely sceptical and Lewis felt his lips twitch upwards as he waited for Poppy's reaction.

"What do you say to Warren?" Ivy prompted.

"Thank you," she said, frowning. "I thought you meant a proper present."

"Aren't biscuits a proper present?" Warren asked, a flicker of amusement in his eyes.

"No, because they're not wrapped up. And because they'll be gone when I eat them."

"The popcorn is all gone," Warren pointed out. "And that was a present."

She stared at him for a moment, considering his words. "The popcorn was wrapped up in nice paper."

"I see." Warren scratched his head. "You know, I think maybe I have a wrapped present for you. I wonder where I would have put it." He made a show of looking in several cupboards, much to Poppy's delight. Finally, he pulled out a present wrapped in shiny red paper. "That looks more like a proper present, doesn't it?"

Poppy's eyes were wide as she took it from him. "Can I open it now?" she asked her mum. When she got the nod from Ivy, she tore at the paper to reveal an apron and baking set. "Can I really bake with it?" she asked. "Can I be a chef like you?"

"Yep," Warren said. "I'll teach you everything I know."

"Can you show me how to bake a cake?"

"Of course. Every chef needs to know how to bake a cake."

"Can you show me now?"

"Not today." He chuckled. "Another day."

Poppy grinned at her mum before turning back to Warren. "Can you help me put the apron on?"

"I can." He plucked her off the counter and helped her with the apron before they sifted through the utensils in her set, discussing what each of them was for.

With a sigh, Lewis shifted his gaze to Ivy. "What did you want to talk to me about?"

She gave a small shake of her head and took his elbow to pull him away from Warren and Poppy.

"I wanted to talk to you about the woman who you took to your parents' place for Christmas dinner."

"Erin. What about her?"

"Why did you take a hotel guest to your parents' place?"

He shrugged. Admittedly, it was a bit of an odd situation, but it had felt right to take her with him and he'd enjoyed having her there. "We've been spending time together. I like her."

"Do you even know her?"

He raised an eyebrow, fairly sure he knew what was coming. "Obviously I haven't known her for long, but I really like her."

Ivy rubbed at her collarbone. "I don't want to be negative, but something about her feels off to me." She glanced at Poppy, then met Lewis's gaze again. "Don't you find it a little strange that she came here alone?"

Lewis opened his mouth, but Ivy kept talking.

"She doesn't seem particularly heartbroken for a woman who was dumped by her fiancé a week ago."

"Oh, yeah. That's not actually true."

Ivy wrinkled her nose. "What?"

"She was never engaged."

"So she just made that up?"

"Not really. Jenny misunderstood and she couldn't be bothered to correct her."

"Oh, my gosh." There was a whine to her voice as she placed a hand over her forehead. "Lewis!"

"What?" he asked, though he knew exactly what was going through her mind.

"You can't be serious. You can't actually be fooled by her little act."

"We've just been hanging out together. Where's the harm in that?"

"She's playing you!" she snapped. "Surely you can see that. No one would genuinely come on their own for a romantic couple's getaway."

"Her parents bought it for her," he said weakly.

She shook her head in an exaggerated motion. "I'm sorry, but I think you're being very naïve."

"I think you're being very loud," Warren said, wandering over to them, leaving Poppy to examine her Christmas gift alone. "What's your problem with Erin?" he asked Ivy. "She seems nice."

"She seems like a fraud, more like," Ivy hissed.

"Don't be dramatic," Warren said, then looked at Lewis. "Have you kissed her with tongue yet?"

He only managed a quick shake of the head before Ivy jumped in.

"You've kissed her *without* tongue? Are you serious? I can't believe you."

"I kissed her under the mistletoe. You know that because you pointed out the mistletoe."

"You're right." She stared in disbelief. "I made the joke about the decorations. I can't believe I encouraged you. If I'd realised she'd lied about her fiancé, I would have never encouraged you."

"It was only a kiss under the mistletoe," Lewis said. "What's the big deal?"

"Seriously?" Ivy spat. "Is no one seeing what I'm seeing here? This woman has turned up at the hotel for a couple's retreat with a bunch of lies about an ex-fiancé..."

"It was a misunderstanding, not a lie," Lewis said, but Ivy didn't seem to hear him.

"After a couple of days she has you so starry-eyed that you're kissing her under the mistletoe and taking her home to meet your family."

"She'd actually already met them before today," he said.

"It's Christmas," Warren said. "Let him have some fun."

"I'm fine with him having fun. All for it, in fact, but do you really not see what she's up to?"

"I don't," Lewis said defiantly, while ignoring the swirl of doubt that stirred in his gut.

"Obviously, she's read about you. She probably knows everything about you and she's come here with her flimsy story about the hotel stay being a gift from her parents." Ivy's nostrils flared. "Why on earth would her parents buy her a gift for a couple? It doesn't even make sense."

Lewis opened his mouth but didn't have an answer. She had a point – it didn't make much sense. He'd believed Erin, though. He hadn't doubted her story for a minute.

Not until now, anyway. Was he being an idiot? Shouldn't he know better than to be so trusting?

"I think she's genuine," he mumbled.

Ivy glared at him. "And I'm telling you, she's not."

"Because she couldn't possibly just like spending time with me?" he said bitterly. "There has to be some ulterior motive."

Her eyes filled with sorrow, and he felt suddenly defeated. Why did everything have to be so complicated?

"Sorry." Ivy put a hand on his arm. "You know I think anyone would be lucky to have you, but I also don't want to see you get hurt again. I'm only looking out for you."

"It's fine," he said. "I'm not going to get hurt. She's good company and I enjoy hanging out with her, but she's a hotel guest and she'll leave in a couple of days, anyway."

The thought of her being gone soon made his chest

constrict, which made him think that Ivy might have a point after all.

By spending so much time with Erin, he was probably setting himself up to get hurt again.

He also knew that the prospect of getting hurt wouldn't stop him from spending as much time as possible with her before she left.

Chapter Twenty-Four

When the Scottish couple went up to their room and Mr and Mrs Ward left the lounge for an evening walk, the Cockney couple tried to tempt Erin into propping up the bar with them. She politely declined, telling them she was heading to bed soon.

Then she was sitting alone in the lounge with only the quiet Christmas music for company. Maybe she should go to bed and not hang around waiting to see if Lewis reappeared.

The young waitress, Kate, wandered over with Molly, and the placid dog settled down beside the fire.

"You don't mind dogs, do you?" she asked. "I'm just going to leave her here for a few minutes, but I'll be right back."

"It's fine," Erin said. "It doesn't seem as though she's going to bother me much." Molly had settled her head on her paws and looked utterly content.

Once Kate left, Erin moved to sit on the floor beside Molly, her back against the couch as she ran her hand over the dog's shiny coat.

Ivy appeared before long, with Poppy trailing behind her.

"Can we stay longer so I can play with the doggy?" Poppy asked, skipping over to Erin and crouching beside Molly.

"No," Ivy replied, her eyes never meeting Erin's. "We need to go now if you want to play with your new toys again before bed. Come on." She held Poppy's coat out and the little girl ambled over to her.

"Can I come and play with Molly tomorrow?"

"Maybe. I don't know. You'll have a lot of time to play with her, though. Goodnight," she said curtly to Erin when they started for the door.

"Night," Erin replied, then watched as Ivy stopped at the door. She took a few steps back towards Erin. "How long are you staying for?" she asked, her polite smile looking painfully forced.

A cool ripple of dread trickled over Erin's spine at the thought of leaving. "Two more nights."

"Where is it you're from?" Ivy asked.

"London."

Ivy nodded. "Enjoy the rest of your stay."

Once they'd gone, Erin was left to contemplate the coolness in Ivy's eyes and the undercurrent of anger beneath her words. It was obvious what the problem was, but that didn't mean it didn't bother Erin.

"All on your own?" Lewis's voice broke her thoughts and made her smile.

"Story of my life," she told him jokingly.

"I didn't mean it like that." He sat beside her on the floor, reaching across her legs to stroke Molly. "I was only thinking it was rare to get you to myself around here."

He sat so close that his hip and shoulder nestled against hers, which was almost enough of a distraction to make her forget the awkward atmosphere with Ivy.

Almost, but not quite.

"I get the feeling I might be treading on Ivy's toes," she said hesitantly.

His brow wrinkled. "What do you mean?"

"I don't think she likes me spending time with you."

"Oh. *That.* It's not that you're treading on her toes. She isn't jealous of us spending time together."

"Are you sure? Because that's the vibe I was getting."

He tilted his head. "She thought it was odd that you weren't upset about your recent breakup..."

Erin winced. "I was about to put her straight about that earlier, but you and Poppy interrupted the conversation."

"I just explained it to her."

"She still didn't seem happy with me," Erin told him.

"No." His tone stayed even. "Because now she thinks you're a big fat liar."

Erin gave him a shove, and they both laughed. "Was there ever anything between the two of you?" Erin asked eventually.

"No," he replied in a rush. "Well, there was a drunken snog when we were sixteen, which left us pretty awkward around each other for a few weeks, until we agreed to pretend it had never happened and continue being friends." Slowly, he reached for her hand and entwined their fingers. "I promise she isn't jealous."

"I can see you believe that," Erin said, running her thumb across his palm. "But I can't help but think you might be too close to the situation to see what's really going on."

"It's really not like that with us," he said.

Erin was unconvinced, but there was no point pressing the matter.

"We're really close as friends," he went on. "But that's all. If she has an issue with me spending time with you, it's only because you're a hotel guest and you're leaving again in a couple of days. She's worried because she can see how much I like you and she thinks I'm going to be upset when you go back home."

"Oh." His honesty took Erin by surprise.

"She might be right," he added, his voice so soft it was barely a whisper, but the words still made her insides quiver.

"I really like spending time with you," she whispered back. "I've had such a brilliant time, and that's mostly down to you."

"I'm glad." The corners of his lips pulled upwards. "I'm also glad someone keeps stringing mistletoe up in this room."

With a wide smile, Erin looked overhead. "That's just tinsel."

"Is it?" Lewis asked, eyes sparkling with mirth. "I always get those two confused."

Her eyes came back to his face and she caught the hunger in his eyes.

When his hand came up to cup her cheek, she felt a wave of desire wash through her. Her heart thudded enthusiastically when their lips met. The kiss was soft and delicious and made Erin's insides quiver even more.

The quiet hum of a moan that escaped her seemed to be all the encouragement Lewis needed, and he upped the tempo, pushing his hands into her hair as his tongue probed her mouth in the most intoxicating way. When her breathing became uneven, he pulled back, then seemed to change his mind and kissed her again.

As her hand roamed over the front of his shirt from his chest to his firm stomach, she drew a groan from him, which was entirely inappropriate for a public place.

"Someone might come in," she told him, drawing back.

"I don't care," he murmured while kissing her neck.

She beamed. "I think you might when Mr and Mrs Ward arrive back from their walk to find us all over each other in the middle of the lounge."

There was a teasing glint in his eyes when he met her gaze. "Those two love a bit of gossip. It'd be the highlight of their stay."

She set her lips against his for one last tender kiss. "Well, *I'd* be mortified."

He screwed his nose up in mock annoyance.

"I think I'm going to head up to my room," Erin said.

"Need an escort?" he asked at the exact moment she realised her statement had sounded like an invitation.

"I'm okay," she said, despite not being sure that was true since he seemed to have left her legs in an entirely jelly-like state.

"Sorry," he said. "I didn't mean to sound so forward."

She smiled gently, while she fought a mental battle over whether to throw caution into the wind and take him up to her room. It was very tempting and would surely be the perfect end to a wonderful day, but her mind seemed to be stuck on Lewis's comment about him getting hurt when she went home.

Except, she suspected it was her who was going to end up hurt. She was falling for him so quickly that she felt out of control. For someone who lived their life in full control, it wasn't a pleasant feeling.

No, she needed to go back to her room alone and try and get her thoughts in order.

She stood, happy to find her legs still functioned. "It's been a long day," she said. "I just need to..."

"Yes. Of course. I didn't mean to make you uncomfortable."

"You didn't." She reached up and placed her hand on his cheek. "This might have been my favourite Christmas Day ever."

"Yeah?" he asked eagerly.

"Possibly." She shrugged. "There was that Christmas when I was six and I got the Barbie Dreamhouse."

"Hard to top that," he said, the dimples deepening in his cheeks.

Softly, she kissed him, then took a step away.

"I'll see you tomorrow," she said, then engaged all her willpower to keep from changing her mind and taking him upstairs with her.

Chapter Twenty-Five

After sleeping late on Boxing Day, Erin skipped breakfast and decided on a ramble around the countryside. Getting out for some exercise and fresh air felt energising after so many days of overindulging in food and alcohol. It also meant she had a couple of hours which weren't spent wondering if she was about to bump into Lewis, and how she would act around him when she did.

Their kiss the previous evening had shifted things. She couldn't brush it off as a quick peck under the mistletoe any more, but she wasn't sure how to view it. Probably as an indulgent Christmas kiss between two people who enjoy each other's company. Considering she was going back to London the following day, that was all it realistically could be.

Which meant there was absolutely no reason to feel nervous around him.

Apparently, her stomach didn't get the memo and turned a somersault when she set eyes on him the moment she arrived back in the hotel after her bracing walk. The cold had made her eyes water and the gusts up on the hills had whipped at her hair. She must look a state, but the hunger in Lewis's gaze when he raked his eyes over her told a different story. Her stomach fizzed wildly and her fingers felt shaky as she fumbled at the buttons of her coat.

Lewis handed a clipboard to the colleague he'd been chatting to before striding towards Erin.

"I was wondering where you'd got to," he said. "I didn't see you at breakfast."

"I gave it a miss," she said, unravelling her scarf. "I was still full from yesterday." She blew into her icy hands and rubbed them together. "I've been for a walk. The countryside around here is stunning."

"It is." He frowned. "Sorry, I didn't mean to sound as though I was keeping tabs on your whereabouts."

"You didn't," she told him with a reassuring smile. It was actually nice that he'd been thinking about her, since her thoughts that morning had mostly revolved around him.

"Also..." He leaned closer. "I hope I didn't make you uncomfortable at all yesterday... You're a guest at the hotel and I'd never want you to feel awkward or anything."

She smiled at his bashfulness. "You didn't make me uncomfortable. Yesterday was lovely." She lowered her voice. "All of it."

His shoulders relaxed. "Good."

Erin took a deep breath and gathered her courage. "Do you, by any chance, have a lunch break coming up?"

"I could probably arrange one," he said happily. "What did you have in mind?"

"There's a cafe down the road which tempted me. It looks all quaint and cosy."

"The Toastie Tea shop?" He nodded. "The food is great, and they serve tea in beautiful old china tea sets."

"So you're up for it?" she asked, quashing a pang of nerves.

"Yes." He glanced across the room at his colleague, who was staring at the clipboard in her hands. "Just give me five minutes."

"We can make it later if you're busy. I'm not in any rush."

"It's fine. We were just trying to figure out how to rearrange the furniture for the quiz night this evening, but I think we have it all well planned out." He held up his hand as he backed away. "Five minutes."

It didn't even take that long before he was back again. Erin hadn't even warmed up enough to remove her coat, so only had to button it up when they stepped outside.

"I think it might snow," she said. "I saw a few snowflakes while I was out for my walk."

"There were a few flakes when I took Molly for a walk first thing, too."

She turned her head to him. "How does it feel to be a dog owner? And where is Molly?"

"Asleep in the office." He shoved his hands in his pockets. "For a border collie she's surprisingly docile. I'm guessing since she had an elderly owner, she had a lazy life. She definitely wasn't keen to wake up at six o'clock this morning when I wanted to leave for work."

"Six o'clock? On Boxing Day?" Erin wasn't sure whether to be impressed by his dedication or concerned about the hotel owner taking advantage of him. "Was that really necessary?"

His shoulders tensed, but maybe that was because of the cold rather than the question. "I had a few things to do and I find it's easier to get things done while most people are still sleeping. Not that it really worked out today since I ended up out with Molly for almost two hours."

"So your dad was right?" Erin said with a cheeky grin. "The dog forces you to work less."

"The dog made me late for work," Lewis said with a slight eye roll.

A dainty bell rang above the door to the cafe when he pushed it open. The warmth of the place was wonderful – not just the temperature but the gorgeous decor of blue and white checked tablecloths and dainty chinaware on display on a vintage dresser at the back of the room.

Unsurprisingly, Lewis knew the middle-aged owner and chatted away as she showed them to a table by the window. Erin ordered soup while Lewis opted for one of the speciality toasted sandwiches. They shared a pot of tea which was delivered to their table almost immediately with dainty cups and saucers.

"This is such a cute cafe," Erin remarked, soaking in the atmosphere. A few Christmas decorations were dotted around – beautiful glass baubles dangled from the ornate light sconces on the walls, and sprigs of holly adorned the dresser. As Erin's eyes scanned the walls, her gaze snagged on the framed oil paintings. "Are these local scenes?" she asked, pointing to the picture nearest to them.

"Yes." Lewis nodded. "The artist is the brother of the cafe owner. I love his work."

"They're gorgeous." It took Erin a moment to drag her gaze from the countryside scene with rolling hills and dotted sheep penned in by a dry-stone wall. There was a crispness to the picture, which gave the impression it was a chilly day and made her think of her morning walk. The price tag beside the picture was hefty, but she could already visualise it hanging in her living room back at her flat.

"The quiz should be fun this evening," Lewis said, breaking her thoughts as he poured them both tea.

"I'm not sure I'm going to join. It's teams of four, isn't it? I'll be an odd number for whoever I team up with."

He shook his head. "Four to six, but we're not strict. Also, Carla mentioned recruiting you for her team. I don't think you'll have much choice."

"Really?" Erin felt a pang of excitement about it.

Lewis smiled gently. "I think it's you and my sisters and Warren."

"The chef?"

"Yeah. He reckons he's not staying for the quiz, but I think he underestimates how persistent Carla is when she wants something."

"I'm kind of looking forward to it now," Erin said, then leaned back in her seat when their food arrived.

The soup was perfect and did a great job of warming Erin up. Conversation flowed seamlessly, and Erin tried not to dwell on the thought of leaving the next day. Her time in the Cotswolds had gone far too quickly and her stomach twisted into a knot at the thought that it was almost over.

Lewis had barely finished his sandwich when his phone rang. He winced at the screen, then offered Erin an apologetic smile as he answered it and had a short conversation about the whereabouts of extra chairs.

"Is the hotel falling apart without you?" Erin asked when he ended the call.

"Apparently," he said with a sigh.

"Do you need to get back?"

"I probably should. Sorry." He waved at the owner and she went to get the bill.

"Are you the general manager?" Erin asked. She assumed so, but there was nothing about his staff uniform that distinguished him from the rest of the staff.

His eyebrows shot up, and it took a moment for him to answer with an uncertain nod. "I think general dogsbody might be a more fitting job description, but yes, I manage the hotel."

The bill arrived and Lewis reached for his wallet, but Erin insisted she was paying. "I'd like this painting as well, please," she told the smiley woman with the credit card reader in her hand.

"It's a lovely one," she said. "That's a great choice. I'll wrap it for you." After plucking it from the wall, she took it back to the counter.

"Why are you looking at me like that?" Erin asked when she caught Lewis staring at her.

His mouth twitched upwards at the corners, taking the intensity out of his features. "I really like that painting too," he told her. "I have a similar one in my living room."

"We must have the same taste in art," she said, then felt her features slip into a frown. Knowing that Lewis had a similar painting would ensure that she thought of him every time she looked at it. She had a horrible feeling it would make her new purchase bittersweet.

When Lewis reached across the table and touched her hand, it pulled her from her thoughts.

"You'll be back home tomorrow," he said with a nervous smile.

"I was just thinking about that."

"Are you going straight back to work?"

The thought of work was like a bucket of cold water over her head. Not that she disliked her job, but it really made her think about getting back to the realities of her life, which suddenly felt extremely far away from the beautiful Cotswolds. And Lewis.

She swallowed the lump in her throat. "I'm only supposed to work a couple of days this week and I can do it from home. There's nothing urgent, so I can probably also get away with taking extra holiday days." She paused, focusing on the way Lewis's hand had remained covering hers -- his thumb rubbing enticing circles on her palm.

"I was wondering," he said quietly. "Would you like to stay in touch?"

Joy blossomed in her chest. "Yes. I'd really like that."

"I've been thinking about a trip to London." His smile brightened his eyes. "If you'd be up for a visitor?"

Erin's stomach turned a somersault. "I'd love a visitor."

She was still beaming when the woman arrived back with her picture; all wrapped up in bubble wrap and in a paper bag.

"Enjoy the rest of your day," she told them, and gave Lewis a pat on the arm before moving away again.

They wandered back to the hotel in a pleasant silence and Erin felt a warm glow in her belly the whole way. Just before the entrance, Lewis stopped her with a hand on her arm, and she automatically turned to face him as she waited for what he was going to say.

He didn't speak, but held out a hand, leaving Erin wondering what he was doing. At least until she spotted the large, fluffy snowflake which settled on his palm before dissolving a moment later. She tipped her head back at the same time as Lewis.

"Now it's properly snowing," he stated happily.

The sky had turned a hazy shade of pale grey and snowflakes whirled down around them.

"So pretty," she whispered, and only then noticed that Lewis had shifted so his face was mere centimetres from hers.

"You *are,*" he said, eyebrows waggling. "I agree wholeheartedly."

She beamed at his flirting and felt a wave of contentment wash over her as he caught her lips in a soft kiss. They stayed there for one perfect moment, taking warmth from each other's lips as the snow came down around them. By the time they pulled apart, Lewis had several flecks of snow in his hair and Erin assumed her hat was turning spotty too.

"Hey, Lewis!" a voice boomed from the opposite side of the road.

He raised a hand to wave at the guy as he gave a nod of acknowledgment.

"Pub tonight?" The guy pointed along the road. "The usual crowd will be there."

"I'm working," Lewis replied.

"Yeah, yeah. You're too good for us these days, aren't you?" His tone was jovial, but Lewis's tight smile was all tension.

"I'll catch up with you another time," Lewis called out before taking Erin's hand and heading into the hotel.

"Who was that?" Erin asked.

"An old schoolfriend." He didn't elaborate and Erin didn't have time to ask questions before the woman behind the reception desk hurried over to Lewis.

"I couldn't find the chair covers," she said. "I looked all over."

"They're in a box near the spare chairs," Lewis said with an impatient undertone.

"There are a lot of boxes down in the storeroom."

"I know, but it's labelled."

"I can't find it."

Lewis's smile was as tight as it had been for his old schoolfriend. "I'll go and look for them in a minute."

While the woman walked away again, Erin lowered her voice. "Sometimes I get assigned an intern at work and I swear they mostly just cause me more work."

"I spend a lot of time thinking it would probably just be easier to do everything myself," he told her quietly.

She pulled her hat from her head and swiped the water droplets from it. "It seems you have resorted to doing most things yourself," she quipped. "I hope you're well paid." She meant it as a joke, but she was suddenly curious. He really did seem to do a heck of a lot of work. And he was always there, though maybe that was because of the busy Christmas season. "What is the pay like for a general dogsbody in a boutique hotel?" she asked, when she caught him staring at her with an odd look.

She smiled at her little joke, but he didn't seem amused. In fact, he seemed entirely ill at ease.

He glanced across the room, tipping his head as though some invisible person had called out to him. "I'll be back in a minute," he muttered before he walked away.

Except he wasn't back again in a minute, and after ten minutes of waiting around in the lounge, Erin gave up and went up to her room.

[illegible]

Chapter Twenty-Six

Lewis's blood pulsed hard in his veins when he strode through the hotel, making a beeline for the kitchen and purposely avoiding eye contact with anyone along the way.

"Where's Warren?" he asked Jamie, who was busy loading the dishwasher at the back of the kitchen. The teenager pointed to the food storage area.

"I'm here," Warren said, wandering out. A frown wrinkled his brow. "What's up with you? I thought you were going out for a romantic lunch. Why do you look like you want to start a fight?"

"I don't," Lewis said automatically, then realised it wasn't entirely true. His instinct had been to come and talk everything through with Warren, but now he was here, he wasn't sure he did want to talk. He'd never seen the appeal of fighting, but he wouldn't mind hitting something now if it meant getting rid of some of the adrenaline pumping through his system.

"What's going on?" Warren lowered his voice and moved to the opposite side of the kitchen to where Jamie was working.

"Nothing." Lewis gave a small shake of his head. "How was the lunch service?"

"Fine." Warren's brow wrinkled. "Did you think we wouldn't be able to cope without you around to micromanage everything?"

"I don't micromanage," Lewis said through gritted teeth. "But if I do, it's because I need to. Today I asked Helen to sort out the spare chairs for this evening and she can't even manage that."

"Why not?"

Lewis rubbed his hand across his forehead. "She can't find the covers for them."

"Do the chairs really need the covers?"

"Yes."

"Are you sure? It's a quiz, not a wedding reception."

"I realise that." He couldn't be bothered to get into how unkempt the chairs looked without the covers. "It doesn't even matter. I'll go and find them myself."

"You know what your problem is?" Warren stalked over to the doors which led to the dining room. "You're too nice." As the door swung open, Warren's eyes did a sweep of the room before he called Helen over. "Go back downstairs and look for the chair covers again," he told her.

"I couldn't find them," she replied.

Warren tilted his head impatiently while Lewis hung back, out of sight. "So you think it's appropriate to run back to Lewis and ask him to do your job for you?"

"He knows where they are," she complained. "And I don't."

"I'm assuming he told you where they are..."

"He just said in the storeroom--"

"So go and look in the storeroom. And don't stop looking until you find them. Because if Lewis has to do your work and his own, then there really isn't much point in you working here. Either find the chair covers, or go home and start looking for a new job." He let the door swing and walked back to Lewis. "That's how you effectively manage staff."

"No," Lewis countered. "That's how you traumatise staff, so that I have to spend the afternoon placating them while they cry in my office." There was barely a week went by that Warren didn't reduce someone to tears.

"She'll get over it," he said flippantly. "Now tell me what's really going on with you."

Lewis fought the urge to go after Helen. "Nothing."

"How was lunch with Erin?"

"Fine." He frowned and his blood pumped harder.

"I'm guessing it wasn't really fine, or you wouldn't be gritting your teeth so hard."

"She leaves tomorrow, so it's not as though it was ever going to go anywhere."

"You could keep in touch," Warren suggested. "Maybe visit her..."

Half an hour ago he'd been excited by exactly that prospect, but now it felt unrealistic. "Maybe Ivy has a point," he said, folding his arms across his chest. "I don't even know Erin properly. It's kind of weird that she came here alone... and the thing with her saying she was engaged is kind of fishy."

"I thought you said it was just a misunderstanding."

"I did, but I hardly know her. And since she's leaving tomorrow, I don't have time to get to know her to see if there might really be something between us. And it doesn't matter, anyway. I don't have time for a relationship and definitely not a long distance one."

When he ran out of steam, Warren stared at him for a long moment. "You need to take more time off," he finally said.

"Right, okay." Lewis rolled his eyes. "So you're going to give me lifestyle advice now, as well as telling me where I'm going wrong with my hotel management style?"

"You work too much, and you don't sleep enough."

"You've been working just as much as me for the past couple of weeks," he pointed out.

Warren shook his head. "I arrive at least a few hours later than you and I leave earlier than you. Plus, I have time off booked for the new year when things are quieter around here. I have a life outside of this hotel, but I'm not sure you can say the same. You're obsessed with this place and it's not healthy."

"I have a life," Lewis growled, feeling his anger levels rise. "I never asked for your advice."

"Maybe not, but you came in here looking for an argument."

"No, I didn't." That might be a lie. Maybe he had been looking for someone to take his anger out on.

"Well, I have stuff to do, so get out of my kitchen now."

"*Your* kitchen?" Lewis scoffed.

"Yes." His smile was all amusement. "You might be the manager of the hotel, but in this kitchen, I'm the boss. Unless, of course, you fancy making dinner for all the guests tonight?"

Lewis straightened his shoulders but had no argument. It didn't matter what the hierarchy was with the hotel staff, Warren was the one person he couldn't afford to upset.

He walked out feeling just as annoyed with the world as he had when he'd walked in.

Getting changed for dinner was a luxury that felt completely indulgent to Erin, but one she was going to miss when she was back eating dinner on her couch tomorrow.

The three-course meal in the dining room was as delicious as ever, despite the uneasy feeling at the thought that Lewis was avoiding her. She'd swear that was what was happening. She hadn't seen him all afternoon, and he was still nowhere to be seen over dinner, which was a first.

Erin was sure he was hovering in the background somewhere – keeping an eye on things. At one point, she could've sworn she heard his voice drifting from the kitchen, but maybe she was imagining it.

Only when she moved to the lounge, after dinner, did she spot him crouched beside the fire, giving Molly a rub down. Mr and Mrs Ward sat nearby and he chatted easily with them.

He didn't spot Erin until he stood. His smile slipped before his features recovered and morphed into polite and professional. Given the way he'd kissed her at lunchtime, polite and professional felt like a slap to the face.

"How was dinner?" he asked pleasantly.

"Delicious, as always."

"Glad to hear it. I'll tell the chef." When he went to pass her, she stopped him with a hand on his arm.

"Have I offended you?" she asked.

"Offended me?" he asked with unconvincing surprise. "No. Of course not. Why?"

"Because you disappeared on me earlier and you seem to have been avoiding me since then."

"I'm not avoiding you. I just have a lot to do. It's busy around here."

Erin could have let him go and left it at that. She *should* leave it at that. This was exactly why she enjoyed being single – so she didn't have to deal with other people's drama. Drama was the last thing she needed. As was spending her time wondering what she'd said or done wrong.

Except, she also didn't want things to be stilted between them. If she'd said something wrong, she'd rather just know.

"Was it because I asked what the pay is like here?" That was the point at which he'd exited the conversation, but she couldn't see why that would be offensive.

His eyebrows rose slowly. "Are you seriously surprised that I was unimpressed by you asking how much I earn?"

"I didn't ask how much you earn," she said, shaking her head. "I only wondered––"

He cut her off. "You wondered if hotel work pays well?"

"Yes." She held his gaze. "I don't know why you're so affronted by that."

He huffed out a humourless laugh. "I realise I don't actually know you very well, but I just didn't imagine you were the sort of person to judge a person by their bank balance or how much they earn."

"Good," she said, not breaking his fierce gaze. "I'm definitely not the sort of person to judge someone by their income."

"And yet, after just a few days, you're asking me how much I earn."

"No." Part of her wanted to laugh at the misunderstanding, while another part of her was annoyed with him for jumping to conclusions and thinking the worst of her. As she caught Mr and Mrs Ward looking at them curiously, she pulled Lewis to the edge of the room. "I didn't ask how much you earn. I asked if you were well paid."

"It's kind of the same thing."

"No, it's not," she snapped. "I asked because I see that you work hard. You seem to run the place with no input from the owners. In fact, everyone here seems to work tirelessly. I also noticed that most of the staff members are young. I only wondered if you are appropriately compensated for your hard work. Or if the owners are employing young staff so they don't need to pay them much, and you're all running around like crazy while the owners are relaxing at home and reaping all the rewards."

She paused and took a breath. "Which is of course how the world works, but my point is, I was curious about how the hotel is run and wasn't prying into your financial situation."

Lewis held her gaze for a moment before his shoulders drooped. "Sorry."

"It doesn't matter," Erin said. "We barely know each other and things don't need to be weird just because we kissed a couple of times. It's Christmas, and we got carried away in the moment, that's all." A lump rose in her throat and she swallowed hard. "I'm just surprised you'd assume the worst of someone."

He sighed heavily and looked exhausted. "I'm sorry. I jumped to conclusions and I shouldn't have..." He trailed off as the front door opened and his sisters walked in.

"It honestly doesn't matter," Erin said quickly. "I don't want things to be awkward between us, that's all."

He nodded, and then Carla was in front of him, flinging her arms around him and becoming the focus of the conversation.

Which was quite convenient. Erin just wanted to enjoy her last night at the hotel and not get dragged down by Lewis's bad mood.

Chapter Twenty-Seven

As Erin settled herself at a table with Anna and Carla, she kept an eye out for Lewis, who'd been pulled away from them by a colleague asking him something about wine. When he returned to the lounge, he caught her eye and gave her a meaningful look before almost immediately being pulled into a conversation with an older couple who'd just arrived.

"I'm messaging Warren again," Carla said, while she tapped manically at her phone screen.

Anna rested her elbow on the table and settled her chin on her palm. "Maybe the fact that he's ignoring your messages might mean he doesn't want to be on our quiz team."

"He doesn't get a choice. We need him."

"I should probably point out that I might not be much help with the quiz," Erin said. "In case you're picking your team based on any kind of ability."

Carla shook her head. "We picked you because you're fun. I just want Warren because I know there's going to be a food and drinks round. Also, because it never hurts to have a bit of eye candy at the table."

Anna turned her nose up. "Are you serious?"

"Yeah. I like pretty things."

"Why do you keep messaging me?" The low voice made all of them look up.

"Hello, Warren," Carla said sweetly. "Lovely evening to you, too."

"Seriously." He thrust his phone at her. "What's this all about? And why do you think it's okay to harass me while I'm working?"

"If you'd have replied to my first message, I wouldn't have needed to keep bothering you," Carla told him. "Not that it matters now. You're here, that's all that matters. You're on our quiz team."

"I'm not joining the quiz."

"Just sit down." Carla patted the seat beside her. "You may as well."

"I've just finished my shift. Do you seriously think I want to hang around at work when I'm not working? Especially for a quiz night. Do I seem like a quiz kind of person?"

Erin caught Anna's eye and clamped her lips together to keep from laughing at the chef's gruff tone.

With her head cocked, Carla stared him down. "There's a food and drinks category. Just stay and help us out with that."

His eyebrows inched upwards, and he looked thoughtful for a moment. "All right," he said, pulling out the chair beside Carla.

"Wait." Carla stuck an arm out to block him. "Can you grab us drinks before you sit down?"

"I see. You just want me on your team for my foodie knowledge and so you can use me as a waiter?"

"No, I only thought of that now," Carla told him, eyes twinkling.

"I'll fetch your drinks on one condition," Warren said, leaning in.

Carla pursed her lips. "What is it?"

He wriggled his eyebrows. "I get to choose your drinks to match your personalities."

"That should be fun." Carla's eyes sparkled. "We accept your terms!"

Chuckling, he walked out of the lounge, but Carla's eyes stayed on him the whole way.

"Let's take a quick opinion poll," she said when she returned her attention to the table. "What do you think about me asking him out?"

"Warren?" Anna's big brown eyes widened dramatically. "You want to ask Warren out?"

"I think he's hot in a rough-and-ready kind of way." Carla's eyes sparkled even more. "Also, don't judge me, but the other day I went in the kitchen when he was busy and he shouted at me to get out. Except it was more of a growl than a shout and the look in his eyes got my lady parts all excited."

Anna covered her face with a hand. "I can't believe you just said that out loud."

"I may have a thing for angry men." She scrunched her nose up and grinned at Erin. "Like I say, don't judge me."

"I think he seems nice," Erin said, glancing behind her to check he wasn't coming back. "A what-you-see-is-what-you-get kind of person."

"Simple?" Carla said cheekily.

Erin smiled, happy that the light-hearted conversation distracted her from thinking about the situation with Lewis. "That's not what I meant."

"I think he's probably actually quite complex," Anna said, a faraway quality to her voice.

"Warren?" Carla jutted her chin out. "Are we talking about the same person?"

Anna's cheeks flushed. "You can't ask him out, anyway. He's Lewis's best friend."

"I don't think there's a law about that. And I don't think Lewis would care."

"Lewis would definitely care."

Carla leaned close to her sister. "It seems as though *you* care," she said teasingly.

"Why would I care? Apart from the fact that I'd get stuck in the middle of all your drama, as usual."

"You've gone red." Carla nudged her sister's elbow, causing her chin to fall from its perch. "You want him for yourself, don't you?"

"No!" Anna's head darted around to check for Warren. "Can you shut up?"

"I won't ask him out then," Carla said. "Not for myself, anyway. I'll ask him out for you, if you want?"

"I don't want to go out with Warren," Anna hissed. "Can you please not embarrass me?"

"You'd make a weird couple." Carla's eyes went to Warren when he walked back in. "He's all burly and masculine, and you're dainty and mouselike."

"Thanks a lot," Anna murmured.

"It's a compliment. I like mice."

Erin snorted a laugh at that. "Sorry," she said when they both looked at her. "Your teasing is just so sweet and affectionate. When me and my sister tease each other, it's mean and bitchy."

"Carla's mean too," Anna insisted, then went quiet as Warren arrived back at the table and set the drinks down.

"Wine for the ladies." He deposited a glass of white in front of Erin and Anna.

Carla glared up at him when he moved a pint in front of her. "What's this?"

"Pint of lager," he said flatly.

"How on earth does a pint of lager say anything about my

personality?" Carla demanded. "I was expecting some fruity cocktail or a sophisticated glass of champagne..."

"A pint of lager says you are loud and crude. It's perfectly fitting."

She picked it up and took a long sip, while keeping her eyes on Warren. "What does your drink say about you?"

"It says I'm thirsty and I'm driving." He picked up his Coke and tapped it against Carla's glass at the same moment that Lewis's voice filled the room, welcoming everyone to the quiz night.

The questions weren't exactly high-brow and ranged from geography to literature to Disney characters. Warren was a definite asset to their team and not only with the food questions. His general knowledge made Erin slightly self-conscious about hers, but she felt as though she pitched in enough that it wasn't embarrassing. They came third in the end, and were all enthusiastic about that.

Mostly, Erin was just happy to spend an enjoyable last evening at the hotel. After her words with Lewis earlier, she'd been concerned that she might leave on a sour note.

"I'm going to head up to bed," she announced, fifteen minutes after the quiz had finished. Lewis seemed to be making his way to their table but kept getting caught up chatting with the other guests.

"I was just going to get more drinks," Warren told her. "Stay for one more."

"I have to be up early. I leave tomorrow." She smiled at him as she stood. "What happened to you only staying for the food questions?"

"You weren't going to do very well without me," he said with a cocky grin. "It wouldn't have been very gallant of me to let you struggle alone, would it?"

Erin suspected it was the banter between him and Carla that had kept him from leaving, but she refrained from voicing that opinion. The two of them had kept her amused with their playful conversations, anyway.

"I probably won't see you again," she said, eyes flicking between Carla and Anna. "I leave in the morning."

"Leave your number with Lewis and I'll message you," Carla said as she enveloped her in a hug. "You should come back and visit. Or we'll come for a day out in London."

"That would be great." She felt a little emotional as she hugged them both, then smiled at Warren.

Glancing across the room, she couldn't see Lewis anywhere, but decided it didn't matter. She'd see him in the morning to say goodbye and that would be that.

The heaviness she felt as she trudged up the stairs didn't make any sense. She'd had a fantastic time – way better than she'd anticipated – so she should be grateful and not grappling with an intense sense of despair which seemed to come at her from all angles.

She was almost at her room when the sound of her name stopped her in her tracks.

"Wait a second," Lewis said, hurrying along the corridor. "Every time I tried to come and talk to you, I got interrupted."

"It's fine." She tried her best to look nonchalant as she turned to him, but suspected her emotions were written all over her face. "The quiz was great. It was a lovely atmosphere, as always."

"Thanks." He dismissed the compliment with a flick of his hand. "It didn't feel great to me, though."

"You seemed very confident as the quizmaster."

"I couldn't stop thinking about you," he said, stepping closer. "I was such an idiot today."

"It doesn't matter. Just forget about it."

"It matters to me," Lewis said. "At least let me apologise properly."

"You already apologised," she pointed out. "And it's not a

big deal." That felt like a lie, but she wanted to keep the conversation as light as possible. She never could deal with drama. "I can see why you took what I said the wrong way." She paused, pondering the statement. "Kind of. Actually, not really, but we are British... very impolite to talk about money, isn't it?"

"Look..." Lewis opened his mouth, but footsteps behind them interrupted them.

"Sorry." Jenny winced as she passed them with a bottle of champagne and a pair of flutes in her hand.

Lewis offered her a friendly smile, then called her back at the last moment. "Where are you taking that?" he asked.

"Room fourteen," she said, looking completely uncertain.

Lewis was beside her in two strides and took the bottle and glasses from her. "Would you mind nipping back downstairs and getting another bottle for room fourteen?"

"No," she said in her usual nervous squeak. "I'll do that."

"They'll need an ice bucket too," Lewis called as she scuttled away.

"I forgot," she said. "I'm sorry."

"It's fine." Lewis watched her walk around the corner, then turned to Erin. "I assume you can drink this quickly enough that you don't need an ice bucket?"

"Is that your idea of an apology?" She lifted her eyebrows. "Because if it is, you're very much forgiven."

He gave her a sheepish smile. "I would also like to explain."

She should allow him that, at least.

With a tap of the key card, she opened the door and he followed her inside.

Chapter Twenty-Eight

Inside the bedroom, Lewis paused and gazed around. "I always forget how nice this room is."

"It's gorgeous," Erin agreed.

While Lewis set the glasses on the table by the window and got to work on easing the cork from the bottle, Erin surreptitiously collected up the scattered clothes from the floor and hid them in her suitcase.

The pop of the cork drew her attention, and she moved to stand beside Lewis as he drizzled the fizz into the glasses. She took a seat in the cosy armchair and felt a pang of disappointment at it being her last night in the decadent hotel. She'd miss this room and these beautiful chairs.

"I have a funny story for you," Lewis said, passing her a glass and then taking the other seat.

"I do like a funny story." She clinked her glass against his and took a sip. "I thought you wanted to explain about the misunderstanding earlier, though."

"The funny story and the explanation are the same."

"Okay."

He set his glass down and stared out of the window for a moment. "It involves socks," he said eventually.

"As does every good story," Erin said, making his face break into a glorious smile. The sight of it swept her tension away, and she felt her muscles relax against the chair.

"I'll set the scene," he said dramatically. "It was two years ago, and somehow I had scored myself a hot girlfriend. Don't ask me how, but I swear she was very attractive, and she was my girlfriend."

Erin shook her head at his self-deprecation. Clearly, he genuinely didn't think he was worthy of an attractive girlfriend. Which was ridiculous – he was a very good-looking guy and a total sweetheart too. Who wouldn't want him?

"We'd only been together for a few months," he went on, "but I thought things were progressing nicely. Everything was going well as far as I was concerned. Christmas was coming up, so I was trying to think of what to give her." He picked his drink up, but only held it in his hand. "She was one of those people who was always complaining she was cold. With hindsight, I can say her low body temperature is most likely due to her being a cold-hearted bitch." He grinned mischievously. "But at the time I felt bad for her for always being cold."

"Is this where the socks come in?" Erin asked.

"Yes. I bought her a pair of socks for Christmas, but before you think I'm a terrible gift giver who absolutely deserved to be dumped on Christmas Day, I'd like to plead my case."

"I'm listening," Erin said, thoroughly amused by his storytelling.

"I'm not talking about a multipack of cotton socks from Debenhams, I'm talking pure wool. They were handmade locally. So it was supporting a local business, and the wool came from local sheep." He nodded vigorously and Erin stifled a laugh. "The sheep live just down the road and the wool they produce would keep even the coldest ice queen warm. *And,*" he said quickly, as though she might be about to interrupt. "The socks had a sheep pattern." His eyes widened. "How do you knit a sheep pattern into socks? That's some skill if you ask me. *And,*" he said again. "They weren't cheap. They were probably the finest socks money could buy."

"I'm guessing your ice queen didn't appreciate them?"

"No." A flicker of sorrow crept into his smile. "She split up with me on Christmas Day after I gave her the socks. In front of my family, I might add. She was absolutely disgusted with me for having wasted three months of her life."

"What a bitch," Erin said. "I know it's a cliche, but it really sounds as though you're better off without her."

"I am," he said, his smile still a little strained. "I don't want to spend my life with someone who can't appreciate a good quality pair of socks."

"Not many people do," Erin said dryly.

Lewis put his glass down and ran a hand through his hair. "Anyway, I suppose maybe I've been left with some unresolved issues about money."

"That makes sense," Erin said. "If it makes you feel better, I really think the socks sound like an excellent gift."

"They had a *sheep pattern,*" he said, with the faintest sparkle in his eyes. "Also..." His features turned serious again. "My family just aren't extravagant gift givers. No one cares how much we spend. You saw us. We buy each other quirky, silly stuff or something you know the person would like... that's how we choose gifts. Not by the price tag. My ex was all into designer stuff. And the humiliating thing was that lots of people had told me we weren't right for each other." He paused and dragged in a breath. "I really didn't see it until she was hitting me around the head with a pair of socks."

Erin couldn't help but laugh. "Did she actually hit you with them?"

"She really did. But those local sheep are as soft as clouds, so the joke was on her."

"Stop it," Erin said, when more laughter bubbled out of her.

"I can't. I promised you a funny story involving socks, so that's what you're getting."

She sucked in a breath to dispel her giggles. Leaning forward in her chair, Erin reached for his hand. "Your ex sounds like a complete idiot and I think you can do way better."

"I like to think so." His fingers softly stroked the back of her hand and Erin reminded herself she shouldn't be getting any more involved. They'd had a nice flirtation and a couple of admittedly knee-quivering kisses, but that was all.

"I also wanted to mention something else about our conversation earlier," Lewis murmured.

She nodded for him to continue.

"You implied that us kissing didn't mean anything." He kept his attention firmly on their intertwined fingers. "Which is absolutely fine... but I wanted you to know that it meant something to me." Slowly his eyes came up to meet hers. "These last few days with you have meant a lot to me. And I know we don't really know each other properly, but I also feel as though I know you."

Erin swallowed the lump in her throat while she searched for a response. Honesty was probably the best approach. "It meant something to me too," she admitted. "The kiss and the time we spent together. It definitely meant something. I shouldn't have said otherwise, but..."

"But?"

"I leave tomorrow."

"Yeah." He reached for her hand again. "I wish you weren't leaving, but I also meant what I said earlier about keeping in touch. If you want to?"

While her brain screamed at her, insisting she was adding

complications to her life that she really didn't need, her heart had other ideas.

"I'd like to see you again," she said, shifting to meet him halfway when he leaned closer.

As soon as their lips met, all logical arguments were silenced. There was no way she could go back to her life tomorrow without a backwards glance. She wanted Lewis in her life, even if some part of her insisted it was a risk. The kiss deepened and a moment later, she was in his lap and kissing him frantically.

The first time Lewis's phone buzzed in his pocket, Erin followed his lead in pretending not to notice it. The second time, he grimaced while he shifted to retrieve it.

"Do you need to get back to work?" Erin asked, trying not to show her disappointment.

"No. It's only Warren wanting me to save him from my sisters."

"He seemed to enjoy the banter earlier."

He placed the phone on the table. "He does enjoy it. He just likes to complain."

"So you don't need to rush off?"

"Definitely not," he said, then grazed his lips tantalisingly over hers.

She let her lips linger on his for a moment before pulling back again. Gently, she ran her fingers through his hair. "How long do I get you for, before you have to go and deal with hotel business?"

"How long would you like me for?" he asked, quirking an eyebrow.

Her pulse skittered as she trailed a hand down his shirt. "All night?" When he didn't reply immediately, she felt completely self-conscious. "Sorry. Was that too forward?"

"No." He reached for his phone. "Warren seems to think he can run the place better than me, anyway."

Erin smiled while he tapped out a message. “He’s really going to wish he’d left straight after his shift.”

“He won’t mind.” Lewis hit send and put the phone aside. “He’s been nagging me to take time off.”

“That’ll teach him,” Erin said. Worried that she was squashing Lewis, she tried to shift her weight, but he slipped his arms around her and clamped her against him.

“Don’t try and wriggle away now,” he teased.

“I wasn’t.” She put a hand on his cheek to draw him close again. With his body pressed against hers, she felt butterflies take flight throughout her entire body.

Maybe she was being too impulsive, but she wasn’t going to deny herself a night of pleasure just because she didn’t know what the future held for them. She’d always been good at living in the moment, and she wasn’t about to stop now. Especially not when she unbuttoned his shirt to find his flawless, taut skin over some clearly defined muscles.

She definitely wasn’t about to deny herself that.

Chapter Twenty-Nine

With her body still thrumming, Erin relaxed into the feeling of bliss and was on the verge of sleep when Lewis eased his arm from under her head. She'd been curled into his chest and had felt utterly content, but she supposed not everyone was a cuddly sleeper.

"Sorry," he whispered, pulling her back from the edge of sleep. When she realised he wasn't just untangling himself in order to sleep but to retrieve his clothes, she felt a jolt of something unpleasant deep in her stomach.

Disappointment.

The thing she tried so hard to avoid and the reason she was happily single. Being alone meant she didn't have to worry about people disappointing her.

"You're going?" Maybe she was misunderstanding the situation. Perhaps he was only pulling on his boxers to go to the bathroom.

"I'm really sorry," he said again. "I had a message from Warren."

"Surely you don't need to work now. It's not a twenty-four-hour reception desk, is it?"

"No." He pulled his jeans on, then plucked his shirt from the floor.

Another pang of disappointment hit. Telling her he'd had a message from Warren was probably just an excuse because he didn't want to stay over. He'd had his fun and now he was off. It seemed out of character, but she'd known him for less than a week, so maybe she didn't really know his character.

"He fed Molly and let her out before he left," Lewis said, fully dressed. "But he left her asleep in the lounge."

That was at least a better excuse than having to work. "Okay."

"I'm the worst pet owner ever. I've only had her a day and I forgot about her." He smiled down at Erin. "I can't leave her in the lounge all night."

"No. Of course not."

"Sorry," he said again, and gave her a lingering kiss before he dashed away.

Left alone, Erin switched the lamp off and turned onto her back, then let out a frustrated sigh. This was the problem with getting attached to people. Previously, the glorious four-poster bed had felt luxurious, but now it felt big and empty, and it was her own stupid fault for getting carried away and making her happiness dependent on someone else.

In the darkness, her mind filled with images of the last couple of hours, and she cursed herself again. Her lack of sex life in the past few years hadn't bothered her at all, but she was fairly sure those intimate moments with Lewis would haunt her for a while.

She was feeling dejected when a gentle tap came at the door five minutes later.

"Erin," Lewis said against the door. Switching the lamp back on, she glanced around.

His phone was on the bedside table, as was his wallet.

"Hang on." Considering he'd just seen her naked, it felt a

little odd to worry about putting clothes on to hand over his stuff, but she hurried to put her knickers and bra on.

She only opened the door a crack. Given how late it was, she couldn't imagine many guests were roaming the halls, but she didn't want to risk being caught in her underwear.

"I'll talk to you in the morning," she said, handing over his things.

The bright light in the corridor dazzled her, but she still caught the way Lewis's brow wrinkled. "What?"

"You'll be around in the morning before I leave, won't you?"

"Yeah, but..." He looked down at his phone and wallet.

"Did you forget something else?" Her gaze swept over the room, but she couldn't spot anything.

"I didn't *forget* my stuff," he said quietly. "I left it while I nipped downstairs to get Molly."

Her hand relaxed on the door handle. "You were coming back?"

"Yes. But if you want me to go, that's fine."

"No." She felt a rush of relief flood her veins. "You can stay. I just thought you were leaving..."

"I didn't want to leave Molly downstairs on her own. She can sleep in here if that's okay. I brought her bed up." He reached beside the door for it.

Erin opened the door wider and Molly brushed past her legs before setting off to sniff at every corner of the room. Eventually, she settled herself beside the radiator where Lewis placed her bed.

A moment later, he was slipping his arms around Erin's waist. "I thought you knew I was coming back. Did you really think I'd have sex with you and then leave?"

Now that he was in front of her, the notion seemed ridiculous, but only a few minutes earlier she'd completely believed that was what he'd done. She rested her forehead against his. "I don't do flings and stuff, so I'm not sure what the etiquette is."

"I don't know what the etiquette is either." He pulled her hips flush against him. "I just know I want to spend the whole night cuddled up with you. And I don't want this to just be a fling."

As her stomach fluttered, she closed her eyes and kissed him softly, savouring the feel and the taste of him. "I'm leaving tomorrow," she said after a moment. "And I'm not sure how realistic a long-distance relationship is. Especially not with your crazy working hours."

"I'll take time off," he said. "But I also had an idea I wanted to run by you..."

"What is it?"

Stepping away from her, he kicked his shoes off while unbuttoning his shirt. "How about you don't leave tomorrow?"

"What?" Her eyebrows lifted.

He removed his jeans, then looked at her in amusement. "Is it me casually stripping off that's making you look so surprised, or the idea of staying longer?"

"I'm totally on board with you casually stripping off," she said, moving into his arms again.

"And how do you feel about extending your stay?"

"I don't know." She certainly had a lot of pleasant feelings about him wanting her to stay longer.

"Is there a reason you definitely need to leave?" he asked. "Didn't you say you don't have to go back to work until January?"

She gave a gentle shake of the head. "I'm supposed to work a couple of days this week, but I could also get away with not."

"Okay, so theoretically, you could stay longer?"

"I suppose, theoretically, I could. This hotel room is only booked until tomorrow, though."

"That *is* a small issue," Lewis said, frowning. "The room has another booking from tomorrow. But I can check and see if there's another room free. If not..." He trailed off, looking unsure of himself.

"*If not?*"

"I was thinking you could stay at my place, but I suspect that might freak you out."

"I would definitely like to *see* your place," she said. "But I think I'd feel more comfortable moving to another room in the hotel if there's one available."

"I'll check in the morning."

Erin swallowed hard as she waged an internal battle. On the one hand, she really hated the thought of leaving tomorrow, but at the same time, staying felt indulgent and spontaneous. Most of all, it felt like taking a risk which she wasn't sure she wanted to take.

"What's wrong?" Lewis asked.

"It just all feels a little overwhelming. I'm not sure where this is heading and whether staying longer is just dragging things out and avoiding the inevitable."

"I already told you I don't just see this as a fling. I've had such a great time the last few days and I want to keep getting to know you and see where this leads."

"I feel the same, but ultimately I'm not sure where it can lead since you live here and I live in London."

"It's only a couple of hours away, so not completely insurmountable." He sighed lightly and gave her a soft kiss. "Look, I don't know what will happen, but I don't want this to end yet. Can you just stay for a few more days and enjoy the time together? After that we can figure out the next move – if we want there to be a next move."

"Okay." She drew in a breath and nodded decisively. Since she really couldn't imagine saying goodbye to him tomorrow, his plan felt like the only option.

She'd stay a few more days to give them time to get to know each other better.

Chapter Thirty

Briefly, Erin wondered if she'd dreamt her night with Lewis. He wasn't beside her in the bed when she woke, and as she looked groggily around the room, there was no evidence that he or Molly had been there.

Someone was knocking lightly on the door.

"Who is it?" she asked while checking the time to make sure she wasn't supposed to have checked out already.

"Lewis," he said through the door.

"Hang on a second." After some scrambling around, she pulled on underwear and a vest top, then remained behind the door when she opened it.

"You could've opened it naked," he said with a wicked grin.

She pulled him inside and only just managed to close the door before his arms were around her and he was kissing her hungrily.

"Good morning," he purred when he finally pulled back.

"Good morning." Her chest fluttered with joy at being in his arms. "You smell good," she said, as she took in his crisp work shirt and fresh appearance. "You've showered and everything, haven't you?"

"I took Molly for a walk and nipped home to shower and change."

Erin frowned. "How long have you been up?"

"A while," he said with a shrug. "Did you sleep well?"

"Very well." With her arms draped around his neck, she ran her fingers through his hair.

"I checked and room eight is free, so I booked you into it for the next week."

"*A week?* I can't stay for another week."

"Why not? You said you don't need to be back at work until January."

"I don't, but I'm not sure I can stay for a week."

"There's a party here on New Year's Eve. You should stay for that."

"I'm supposed to be at a party with my friends." Not that they'd mind if she cancelled. Spending the evening with Lewis was a tempting alternative.

"The room is reserved for you for a week," he said. "Just see how you feel. You don't need to decide now."

She gave him a soft kiss, then stopped abruptly. "How much do the rooms cost?" she blurted out. Not that it really mattered. She was happy to treat herself.

"I'll take care of it," Lewis said.

"No, you won't." She gave a firm shake of the head. "I can pay for myself. I only wondered, that's all. The hotel isn't cheap, is it?"

"No. But it's quieter now that the Christmas guests will be leaving. Since the room would have been empty, I can heavily discount it."

"That would be nice." She tightened her arms around him, pulling him closer. "I'm definitely okay with a discount." With her forehead resting against his, she felt a sudden burst of nerves hit her stomach. "This all feels a bit surreal," she told him shyly. "I don't do stuff like this." She shook her head. "Am I really doing this?" Another thought hit her. "What are the other staff going to think?" She knew one of them definitely wouldn't be happy.

"Ivy isn't working much over the next week, if that's who you're worried about. But they'll just think you're staying longer because you're enjoying yourself so much and want to explore the area more."

Which wasn't even a lie. It just wasn't only the Cotswolds she wanted to explore, she thought as he pressed his lips to hers for a tender kiss.

"I'm really glad you're staying longer," he said, breaking the kiss too soon.

"You have to work now, don't you?" she asked.

"I have to get a few things done this morning." He pulled a key card from his back pocket. "But you need to pack and move to room eight, anyway. I should be able to take the afternoon off. We can go out somewhere."

"That sounds perfect." She took the key from him. "I'd really love to see your house."

"Let's go there this afternoon then," he said and gave her a hasty kiss before he left.

It ended up being the middle of the afternoon before Lewis could get away from work, but Erin had kept herself amused in the lounge, alternating between reading a mystery novel and messaging with her friends and family. Her mum called her as soon as she heard her plans to stay a little longer at the hotel. Eagerly, she asked questions about Lewis, which Erin answered in a nervous whisper while scanning the room in case he or any of the rest of the staff appeared.

When he finally came looking for her, he was full of apologies. His promise to take the rest of the day off placated her and they set off for the five-minute walk to his place.

She was certain the chocolate box cottage on the outskirts of the village always looked beautiful, but with the dusting of snow, it was like something from a postcard. The thatched roof gave a quaint yet simultaneously sturdy air, while the ivy which crept all around the green front door gave it a fairy tale quality.

"It's gorgeous," Erin said, drifting through the front gate when Lewis unlatched it and set off along the paved front path. "This is really yours?"

Grinning, he looked back at her. "Yes."

"It's beautiful," she whispered. "And I guess it's true what they say – hard work really does pay off."

A muscle in his jaw twitched, and he looked as though he were about to comment before he clamped his mouth shut.

"I'll bet it's just one big rundown mess inside," she teased as she caught up to him and Molly.

"Absolutely." One corner of his lips quirked upwards as he slipped his key into the door. "It's an absolute disgrace."

It wasn't, of course. The inside was as picture perfect as the outside and Erin wandered from room to room, taking it all in with wide eyes. Everything looked new – from the paintwork to the plush carpets to the sumptuous cream couch.

The farmhouse-style kitchen overlooked a long garden with a sturdy oak tree in the middle and a beautiful dry-stone wall around the border. Erin spent a few minutes staring out before leaving Lewis to make hot drinks and wandering back to the living room with Molly at her heels.

At the fireplace, she stopped and stared at the painting hanging above the mantelpiece.

"Now I know why you were amused by my choice of painting," she remarked when Lewis arrived behind her and snaked his arms around her waist. "It's not just similar, it's exactly the same."

"Not to brag, but mine's bigger," he said, holding her tightly against his chest. "And it's the same view, but there are subtle differences."

"I'll have to bring mine over and we can play spot the difference." They moved to the couch and she sank into it, curling her legs under her while she sipped at her tea. "It's really a lovely house," she told him. "I don't know how you can bring yourself to spend so much time at work when you could be chilling out here."

His cheek twitched again, and he picked up his drink. "I guess I'm one of those people who isn't very good at relaxing. Life feels easier when I'm busy."

Erin blew on her tea. She never really understood people who couldn't slow down. Even though she thoroughly enjoyed her job, she was always happy to get home. If she had a home as perfect as Lewis's, she was sure she'd begrudge ever having to leave it.

"This actually makes me contemplate moving out of the city," she said without thought. "A place in the sticks is suddenly very appealing."

The way Lewis fell silent made her self-conscious.

"Don't worry," she said feebly. "I'm not about to suggest moving in together even though I am completely head over heels in love with your house."

It drew a small smile from him, but hadn't lightened the atmosphere as she'd hoped.

"I actually love London," she said, trying to dispel any fear he had that she really might suggest moving in with him. "My flat isn't as perfect as this place, but I love it."

"Yeah?" He leaned on the arm of the couch. "What's it like?"

"It's small, but cosy." A smile spread over her face at the thought of it. "My furniture is mostly brightly coloured and mismatched, but everything has a story behind it."

"There aren't a lot of bright colours around here," he pointed out. "It's a lot of beige and grey."

"You have lovely pictures," she said, looking around. As well as the oil painting above the fireplace, there was a selection of other enchanting landscapes. "Are they all by local artists?" She thought of the jewellery he'd bought his sisters from a local jeweller and his story about the socks for his ex-girlfriend.

"Mostly," he said, his eyebrows pulling together as he looked from one picture to the next.

"You really love where you live, don't you?"

"Yes." He gave a subtle nod. "It's hard not to when you live in one of the UK's most desirable places to live."

"I'm not sure that's true. Most people want what they don't have. The grass is greener elsewhere and all that."

A smile pulled at his lips. "I like where I am."

"That's good." Except her mind insisted on jumping ahead, questioning what that would mean for them if they kept seeing each other. One of them would have to make a change if they ever wanted more than a long-distance relationship.

Taking a sip of her tea, she pushed the thought aside. She'd known Lewis for a week and while she could absolutely imagine a future with him, she really didn't need to get herself into a tizzy, wondering exactly what that future would look like.

"Have you eaten today?" she asked when Lewis's stomach growled.

He looked thoughtful. "I'm not sure."

"Have you got any food in? We could cook something."

"Probably not, but we could go shopping, or order a takeaway."

"Let's go shopping," she said, enjoying the idea of wandering around the supermarket with him and then pottering around his homely kitchen.

After all their lovely, romantic trips over the last few days, doing something mundane felt like a pleasant change.

Chapter Thirty-One

With Erin there, Lewis felt more at home in his cottage than ever before. Cooking together reminded him why he'd fallen in love with the cottage. The domestic scene was exactly what he'd imagined when he'd first viewed the place. It hadn't occurred to him back then that he'd end up too busy working to appreciate his beautiful home.

When Erin muttered about going back to the hotel after dinner, he pointed out that she hadn't seen the upstairs of the cottage. She didn't need much convincing to stay the night after that.

Waking with her sprawled beside him brought an instant smile to his lips and even enticed him to doze for an hour, which wasn't like him. Usually, he bounced out of bed as soon as he woke.

Leaving Erin fast asleep, he pulled on comfy clothes and went to fire up the coffee machine. Molly opened one eye when he passed her curled up in the hallway downstairs, but didn't seem at all interested in getting up yet.

With a mug of steaming black coffee, he went to the lounge and settled himself on the couch before opening his laptop. He responded to a few emails and then glanced overhead when a floorboard groaned. The click of a door told him Erin was awake and in the bathroom. He set the laptop aside and rested his head back on the couch, basking in the warm glow of having met someone who he felt so comfortable around.

His forehead creased in a frown, and he contemplated all the moments the previous day when he'd opened his mouth to be completely honest with her and hadn't found the words.

Despite feeling so comfortable around her, he was holding back.

He was hiding something huge and he knew he needed to find a way to share everything with her. Especially since she'd extended her stay so they could get to know each other better.

If it caused an issue between them, surely it was better to find out sooner rather than later.

Erin's plans to get up and make coffee were thwarted when she rolled over to find Lewis's side of the bed empty. The scent of coffee permeated the air as she padded down the stairs.

"Morning," Lewis said, smiling at her from the couch. At least he didn't look as though he'd been up too long. He was wearing jogging bottoms and a T-shirt, his hair giving off definite bedhead vibes.

"I wanted to get up before you," she said, cuddling up beside him.

"Why?"

"So that you could relax and be lazy for once while I made breakfast."

"I only made coffee, so breakfast is still a possibility."

"Good. How do you feel about French toast?"

Wrapping his arms around her, he nodded. "Sounds perfect.

Especially since I'm fairly sure I have all the ingredients so I won't need to venture to the shop."

"Great." She kissed him lightly and marvelled at how natural it felt, as though it was something they'd been doing for years and not only a few days. When she peeled herself away from him, he scratched the bridge of his nose. "Why do you look so pensive?" she asked.

He shifted his fingers and rubbed at his forehead. "I was just thinking..."

"About something serious, by the look of it." Curious, she sank back down onto the couch. "Are you okay?"

After pressing his palm into his eye, he broke into a slow smile. "I'm fine. It just occurred to me that I don't know exactly what you need for French toast. I feel as though it's one of those things that everyone has their own recipe for."

"Bread, eggs and milk will suffice," she said, amused. "Cinnamon would be great if you have some."

"I reckon I have all of that." He stood and pulled her up with him. "I'll have a look. There's a pot of coffee if you want some."

"I'd love some." She helped herself while Lewis rifled through the cupboards for breakfast ingredients. The hot coffee was wonderful but highlighted that it wasn't warm enough for her to be wandering about in underwear and a T-shirt.

"I really love your kitchen," she told Lewis as he deposited eggs and milk on the sideboard. "But I'm not convinced about the wisdom of the tiled floor. It's freezing."

"I know," he agreed. "I tend to view it as cold therapy and assume it has similar effects as an ice bath. Certainly wakes me up in the mornings."

"I wish I had my fluffy socks with me. My feet might turn to ice while I cook breakfast. Maybe I'll put on a few pairs of your socks."

"There's also a really lovely woollen pair," he said blithely. "With a sheep pattern and everything."

"Are you serious?"

"No." He laughed. "Of course I'm not serious."

"For a second there, I really thought you still had them."

"I still have them," he said. "I just wasn't seriously thinking that you'd wear them."

"You kept them?"

"Yeah. Which you're making me feel weird about. It's not something I put a lot of thought into. I just shoved them into the back of a cupboard."

"Can I see them?"

He eyed her with gentle amusement. "It's a pair of socks."

"I know! I want to see them."

"Okay."

They wandered back up to his bedroom and Erin sat on the bed while Lewis rooted through the wardrobe.

"Here," he said, flinging them at her.

"They're *nice,*" she said emphatically. The pattern was gorgeous and they were wonderfully thick while also luxuriously soft. Not the scratchy sheep's wool she'd been expecting. "Is it weird if I wear them?"

"You want to wear my ex-girlfriend's socks?"

"She didn't accept the gift, did she? Technically they were never hers."

He shrugged. "I don't mind, if you don't."

She lifted her foot to put one on and then the other. "I love them," she declared. "I'm going to be much cosier cooking breakfast now." She went to pick up her jeans, but stopped when she realised Lewis had gone quiet.

From across the room, he gazed at her intently.

"Oh, no," she said. "Am I really weird?" She looked down at her feet, now snug in the lovely socks. "Should I take them off?"

Slowly, he crossed the room and took her face in his hands.

Then his lips melted against hers and he kissed her with an intensity that she felt all the way to her cosy toes.

"You're not weird," he said between kisses. "You're perfect."

He walked her backwards until the backs of her legs hit the bed. Then he kept going and they fell onto the bed amid a shriek of laughter.

"You don't mind delaying breakfast, do you?" Lewis asked with a wicked glint in his eyes.

"Not at all. Just as long as you're not going to make me take these socks off."

"Okay, *now* you're being weird," he said playfully. "The socks are coming off."

"Nope," she declared, then shrieked again as he tickled her ribs.

Chapter Thirty-Two

The thing about opening up to Erin about the weird events of his life in the past few years was that it would inject a dose of reality into their relationship which Lewis wasn't sure he was ready for. Things were great, so why not just let them continue to be great for a little while longer?

He'd been certain he'd tell her after breakfast, but when they ended up back in his bed, and breakfast had turned into lunch, the subject of his life felt like something he could raise later.

In the afternoon they moseyed back to the hotel and he ended up working until the evening. After that they took food up to her room and things had once again felt perfect enough for him to keep his thoughts to himself.

He'd tell her everything soon, though. He'd tell her and he'd realise that it wasn't a big deal and everything would continue as it had between them. That's what he told himself while he tried to concentrate on the office work he needed to get done before Erin got up.

Once again, he'd left her sleeping, and crept away to hole up in the office. Molly was snoozing in the corner when Erin messaged to say she didn't enjoy waking up without him. He replied quickly with a promise that he'd make sure to be there tomorrow.

Ten minutes later, he wandered through to the dining room and smiled at her across the room. He supposed most of the staff had noticed something going on with them, but it didn't stop him from being as discreet as possible.

He still had a few things to be getting on with in the office, but he lingered behind the bar, checking stock and making sure everything was in order. It was ridiculous how he couldn't seem to get enough of Erin's company and was finding any excuse to stay close to the dining room while she ate her breakfast.

He caught her eye and flashed her a flirty smile before deciding he really should get the office work done. If he got that out of the way, he'd have the afternoon free to spend with Erin.

"What the heck?" Ivy's voice was a mixture of confused and annoyed.

Lewis sighed as he looked up to find her staring across the room at Erin.

"You're early," he remarked. She shouldn't be at work for another couple of hours, and he'd planned to intercept her and explain about Erin still being there.

She completely ignored Lewis's remark, but at least shifted her gaze away from Erin. "Why is she still here?"

"She decided to stay longer."

"Are you serious?" Ivy's shoulders tensed. "She just spontaneously decided to extend her stay?"

"No." Her mocking tone immediately put him on the defensive. "She decided to stay longer because I asked her to."

Ivy pressed her palm to her forehead. "What were you thinking?"

"I was thinking I like her and want to spend more time with her."

"Oh, Lewis," she said, both her tone and the tilt of her head annoyingly condescending.

"I've been having a really great time with her."

"You've slept with her, haven't you?" she asked quietly.

He blew out an exasperated breath. "I hope you're not actually expecting an answer to that."

"That means you have then," she said, planting her hands on her hips.

"I can't figure out why this is such an issue for you." He paused. "Unless..."

"Unless what?"

He gave a half-hearted shrug. "Erin was concerned she was treading on your toes."

"What?"

He nodded. "She thought you were jealous of her getting close to me."

It was petty, but he'd mostly only said it to annoy her. He fully expected her to laugh hysterically while telling him how absurd the suggestion was.

He absolutely hadn't anticipated the way her eyes filled with tears. Ivy hardly ever got upset. Or showed it anyway.

Lewis opened his mouth to speak but only managed a questioning grunt. He had no idea what was going on. There was no way Ivy had feelings for him. He'd have noticed that.

Calmly, she turned and walked away through the staff door, leaving Lewis to try and figure out what had just happened.

He cast a quick glance in Erin's direction, but she was chatting to Kate, who was clearing her plate.

After taking a deep breath, he went into the hall at the back. Just in time to see the office door close at the other end of the hallway. At least Ivy hadn't gone far.

"I'm sorry," he said automatically when he found her on the office couch with Molly nudging her hands from her face while she sobbed into them.

Her shoulders were shaking when he sat beside her and put his arms around her. In fact, her whole body was trembling as she leaned into his embrace and rested her head against his chest.

For a couple of minutes, she cried softly while he rubbed her back and Molly sat alert in front of them.

"Just to be clear," he said, when she calmed down a little. "I don't know what's going on here."

That got a small laugh from her and she straightened up to wipe at her cheeks with her sleeves. "I know you don't."

"What is going on?"

"I've just spent far too much time with my family," she said, then inhaled deeply and reached to stroke Molly. "Specifically, my sister and her perfect family, making me feel like a failure."

"Laura?" he asked, confused. She was the only sister Ivy had, but they got on well. And they didn't see each other too often since Laura lived in Manchester. "What happened?"

She gave a dismissive flick of her hand as more tears flooded her eyes. "Nothing happened, but she always seems to have everything together. The four of them are like this perfect little family unit, and everything always seems so easy for her." Tears trickled down her cheeks. "Yesterday, Laura's youngest asked Poppy why she doesn't have a daddy. Poppy came and asked me the same question. How am I supposed to explain that she *does* have a daddy, but he doesn't want to know her and would actually prefer it if she didn't exist?"

"You knew these questions were going to come up at some point," he said, continuing to rub her back.

"Yes, but until now Poppy's been so accepting of not having a dad. It threw me that she suddenly wants to know *why* she doesn't. I don't know how much to tell her. I feel as though I fobbed her off and didn't explain properly."

"She's six," Lewis pointed out. "I think it's fine not to give her all the details yet."

"You're right, and I know that really. I just seem to question myself constantly."

"I guess that's normal." He pursed his lips when they descended into silence. "So you being upset has nothing to do with what I said before?" As much as he'd like to just let that issue slide, he thought he should probably address it.

She rolled her eyes. "I'm not in love with you if that's what you're worried about. I realised we were never meant to be anything more than friends that time you ungracefully stuck your tongue down my throat when we were teenagers."

"As I recall, you were pretty ungraceful with your tongue, too."

She smiled as she ran her fingers under her eyes, catching the leftover tears. "I'll be honest, sometimes I wish there was more between us."

His eyebrows shot up.

"I only mean hypothetically. When I watch you with Poppy, I think it would be nice for her to have more family other than just me."

"She has more family."

"Yes, but you know what I mean. Some sort of father figure."

"Poppy seems to be doing fine without one so far. You're an amazing mum and you're doing a brilliant job raising her."

"Are you trying to make me cry again?" She drew in a steady breath. "If I'm really honest, I don't think Poppy needs a father figure, but maybe *I'd* like to have someone."

"Why do you say that as though it's a terrible thing?"

"Because I've spent the last six years focussing on Poppy and it feels weird to think about what I want out of life." She tapped the arm of the couch. "Don't laugh at me, but I recently downloaded a dating app."

"That's good. You should do something for yourself."

"It's not going great so far. I got stuck with writing my bio. I don't have a lot to say about myself except that I have a daughter, and I'm not sure how many men are going to be attracted by a single mother harping on about her kid."

"I think there's a lot more to you than the fact that you're a mother."

"It doesn't feel like it most of the time." She rubbed at her forehead. "Anyway, tell me what's going on with you and Erin. I take it you really like her?"

He couldn't help the way his face cracked into a smile. "I really do. And I know you'll say I hardly know her, but I can really imagine this turning into something long term."

She gave a resigned sigh. "Do you really think she's genuine?"

He hesitated. While he was almost certain she was genuine, there was a tiny seed of doubt in his head that refused to go away. "Yes," he said firmly. The doubt might not go away, but he could do his best to ignore it.

"Does she know about your situation? Have you discussed it with her, I mean?"

He grimaced. "Not yet, but I will soon."

"If you see this being a long-term thing, then you really should talk to her about it. Also, bringing it up with her is probably a good way to find out if she already knows."

"I'm going to talk to her about it soon, but I really can't see it changing anything." That's what he'd keep telling himself.

"You know I want you to be happy." She gave his hand a squeeze. "I'm worried about you, that's all."

"Will it make it better if I tell you I took time off yesterday and the day before?"

She gave a dramatic and mocking gasp. "That's actually good. If she continues to motivate you to take time off, I might come around to her." She checked her watch. "You could take time off today, since I came in early."

"Why *are* you here two hours early?"

"Needed a break from my family," she said lightly. "I love

them, but it was getting a bit much. Plus, since Poppy is more than happy to get extra time with her auntie and cousins, I decided I could make up for all those times I arrive late."

"You're only ever a few minutes late," he pointed out. "And no one cares."

"*I* care. I was always a punctual person before Poppy came along."

"You really don't need to make up for the times you're late. If you needed a break from your family, you could have said you were going into work and spent the two hours doing something for yourself."

"Why didn't I think of that?"

"Not as devious as me, obviously. Go off and do something if you want."

"No, it's fine. I enjoy being at work." She leaned her head on his shoulder. "You created a good atmosphere here."

"We all did," he said, and received a poke in the ribs.

"From time to time, you could just take credit for what you've done for this hotel."

"It's always a team effort," he said, and meant it.

Ivy gave him a look of sheer frustration. "Anyway, I'm here and can handle things. Why don't you go and do something that doesn't involve the hotel?"

"I have a few things to do here first, but I was planning on taking time off this afternoon, if you don't mind."

"I don't believe there's anything you need to do right now that you can't pass off to me or just leave for later. Take the whole day off." She raised an eyebrow. "Maybe you could use the time to have a chat with Erin about everything."

He pouted, because she was right that there was nothing so urgent that he couldn't put it off. And that he should bite the bullet and have what was fast becoming an overdue conversation with Erin.

"It's beautiful outside with the snow," Ivy said. "You could go for a walk."

Molly lifted her chin and barked once, showing her approval of that idea.

"I suppose I have no choice now," Lewis said, giving Ivy a playful shove. "Thanks for that."

"Sorry," she said, but looked thoroughly amused.

He kissed her cheek, happy to see her smiling again.

"Okay," he said to Molly, who was bouncing around in front of him. "We'll find Erin and see if she wants to come for a walk with us."

And he'd find a way to explain everything, and hope it wouldn't change things between them.

Chapter Thirty-Three

Given her state of almost-constant elation, Erin wasn't at all bothered by the look she caught Ivy giving her across the dining room. She focussed on enjoying breakfast and then had a pleasant conversation with the waitress who was starting to feel like a friend.

When Lewis followed Ivy out of the room, Erin decided not to worry about whatever drama she was stirring up and set off up to her room. She'd message Lewis later and ask when he could get off work.

Her sister's call came through as she ascended the stairs, and she was sorely tempted not to answer. As immune as she was feeling to other people's drama, her sister was a different matter. If there was one person who could burst her bubble, it was Zara. Then again, with the mood she was in, she felt invincible. Even Zara couldn't bring her down today.

"Hello!" she said cheerfully as she answered.

"Hi," Zara said, an air of surprise at the edge of her voice, as though confused by Erin's cheerfulness. Then again, Zara never seemed to understand how Erin could be happy with the state of her life. Most likely, she thought it was all an act and assumed that Erin was miserable deep down.

"How's everything?" Erin asked, tapping her key card to open the door of room number eight.

"Fine. Mum said you've extended your stay at the hotel."

"Yes. It's hard to leave this place." She didn't like to mention that it was a man who'd tempted her to stay longer. Zara would surely take it as a sign that she'd been right all along and that Erin needed a man in order to be happy.

"I looked up the hotel online," Zara said. "It does look great. A little out of our price range at the moment. The joys of having a mortgage," she said in a tone that was oddly bragging. "I told mum it was unfair that they were so much more generous with your Christmas gift than mine. But I suppose there has to be some benefit to being a lonely singleton."

Erin rolled her eyes. She was right about her mood being a good buffer – Zara's snipes really couldn't touch her. "It definitely has its perks, but I already knew that."

"Yes, I know. Your carefree life where you can do what you please and don't have to worry about anyone else."

"Were you calling for something specific?" Erin asked pointedly as she paced the room.

"Yes." There was a pause long enough for Erin to wonder what on earth Zara could want. "You know I'm not one to gossip," she said eventually. "But I wondered if you'd met the owner of the hotel."

Erin squeezed her eyes closed, puzzled by the conversation, and wishing Zara would get to the point. "No. Why, is it someone you know?"

"No. But when I did an internet search for the hotel, I found a load of articles about the millionaire owner. I was thinking it'd be just your luck to go off on a couple's trip alone and bag yourself a millionaire."

"I don't think the owner is on site much," she said.

"Makes sense. He's probably off somewhere exotic. He won the lottery, you know?"

"No. I didn't know that."

"At twenty-three. Imagine winning the lottery at twenty-three years old. A big win as well. Not just a few hundred thousand, but actual millions."

"Sounds nice," Erin said, though she wasn't sure that was entirely true. Being financially secure was one thing, but millions would be a lot to manage.

"Mum mentioned you had a crush on one of the hotel staff so I just wanted to check you hadn't been dazzled by some stuck up twenty-something millionaire. Money can't buy you happiness, you know?"

Erin screwed her face up at how pathetic her sister was. How could she be jealous at the *idea* of Erin dating a rich guy? It was just sad. She was also a bit put out that her mum had described it as a crush, which sounded way more trivial than it felt. She decided not to get into it.

"I have to go," Zara said. "But keep an eye out for the owner. Mr Carrington looks a bit dishy in his online photos, but I suppose he can afford to pay for good headshots."

"Mr Carrington?" Erin asked, stopping her pacing at the end of the bed.

"Yes. Lewis Carrington. The guy who won the lottery. You should look him up. It's an interesting story."

"I will," Erin muttered, then sat staring at the phone when her sister ended the call.

Had she really just said...

No, she couldn't have. It made no sense.

Except, as the notion took root in her mind, she realised that it did make sense. It made a lot of sense.

There was a slight tremble to her fingers as she went into her phone. A moment later, she was staring at an article which described how Lewis had won the lottery.

She ripped her gaze from the image of him and tried to get her breathing under control as everything fell easily into place.

The reason Lewis did everything around the hotel was because he owned it.

And the reason everyone seemed to know him was because winning the lottery would have turned him into a local celebrity.

His girlfriend splitting up with him also made a lot more sense now. It hadn't been because her boyfriend gave her socks for Christmas, but because her *millionaire* boyfriend bought her socks. You could see why she might have been expecting more.

After a few minutes, Erin returned to the search engine on her phone. Soon, she was clicking into numerous articles about Lewis Carrington and they all announced the same thing: he'd won twenty-six million pounds on the lottery three years ago, and had immediately bought the hotel.

One article hailed him a hero – saying the hotel had been on the verge of bankruptcy and the staff had been facing unemployment when Lewis swooped in and bought it, saving their livelihoods.

The more she read, the more Erin's heart pounded. Finally, she tossed the phone aside. She'd seen enough.

Enough to know that the sweet, kind man who she'd thought she was falling for, had spent the last week lying to her.

Chapter Thirty-Four

At a guess, she'd say ten minutes had passed when the quiet knock came at her door. Erin hadn't moved from the chair by the window and had been trying to figure out her next move. Confronting Lewis felt like the logical thing to do. She could demand to know why he hadn't told her the truth.

Her mind whizzed back over the last week and she thought of all the opportunities he'd had to tell her, but had chosen not to. Did he think she'd expect elaborate gifts? Or that she'd think differently of him because he had money? Her heart sank as she thought about how he'd spent the whole time keeping secrets.

She'd genuinely thought there could be a future for them.

Now, the last week felt like a scam. He'd said he wanted more than a fling, but he hadn't been honest with her about who he was.

Another tap came at the door, and Lewis called out to her quietly.

Erin held her breath. She'd let him think she wasn't there.

He probably had a key and could let himself in, but she didn't think he'd do that.

Then again, what did she know about him?

Quietly, she waited for the sound of his footsteps retreating. Only then could she properly breathe again. Burying her face in her hands, she took a few deep breaths.

If she talked to him, she was sure he'd have good reasons for having kept his secret. Presumably, he was used to people treating him differently because of his money and had wanted to get to know her without that in the way.

He still should have told her. When she'd extended her stay to give them more time together, he should have told her then.

Now, everything was a mess.

This was why she had no interest in a relationship. She'd been perfectly content with her life, and he'd swooped in and made her want more. But she wasn't a person who always needed more. She was perfectly happy with her lot in life.

That needn't change. She could go back home and it would all be the same. Maybe she'd miss Lewis for a few weeks, but she'd soon forget him.

Tears threatened, but she blinked them away.

Maybe she wouldn't *forget* him, but he could just be a fond memory – possibly even a funny story once she'd gotten over the deceit.

Feeling decisive, she stood and surveyed the room. Then she began shoving things haphazardly into her suitcase and contemplating the chances of being able to sneak out of the hotel without Lewis seeing her.

Her phone rang twice while she was packing and she ignored it both times. Lewis followed up with a message asking where she was. He was going to walk Molly and asked if she wanted to go with them. He told her to call him.

With her heart pounding, she crept to the window, keeping herself out of sight behind the curtain. A few minutes later, Lewis stepped out onto the street with Molly by his side. He ruffled the fur on her head, then set off along the road.

It didn't matter anyway, Erin told herself. It had been a fun holiday romance, but it was over now and it didn't matter.

It didn't matter that she wouldn't see him again, because she had a nice life with good friends and a job which she enjoyed and a flat which was cosy and homely.

She absolutely didn't need Lewis in her life.

A tear slipped down her cheek as she watched him walk away. Once he was out of sight, she pushed the tears from her cheeks and shot into action. He should be gone for half an hour at least, which gave her time to get as far away from Chipping Campden as possible.

After summoning a taxi through her app, she waited at the window until the car pulled up outside. That should give her the best chance of slipping away unnoticed.

She almost made it. The only member of staff she encountered on her way out was Ivy, and she was busy chatting with a couple of women at the front desk.

The taxi driver gave her a friendly smile and took her case from her.

"Where are you going?" Ivy called, stepping outside just as Erin had put a foot in the car.

So close, she thought, her heart absolutely charging. "I'm leaving," she said curtly. "Goodbye."

"Wait!" Ivy rushed towards the car. "What do you mean, you're leaving? Where are you going?"

"I'm going home. Back to London."

"Does Lewis know? Because he was looking for you earlier."

"I guess he'll figure it out." She supposed the good thing about it being Ivy who'd interrupted her getaway was that she probably wouldn't be in any rush to tell him. She could tell him once Erin was long gone and then be there to comfort him.

Erin pushed that thought aside and slipped into the seat.

When she pulled the door closed, she was met with resistance.

"I'm guessing he doesn't know you're leaving?" Ivy asked angrily. "You're just leaving without saying anything?"

"It turns out there's a lot that *he* didn't tell *me,* so I don't think I need to feel too guilty about this one thing." She made a feeble attempt to close the door again, but Ivy had a firm hold.

"What are you talking about?" she asked, fiery determination in her eyes that said Erin wouldn't be going anywhere until she explained.

"I just found out that he owns the hotel," she sniped. "And that he won the lottery."

Ivy stared at her. "You're leaving because of that?"

"Yes."

Ivy rubbed a hand across her forehead. "So you didn't know already?"

"No. He didn't tell me. I spent all this time with him and he didn't think it was worth mentioning." She dragged in a ragged breath. "Does everyone know he was keeping it from me? Have you all been having a laugh behind my back?"

She shook her head. "It wouldn't even be funny, would it? I mean, if you thought he was a millionaire and he was secretly penniless, then I could see your issue but I'm not sure why it matters that you didn't know."

"Because he hasn't been honest with me. I thought he was just a normal guy who works in a hotel."

"He is a normal guy." She frowned. "He's a really good guy. You can't just leave without saying anything."

"I can and I will, and to be honest, I'm surprised you care. You made it pretty clear that you didn't like me spending time with him."

Ivy winced. "Only because I thought you already knew about the money."

"I had no idea."

"I see that now, but I thought you were playing this whole innocent act to get close to him... and get to his money."

"No." Erin bit down on her bottom lip. "I didn't know until an hour ago."

"I don't understand why you're leaving."

"Because he hasn't been honest with me."

"Yes, but about being a millionaire! I feel as though that's fairly easy to forgive."

"But I don't care about the money. It makes absolutely no difference to me. What I care about is being with someone who I can trust and who doesn't keep secrets."

"I totally get what you're saying, and in other circumstances, I'd agree. But it's not a terrible secret, is it... twenty-six million in the bank? Ask him to buy you a few diamonds as an apology and move on!"

Erin almost laughed. *Almost,* but not quite.

"Can you do me a favour?" she said. "I know you don't really like me, but can you please not call Lewis right away? Give me a chance to get on a train before you tell him. When I'm too far away for him to follow."

Ivy looked torn. "Can't you stay and talk to him? I know I haven't been very friendly, but I thought you were another gold digger. If you genuinely didn't know, then you're actually kind of perfect for him. Plus, he's been really happy since he met you, and I'd like him to be happy."

"I just want to get home and sort my head out," Erin said. "Maybe it was only destined to be a fling. We've only known each other for a week, so I can't imagine he'll be that heartbroken." As she said it, she hoped it wasn't true. She hoped she hadn't imagined the connection between them, even if it wasn't destined to go anywhere. She looked pleadingly at Ivy until she removed her hand from the door.

"Get home safely," she whispered as she closed the door.

Erin looked up at the hotel as the car moved away and felt the desperate weight of disappointment pressing on her chest.

Chapter Thirty-Five

There was a bite to the air when Lewis stepped out of the hotel.

"We won't go far," he told Molly, who trotted along by his side. Partly, because it was freezing and partly because he wanted to get back to Erin. Not being able to get hold of her left a twinge of worry in his stomach, despite being fairly sure she was only in the shower. Or possibly taking a nap. They hadn't got all that much sleep the previous nights.

Thinking of their nights together made him want to abandon the walk altogether and find her. But maybe he should give her some space and not crowd her.

He offered a smile to the middle-aged guy he passed, then turned off the main road towards the fields so Molly could properly stretch her legs.

No one was around and he felt his shoulders slowly relax as his body acclimatised to the temperature. After a couple of smaller lanes, they hopped a stile into a large field which glittered white with its blanket of snow.

"Don't go far," he told Molly, unclipping her lead. She didn't seem like a dog who was going to cause him any trouble, but they were still getting used to each other and he could only really hope that she didn't bolt. Chasing her through the countryside didn't sound like his idea of fun.

She sniffed around the stone wall, then trotted a little way in front of him before turning to look back. He could have sworn she was just as concerned about losing him.

"I'm here," he told her. "You can have a run around."

She wagged her tail but maintained her distance a few metres in front of him.

The crisp air felt invigorating now, and it occurred to him that having a reason to get out of the hotel and take in some fresh air wasn't a bad thing at all.

Which was exactly what his dad had thought. Maybe he'd been right. Maybe he'd keep Molly.

The thought came out of nowhere and he buried it again. It had never been that he didn't want a dog, but that he didn't think it was fair to the dog. Realistically, once the novelty wore off, Molly would probably end up lying around the hotel all day while Lewis was too caught up with work to remember to walk her.

They reached the stile at the far end of the field and Lewis glanced back. He could turn back and go and find Erin or continue into the next field.

For him, the choice would have been Erin, but Molly had already slipped through into the next field. Apparently, she was deciding.

"Fine," he said, following her. "We'll do a lap of this field and then head home." Back to Erin.

It was a little crazy how attached he'd become to her in only a week. The thought of her going back to London felt like a boulder in his stomach, but he refused to dwell on it. He'd convince her to stay until the new year and then they'd figure out how to move their relationship forward from there.

He really wanted them to move forward. Which meant he was going to have to put his fears aside and tell her everything.

His phone buzzed in his pocket and he pulled it out to find Ivy's name flashing on the screen.

"I'm walking Molly," he said when he answered. "I told you I wouldn't be long."

"You need to get back here," she said in a tone that made him stop dead.

Fear snaked around his spine. "What's wrong?"

"Erin knows," she said breathlessly. "She just got in a taxi. If you get back here now you can follow her and catch her at the train station."

He was already walking back the way he'd come. Molly followed without needing to be told.

"What do you mean?" he asked Ivy, hoping he'd misunderstood.

"She knows about the money," Ivy said, confirming his fear. "She knows everything and she's upset."

His brain whirred and his heart rate ramped up, but he couldn't think of anything to say. "I'm on my way," he muttered.

He strode at a fast pace all the way back to the hotel.

Ivy stood outside, waiting for him. "I'm sorry," she said weakly.

"Did you tell her?" he shouted, directing all his anger and fear at her.

"No." The sorrow in her eyes made it clear she was telling the truth. "I don't know how she found out but she knows and I'm sorry."

Overwhelmed by his emotions, he had nowhere to direct his anger but at her. "Why are you sorry if you had nothing to do with it?" he growled.

"Because she didn't know before this morning. I really thought she knew, and was only after your money, but she wasn't."

Forcefully, Lewis thrust Molly's lead at Ivy. "Can you look after her?"

"Of course. I checked and the next train doesn't leave for another half hour, so you should catch her."

He checked his pocket for his car key and was about to walk away when he turned and glared at Ivy. "I didn't even want it," he said, his accusing tone illogical and unfair, but he couldn't help it. The whole stupid situation infuriated him. "I didn't want the money. I was perfectly happy and now I don't even understand my life."

"I know." Tears glistened in Ivy's eyes.

"Do you know what I want?" He threw his hands up and paced away from her. "I want to work from nine til five, Monday to Friday, and I want to walk my dog and hang out with my friends and family, and I want to go fishing again." He didn't even know where that had come from because he hadn't been fishing in years and hadn't even noticed he missed it until right then. "I don't want this life," he told her sadly as he felt her arms wrap around him.

"I know," she said again, her voice so quiet.

He sank against her as exhaustion seemed to creep out from his bones and fill his entire body.

"I don't understand why you didn't just tell her yourself," Ivy said when she released him.

"Because..." He stopped, not wanting to waste time having this conversation with Ivy. "I need to find Erin."

"Yes," Ivy agreed, following him to his car. "Once she's got over the shock, and when you explain things properly, you'll sort things out and everything will be fine."

He gave her a grateful smile, then slid into the car, hoping he could get to the train station in time.

If not, he suspected he'd be driving all the way to London.

Chapter Thirty-Six

The train was due to leave in a few minutes, and Erin was impatient. The sooner she was away from Chipping Campden, the better. She just wanted to be back in the comfort of her flat.

A shadow fell across her and she cursed her luck that someone would take the seat next to her when she desperately wanted to be alone.

"Is this seat free?"

Her eyes snapped up, and she felt the usual rush of endorphins at the sight of Lewis. But then the lies came rushing back, and she cast her gaze at the back of the chair in front of her. "It's taken," she said, removing her bag from her lap to plonk it on the free seat.

"Just let me explain," he said, picking up the bag to sit down. "Please."

She couldn't look at him. If she looked at him, she'd start crying at the unfairness of it all. Because she'd thought he was exactly the sort of person she'd like to be with. Stupidly, she'd let herself think that being in a relationship might improve her life.

And all it took was one week for him to let her down and remind her of why she was better off alone.

"Look," she said, amazed by how calm she sounded when inside she was an absolute wreck. "We had a nice time. Nobody promised anyone anything, so I think we can just put all of this behind us and get on with our lives."

"That's really what you want?" His eyes bored into her – she could feel them – but she refused to look at him. "You'd leave without letting me explain?"

"The train is leaving soon," she told him at the sound of a muffled announcement on the platform.

He glanced along the aisle but otherwise made no move to go anywhere. "Can I tell you a story?" he asked, an edge of sorrow in his voice.

Erin didn't reply. She wanted him to leave, and she wanted him to stay, and it was all too confusing.

"Can I tell you a story about a lottery ticket and a pair of socks?"

A lump swelled in her throat and she wished he'd told her the story three days ago. If he'd told her then, she could have been surprised and amused, instead of having to deal with the anger and disappointment she felt now.

"The train is leaving," she said as it moved away from the platform.

"I'll get off at the next station and get the next train back. I really want to tell you the story. And then I'll leave if that's what you want, and you'll never have to see me again."

Her lower lip trembled at the thought of never seeing him again, and she trapped it between her teeth to stop it. "Tell me the story then," she whispered. Since he wasn't going anywhere, she may as well hear him out.

"I'd never played the lottery before," he said, his voice tinged with sadness that didn't fit the story she knew was coming. "I was in a shop in Chipping Campden and they had this deal on chocolate bars. You could buy a surprise bag really cheap because the chocolate was almost at the expiry date. They were in a paper bag, so you didn't know what you'd get. I'd only gone in for a magazine, but I saw the sweets and wanted to buy one for Carla. She's a chocoholic and loves a surprise, so I thought it would be perfect for her."

He paused and took a breath. "They called them a lucky dip, and when I asked the shop assistant for one, she thought I was referring to a Lucky Dip lottery ticket. You know the one where they give you random numbers? She'd printed it before I realised she'd misunderstood. I told her it wasn't a big deal, and I'd pay for the ticket."

When he paused again, Erin risked a glance at him to find him staring straight ahead, lost in thought.

"I shoved it into my wallet and didn't think about it until a couple of weeks later when my mum told me she'd seen on the news that there was twenty-six million in unclaimed lottery winnings and it was someone in our area."

He huffed out a gentle laugh. "She said someone could be walking around with a twenty-six-million-pound ticket in their pocket and have no idea. Or maybe they'd accidentally put it through the wash. Those were her theories. We had a laugh when I told her I had a ticket in my wallet and maybe I was a millionaire. We joked about how we'd spend it and what kind of life we'd have... and then the following day I took it into the shop and found out that I really had won." There was a faraway look in his eyes when he paused again. "But the reality of winning the lottery was nothing like the imaginary scenarios Mum and I had cooked up. As it turns out, we don't spend our time sipping cocktails on yachts in tropical places."

"You could afford a few yachts though, couldn't you?"

He turned, seemingly surprised by her voice. "I could, but when it came down to it, that wasn't something I wanted."

"What did you want?"

"Nothing," he said. "That was the problem. I liked my life as it was. It wasn't anything special, but it was comfortable. Sometimes money only complicates things."

He fell silent, and Erin stared out of the window, trying to get her thoughts in order. "There were no socks in that story," she said dryly.

"Sorry, I forgot that bit. I was wearing socks when I bought the ticket. I think the woman who sold it to me was also wearing socks."

"Not critical to the story, then?"

"No, but you said every good story includes socks, so it seemed like a good way to get your attention."

Erin's cheek twitched, and she wanted so badly to be amused. To carry on as they had been and pretend nothing had changed.

"Why didn't you tell me?" she asked.

"Because people treat me differently when they know. I was enjoying spending time with you and getting to know you without money being an issue."

"I can see why you wouldn't mention it if it was just a fling between us, but you told me it was more. I extended my trip, so we'd have more time to get to know each other. But how could I get to know you when you were hiding things from me? It's not as though it's a small thing. It's huge."

"But you did get to know me. Plain, everyday me. The money doesn't mean anything to me."

"It wouldn't mean anything to me either. What matters are things like trust and honesty. Did you think I'd see you differently because of the money?"

"No," he said without conviction.

"You must have thought it would cause some kind of issue or you'd have told me."

He rubbed at the bridge of his nose. "I should have told you. I'm sorry I didn't."

"I don't understand why you didn't."

"Because," he started, then caught himself and took a breath. "Because Ivy was convinced you already knew about the money."

"You knew I didn't know about it."

"I *thought* you didn't know, but..."

"But what?"

"After I won the money, a lot of people suddenly wanted to be my friend. None of them were genuine, they were only interested in me because of the money. That girlfriend I told you about? I met her at the supermarket. Bumped into her by the tinned goods and it took me three months to figure out that she'd orchestrated that meeting and would never have had any interest in me if it weren't for the money."

"You thought I was after your money?"

"No." He shook his head. "Whenever I was with you, I was sure you were genuine. I thought you were interested in me and that you liked spending time with me. Just for me." He smiled gently. "But every time I thought about telling you the truth, I had this fear that I'd tell you and you wouldn't look completely surprised. I like you so much and I hated the thought that what we had might not be real. So I didn't tell you because that way I could keep things as they were. I really liked how things were between us."

It didn't feel as though much time had passed, but the train was slowing for the next station and Erin felt her stomach twist at the thought of saying goodbye.

"Thank you for explaining," she said curtly.

His hand reached for hers and she savoured the warmth of his fingers, which sent a jolt all the way to her heart. "Am I forgiven?"

With an amazing amount of willpower, she pulled her hand from his and clasped her hands together in her lap. "It's not just a matter of forgiving you," she said, aware that the station was getting closer. "I spent a week getting to know you, but now I'm not sure I know you at all."

"You know me. I didn't lie about who I am."

She shook her head. "I need time to process everything. Maybe we can speak again in a few days."

"That sounds like you're giving me the brush off."

"You lied to me." Her lower lip quivered again as she looked at him. "Not just about the money. You let me think you were a hotel employee when you own the place."

"I'm sorry." This time when he took her hand, she didn't draw away. She refused to look at him though, as a couple of stray tears spilled down her cheeks.

"You need to get off the train," she said eventually. "It's going to leave again in a minute."

"I don't want to leave. Not when you're upset and everything feels unresolved. I don't want to leave things like this."

"The train is going to leave," she told him firmly. "You need to get off."

"Do you own the train?" he asked.

"Of course I don't own the train," she said, aware that she should probably release his hand but unable to bring herself to do it.

"It's not up to you if I get off or stay on, then."

"So you plan on following me to London?"

"Yes," he said as the controller arrived in their carriage. "I think I will."

Erin watched in exasperation as he paid an extortionate amount for a ticket to London.

"Seriously?" she huffed. "Are you planning on stalking me all the way to my flat?"

"No," he said calmly.

"What exactly is your plan?"

"You said you don't know me. So you have from here until London to ask me anything you want. I'll answer honestly."

"Then what?"

"Once we get to London, it's up to you. I can get on the next train back to Chipping Campden and you can never see me again, if that's what you want..."

Once again, it seemed she had no choice but to go along with his plan.

Chapter Thirty-Seven

As much as she'd thought she wanted space to process everything, Erin was glad, in the end, that Lewis stayed on the train. After telling her his story, he wasn't intrusive, but gave her time to let everything sink in. Looking back on her week with him, everything shifted slightly, but having him beside her meant she could get clarification rather than speculating.

"When you had that meeting with the accountant the other day," she started, then left Lewis to fill in the blank since she wasn't sure what her question was.

"Mr Garrett is the accountant for the hotel and also my private financial advisor."

"And do you genuinely dislike him? Because it seemed as though you didn't like him."

"I don't enjoy meeting with him." He paused, seeming to ponder the question. "I was going to say that I don't mind him as a person, but I'm not sure that's true. I guess I don't even like him as a person that much."

"What does he actually do?"

"Helps me decide what to do with the money, then moves it around to the appropriate places."

"So he works for you?"

Lewis nodded slowly.

"Why do you employ someone who you don't enjoy working with?"

His features filled with puzzlement as he cocked his head. "He was the hotel's accountant before I took the place over. He's not a terrible person or anything. And I guess it's a case of 'better the devil you know'."

That didn't make much sense to Erin, but it didn't seem worth lingering over.

"What did you buy?" she asked, changing tack. All she got from Lewis was another puzzled look. "When you won the money, you must have splashed out. What did you buy for yourself that was totally indulgent?"

Creases appeared on the bridge of his nose. "I bought the hotel. That was a pretty significant purchase."

"Yes, but that's more like an investment, isn't it? It's a business transaction, not something indulgent. And was the hotel really something for you?"

"I own it," he stated, misunderstanding her.

"I know, but did you buy it because you wanted to own a hotel, or because the place was failing and the staff were about to lose their jobs? Was owning a hotel something you really wanted?"

"No," he said plainly. "I didn't particularly want the responsibility of owning a hotel. I bought my house, though. That was extravagant."

"It's lovely that you could buy your own house," Erin said. "I'm not sure it counts as particularly indulgent or extravagant. Not when it's also a practical purchase and another good investment."

He sank back in his seat. "I paid off my parents' mortgage, and my sisters let me buy them a flat each, but it was hard work getting my family to agree to that. The people who I wanted to give money to weren't keen to take it, but random people who I'd never met started sending me begging letters. There was a part of me that would have been happy to give it all away, but I also felt I had a responsibility to do some good with it..."

"The kid waiting to see Santa," Erin mused as she recalled the conversation which hadn't meant anything at the time. "You sponsor his football team. You said it was the hotel, but it's you."

He nodded. "I like to support community groups and other local projects. But even twenty-six million isn't endless, so I invest a portion of the money to make sure I can continue to give to worthy causes. But figuring all of that out feels like a full-time job sometimes."

"I'll bet," Erin said, trying to wrap her head around it all but not managing it. It all felt very surreal. "Also, if it's so much work managing the money, why don't you hire a financial advisor who you actually like?"

"I don't know." Lewis looked vaguely confused, as though he'd never even considered the possibility. "Like I said, Mr Garrett was the accountant for the hotel before I took it over, so it made sense to keep him on. And it felt easy to have him advise me with the rest of it, too. I already knew him, so I didn't need to worry about him screwing me over or anything."

"That seems like a flimsy basis to employ someone on."

"Maybe," he agreed with a faraway look in his eyes.

"Did you do anything fun with the money?" Erin asked after a few minutes.

The crease reappeared between his eyebrows. "Not especially. It felt like a burden really quickly. I also had the feeling that everyone was watching me and judging me. I still feel as though people are waiting for me to blow it all, or somehow make a mess of my life because of it."

"I don't understand why you work so much," Erin said. "Surely you could hire a manager to take care of the hotel. At least so you don't need to be there around the clock."

"I could," Lewis said. "But I don't want to be the guy who won the lottery and never worked again. That's not who I am."

"I understand that, but it seems you've gone to the other extreme. You work constantly."

"I don't really know why," he said slowly. "But I didn't earn the money. I guess sometimes it feels as though I need to earn it. Which I realise doesn't make sense."

"It does actually." She paused and another ten minutes passed with them sitting in silence. "I guess you already donate to the dog shelter?" she asked eventually, remembering the odd look in Carla's eyes when she'd mentioned promising them a donation.

He smiled warmly. "My sister has no interest in taking money for herself, but she has no problem begging on behalf of those dogs."

"Did you tell your family not to say anything to me about the money?"

He shook his head. "I didn't have to. Anna realised immediately that you didn't know, and she told the rest of them. They thought it was better if you didn't know until you got to know me. My family really don't talk about it much anyway, so it's not as though they had to bite their tongues constantly."

Erin straightened her spine. "It all sounds quite depressing."

"What does?"

She shrugged. "You won the lottery and when you talk about it, you don't sound happy. It's weird."

"I think about this a lot, and I don't think winning the lottery made me happier."

Erin waited a moment, considering his words. "Are you less happy than you were before?"

His jaw tightened, and she knew the answer before he even spoke. "Possibly." He exhaled a full breath. "Don't get me wrong, I don't hate my life, but the money brought a lot of stress, and whether they're real or not, a lot of expectations.

Also," he added blithely, "when you're a multimillionaire suddenly you can't complain to anybody about anything."

That made her smile. "I suppose you could always hire someone to listen to you complain."

"Yeah," he said, but he didn't sound amused as he massaged his temple. The train was pulling into the station and he stood in the aisle and lifted her case from the rack.

"How do you get home from here?" he asked.

"I'll jump in a taxi." Usually, she'd get the Tube, but she just wanted to get home while encountering as few people as possible.

"I'll walk you to the taxi rank," he told her, then fell quiet as they eased their way off the train and through the station.

The queue for the taxi rank wasn't long, and he stayed by her side when she joined it.

"Tell me what I said to annoy you," she said quietly.

He turned to gaze at her.

"Just tell me. Don't pretend I didn't say something that irritated the heck out of you."

Again, he rubbed at his temple, a pained expression darkening his eyes. "I realise you were joking, but you did what everyone does and offered me a way to solve a problem with money. Everyone thinks they'd have a perfect life if they won the lottery. People are more than happy to tell me what they'd do in my situation, but the truth is there are a lot of problems that money can't help you with. Like..." He stopped and when he spoke again, his voice was calmer, more controlled. "Like what would you do if you suddenly didn't know who to trust? If you couldn't tell who was genuine and who was only pretending to like you because they were interested in your money."

A lump clogged Erin's throat. "I wouldn't tell them," she whispered.

He nodded gravely. "I know I should have told you, but I hope you can at least understand why I didn't."

"Yes," she murmured.

The understanding should have made everything easy, but it was suddenly very clear that it wasn't just about his secret. It was about her, too.

The taxi queue moved forwards and then it was her turn.

"I know I said that I'd get the next train back, and you'd never have to see me again," Lewis said, "but I really want to see you again."

Her heart was pounding as she wrapped her arms around his waist. The driver of the black cab shouted for her to get in and she shouted back for him to wait a minute.

With the scent of Lewis filling her nostrils and the feel of his body in her embrace, she knew for a fact that she couldn't get in that taxi and leave things as they were.

"Do you want to see my flat?" she asked in his ear.

Drawing back, his features creased in surprise.

She smiled faintly. "I want to tell you a story."

"As long as it involves socks, I'm in."

Chapter Thirty-Eight

Lewis remained quiet on the taxi ride and Erin wondered how often he really opened up to people, and if him sharing everything had left him emotionally exhausted. He seemed a little spaced out when she paid for the taxi and lugged her case out onto the road. Stepping out after her, he took the case and carried it the rest of the way up to her flat.

"It's nothing fancy," she said as she opened her front door. "But it suits me."

She felt a jolt of warmth at the familiarity of it. Her plants looked wonderfully healthy and the blanket her friend had crocheted for her was in its usual place draped over the back of the couch – giving a dose of colour to the room, which wasn't lacking in colour, anyway. The sunny yellow curtains matched the selection of orange and yellow cushions on her green velvet couch. She'd carefully chosen everything, and loved the vibe she'd created.

"My neighbour is one of my best friends," she told Lewis, closing the door behind them.

"That's convenient," he said, stopping in the centre of the room to look around. "It's cute."

"Thanks." It felt odd having him in her space. If he was there, then it wasn't just a holiday romance. The thought sent a ripple of unease billowing up her spine. "Do you want a drink? I can put the kettle on."

"Please. Whatever you're having." He sank onto the couch and she went to the kitchen.

When she returned a few minutes later with two cups of tea, he had his head resting on the back of the couch and his eyes closed. Given the steady rise and fall of his chest, she would've sworn he was asleep until he slowly opened his eyes, making it look like a great effort.

"Are you okay?" she asked, setting the steaming mugs on the star-shaped coasters on the coffee table.

"Fine," he said with a smile. "What did you want to tell me?"

She sank beside him on the couch, not sure where to start or what she even wanted to say.

"It's not a story as such," she said. "I just realised that you keeping secrets from me wasn't the only thing that freaked me out. You being secretive also reminded me how complicated relationships are, and how much I could get hurt." She sighed. "My last proper relationship ended badly. With hindsight, it was bad right from the beginning, but I didn't see it. I was with him for four years and when we split up, I had to rebuild my whole life. I swore I'd never be in that position again and wouldn't let myself get hurt like that again."

"I don't want to hurt you," he said. "I wasn't trying to hurt you by not telling you everything."

"I know you weren't."

He ran a hand down his face and looked worn out. "What are you trying to say? Because I get the feeling you just don't want to be in a relationship with me and are trying to politely give me the brush off. Was it just a fling for you?" There was an edge of bitterness to his words which cut right through Erin.

"How would we even have a relationship when we live two

hours apart and you run a business which you never take time off from?"

"I can take time off," he said flatly. "I just never had a good reason to before I met you."

The sweetness of his words went straight to her heart, and she wanted to believe that things could work out between them.

"I need some time to think," she said.

He nodded, but there was a coolness to his tone when he spoke. "You mean you want to get back to your real life and see if you forget about me?"

"No." It actually wasn't a terrible notion, except she knew she wouldn't be able to forget him. She wasn't going to stop thinking about him. That much she knew with certainty.

"I'm not saying I don't want to be with you," she ventured. "But I'm trying to be honest and realistic. I don't know how it's going to work out given our situations and..." She paused and took a breath. "I'm scared."

When she'd split up with her ex, she'd been such a mess for so long and she couldn't face the thought of going through that again.

"Okay." His tone was softer now. "I really want to be with you, so I would like us to figure out a way to make this work."

His eyes drifted around the room, and he rubbed at the back of his neck.

"Are you okay?" she asked, because while he was saying the right things, she had the sense that his mind was somewhere else entirely.

He closed his eyes for a moment. "I should probably go home and give you time to think about everything." He stood abruptly and headed for the door.

"I'm confused," Erin said, a jolt of irritation hitting her. "You just told me you want us to work things out, but you also seem as though you can't get away from me fast enough."

He sighed and his body slumped slightly as he rested his

hand on the back of the couch. "It's not that... I'm sorry. I want us to work things out, but I also don't feel brilliant and if I'm coming down with something, I'd rather be ill at home on my own than at your place."

Erin was off her feet in an instant. Walking around the couch, she registered the sheen of sweat across his forehead. Instinctively, she placed the back of her hand on his cheek.

"You're red hot," she said.

His lips attempted to pull into a smile. "Thank you," he said, but the joke fell flat.

Erin rolled her eyes. "You've got a fever."

"I'll get home and sleep. I'll be fine."

"You can't get on the train if you're ill."

"I'm fairly sure it's not contagious."

"I'm not worried about other people. I'm concerned about you. How long have you been feeling ill for?"

He looked thoughtful. "Since we were on the train. Or before that. Maybe when I argued with Ivy."

"Why did you argue with Ivy?" She shook her head. "Never mind. It doesn't even matter. I'm not letting you leave in this state. You can get into my bed."

"I have to get back for Molly," he said as she led him towards her bedroom.

"Where is she now?"

"With Ivy."

"I'm sure Ivy won't mind taking care of her for longer. Just sleep for an hour or two. You can always get the train back this evening."

He sat on the edge of the bed and pulled his jumper off. "Do you have any painkillers?"

"Yes. What hurts?"

"My head is pounding. Some ibuprofen and a couple of hours' sleep, and I'll be fine."

She eyed him wearily, getting the impression this might be a regular occurrence.

Deciding not to quiz him on it, she went to the bathroom in search of painkillers and came back a few minutes later with a glass of water as well.

"Thanks," Lewis murmured as he knocked the tablets back. "I'm sorry." He lay back on the bed, eyes closing immediately.

Erin could have sworn he was asleep before she even left the room.

She checked on him a couple of times over the next few hours, but he was dead to the world and never even switched position. The third time she walked in, she rested a hand against his forehead, happy to find he was no longer burning up. He didn't stir, and she was about to walk out again when his phone vibrated on the opposite side of the bed.

Ivy was calling him and Erin hesitated over whether she should answer his phone before deciding that Ivy was probably worried about him. Plucking the phone from the bed, she crept back out of the room before swiping her finger across the screen.

"It's Erin," she said on answering.

"He caught up to you then?" Ivy said, a confused undertone to her voice, probably trying to figure out why Erin had answered his phone.

"Yes. He ended up getting the train to London with me."

"Is he there?" Ivy asked. "I've tried calling a few times."

"He's in bed."

Ivy let out a hum of understanding. "You two sorted things out, then?"

"Kind of. We chatted everything through anyway." She grimaced as she realised the picture she'd painted for Ivy. "He's actually ill. That's why he's in bed. I'm a little worried about him and I don't know whether to wake him or let him sleep."

"Did he have a migraine, by any chance?"

"I'm not sure. He had a fever, and he said his head hurt. I got the impression that this wasn't completely unusual."

"No." Ivy's tone was full of sympathy. "I have a theory that it's his body's way of forcing him to stop and rest, but if you suggest that to him, he's likely to bite your head off."

"Thanks for the warning." She perched on the arm of the couch. "What should I do?"

"Let him sleep, if you don't mind."

"I don't mind. I was just worried about him."

"He'll be fine once he's caught up on sleep. When he wakes up, let him know Molly is fine with me."

"I will."

"Thanks for taking care of him," Ivy said quietly.

"No problem," she replied before ending the call.

Quietly, she slipped back into the bedroom and left the phone beside the bed, then she closed the door and left him to sleep for as long as he needed.

Chapter Thirty-Nine

After falling asleep with such a shocking headache, it was a relief to wake up to a clear head. It always was.

Lying in Erin's bed, Lewis tried to piece together the events of the previous day. He was a little fuzzy with the details.

He'd been on the train with Erin, he recalled. They'd gone back to her place to talk, and he distinctly remembered feeling lousy on the taxi journey. Erin had paid the driver, and he hadn't even mustered the energy to offer to pay. And then they'd sat in her living room and she'd explained why she didn't think it would work out between them and he'd struggled to concentrate on her words, never mind argue with them. He fully intended to, though. He wanted to be with her, and he needed to make that clear.

Sitting up, he plucked his phone from the bedside. He'd already assumed that he'd slept all afternoon and all night as well, but it was almost midday now. He groaned in frustration as he ran a hand through his hair while reading the slew of messages from Ivy the previous day. She'd obviously been worried about not being able to contact him, but the messages and calls had stopped early in the evening.

Quickly, he shot off a message saying he was fine and telling her he'd call her shortly. Then he pulled on his clothes, which he had no recollection of taking off, and made a quick stop at the bathroom before following the sound of the radio to the kitchen.

On the way, he noticed the pillow and blankets on the couch and muttered a curse.

"Morning," he said, the dryness of his throat making his voice croaky.

"Hi." Erin spun around. "How are you feeling?"

"Pretty embarrassed, but other than that, I'm fine." He scrubbed at the stubble on his jaw. "I'm sorry. I'm not sure what happened."

"Exhaustion, at a guess." She leaned against the sideboard, her gaze sympathetic. "Do you ever think about not working so much so you can get enough sleep on a regular basis?"

"Have you been speaking to Ivy?" he joked.

"I have actually."

His eyebrows shot up. That explained why her messages and calls had stopped.

"I answered your phone yesterday," Erin said with an apologetic frown.

"It's fine," he told her.

"Ivy said this happens from time to time."

"Not often," he said, despite knowing it happened far more frequently than was normal for a healthy guy in his twenties. And he knew it was down to stress and lack of sleep, but he just didn't seem to be able to slow down.

"Are you hungry?" she asked. "I'm making myself a sandwich if you want one."

"I'm starving. Can I grab a glass of water too?"

"Sit down," she said firmly when he hovered behind her.

"I can help," he insisted.

"You can do as you're told and sit down." Her tone was

menacing enough that he felt a little nervous as he pulled out a seat at the small, round table. Then she smiled sweetly, and he relaxed again.

"You're kind of terrifying sometimes," he told her.

"Only when people don't follow directions." She set a glass of water in front of him and placed her hand against his forehead.

"I feel fine now," he said, while his pulse skittered at the feel of her skin against his.

"Good." She moved back to the sideboard. "I was worried about you."

He gulped the entire glass of water, unable to stop once he'd started. "Sorry you had to sleep on the couch."

"It's fine. I just wasn't sure... well, I didn't know how things stood between us and you were ill..."

"You didn't want to cuddle up to the sick guy?" he teased.

She fell silent, and he watched intently as she pottered around the compact kitchen. An array of house plants on various shelves gave it a lovely, homely feel.

"I owe you money for the taxi," he said when she came to the table with two plates of sandwiches.

She wrinkled her nose. "What?"

"You paid for the taxi from the train station."

"Yes." Her eyebrows gathered together. "I was getting a taxi home. Of course I paid for it." She looked at him as though he was being weird. Which he probably was. When it came to money, he felt as though he never knew what the etiquette was these days. "Did you think I'd expect you to pay because you're rich?"

He shrugged and picked up his sandwich, but didn't take a bite.

"Lewis?" she said, apparently wanting him to answer.

"Sometimes it can be awkward with people." At least it used to be until he gave up on socialising. "When I won the money, I had this group of friends who I'd gone to school with. We'd always go out on Friday nights, but after I won, it got awkward. They always expected I would pay. And it was sort of fine. It wasn't as though I couldn't afford it but..."

"But why should you always have to pay?" she asked, irritation flickering in her eyes. "That's stupid."

"I stopped hanging out with them after a while. That solved the problem." He took a large bite of the ham and cheese sandwich and chewed slowly. "This tastes amazing."

"Your taste buds are just easy to please because you haven't eaten in so long."

"Possibly," he said with a teasing smile.

They ate in silence for a few minutes before Erin spoke again. "Do you remember our conversation yesterday, or were you too spaced out?"

"I remember you giving me excuses about why it wouldn't work out between us."

"They weren't excuses. I was telling you how I felt."

"But I think we can make it work. If you want to."

She hesitated for long enough that he lost his appetite and pushed his plate away with half the sandwich still on it.

"Don't you want to try?" he asked.

"Yes," she said with absolutely no certainty.

"Will you come back with me today?"

Her head shot up, and she stared at him in confusion.

"I need to get back. I was only intending to leave Molly with Ivy for a couple of hours. Also, there's the New Year's party at the hotel tomorrow. But you could come with me. We can celebrate the new year together."

She shook her head so firmly that he knew she wouldn't budge on the subject. "I need space to think everything through."

A knot of disappointment wedged itself under his sternum. "When will I see you again?"

"I don't know. I need to get back to work next week and get back into my routines. But we can talk on the phone and maybe you can take some time off in January and come and visit me."

It felt like a brush off and he wasn't at all convinced that she'd even keep in touch.

"Will you?" she asked, chewing on her bottom lip.

"Will I *what?*"

"Take time off to come and visit me?"

"Yes." He reached across the table and took her hand, hating that she even had to ask. "Of course."

Chapter Forty

When Erin's good friend and neighbour, Jessie, messaged on New Year's Eve asking her to go over to her place early to help get everything set up for the party, she accepted eagerly. A distraction was exactly what she needed. Some time with Jessie and her positive energy would no doubt perk her up.

Since it wouldn't be a huge party, she didn't expect there to be much preparation, so was surprised to see Alicia and Irina there when she arrived. That was great, though. It was always a fun atmosphere when the four of them hung out.

They exchanged hugs and greetings before the girls sat back down in the living room.

"What do we need to do for the party?" Erin asked, not bothering to sit. "We could get straight to the food prep and you can fill me in on your news while we work." Over the last week, the group chat had mainly focused on her, and she was keen to get properly caught up on her friends' lives.

"There's no rush," Jessie said. "We've got ages before anyone arrives."

"We thought we could relax for a while and catch up." Alicia pushed her dark curls over her shoulders.

Erin sank onto the fluffy carpet beside the coffee table. She would rather be busy, but chatting with her friends was fine, too.

"How are you feeling now?" Irina asked with a sympathetic tilt of her head.

"Let's not talk about me," Erin said. "I want to hear everything that you guys have been up to over Christmas."

Her three friends wore similar concerned expressions, and she caught a nervous glance between Jessie and Alicia.

"Wait," Erin said. "Why does this feel like some kind of intervention?"

"It's not," Irina said nervously.

"Well." Jessie grimaced. "It kind of is."

Alicia leaned onto her knees, causing her curls to fall forward again. "We're worried about you."

"No need," Erin said breezily. "I'm fine."

"So what are you going to do about the situation with Lewis?" Jessie asked.

"I've decided not to think about it for now. I just want to enjoy the party, then I'll get back to my normal routines next week. After that, I'll figure out things with Lewis."

"You're going to let him get away, aren't you?" Irina asked sadly.

"To be honest, it was probably just a Christmas fling. Which was great, but we have completely different lives and I'm not sure how a relationship between us would work."

They all stared at her for a moment, then exchanged glances as though silently deciding who would be the one to say what they were thinking.

"It just seems pretty obvious," Alicia said, wincing slightly. "You like each other. So you should date each other and see how things progress from there."

"Yes." She agreed in theory. "But what happens after that? Because I know there's no way he's going to move to London.

He has a business and his family and he has a beautiful house. He won't give all that up."

"You don't know that," Jessie said. "Also, that's not the only option, is it? If things *did* work out."

"Of course it's not." She wasn't an idiot. "If things work out, then of course the obvious solution will be for me to uproot my whole life and live with him."

"You say that as though it's a really terrible notion," Jessie said. "Could you not imagine moving if things worked out between you? I always thought the Cotswolds were an idyllic place to live."

An image flashed into her head of cosy evenings by the fire in Lewis's cottage, and winter mornings in thick wool socks on his cold kitchen tiles.

Yes, she could imagine it, and of course it wasn't terrible.

"I can't do it again," she said, a lump lodging in her throat and making it difficult to speak. "I can't change my life for someone and hope they don't decide to pull the rug out from under me. I can't make my whole life revolve around a guy and hope that I don't get hurt."

There was a sympathetic pause before Alicia spoke. "We completely understand that you're scared of getting hurt again, but this situation is nothing like when you were with your ex."

"Isn't it?" She swiped the tears from her cheeks. "Because I thought everything was great then, until it suddenly wasn't."

"Because you were young," Jessie said gently, "with no life experience, and nothing to compare your relationship to. From what you've told us, it sounds as though you just went along with whatever he wanted because you were so besotted with him."

"You won't end up in that situation again," Alicia said. "Because you're a different person now. You won't blindly make decisions based on some obsession that you've convinced yourself is love. You've got really good at making the right decisions for yourself, but that doesn't mean you always have to be alone. If you want to be in a relationship, and that relationship feels right, trust your instincts."

"And no one is saying you have to make any big decisions right away," Irina continued. "But if spending time with Lewis makes you happy, then spend more time with him. Have a long-distance relationship for a while until you figure out if you want more than that."

Tears spilled down Erin's cheeks and Jessie slipped down to the floor to put an arm around her.

"I know that you're right," Erin said. "It just feels very scary. But like I told you, I'm not giving up on him entirely – he said he'll visit me, so I'll wait and see how things go. For now, can we focus on the party, or talk about you guys or something? You're depressing me."

"I don't think it's the conversation that's depressing you," Jessie said. "I think it's the fact that you're here when you'd rather be with Lewis."

Irina wiggled in her seat. "Can I give her the present now?" she asked, a spark of excitement lighting her eyes.

"What present?" Erin asked suspiciously.

"You sounded so down on the phone yesterday." Irina handed over a plain white envelope. "So we got you something to cheer you up."

Erin guessed what it was before she pulled the train ticket from the envelope.

"You can be with him in a couple of hours," Jessie said, her hand resting between Erin's shoulder blades. "Pack a few things, jump in a taxi and you can be at his place in no time. See the new year in with him."

"Thank you." Erin sighed as she stared at the ticket in her hand. "That's really kind, but I'm just not sure..."

"Oh, come on," Alicia complained with a pout. "If you won't go after him for yourself, please go after him for us. This time next year I would like to be hanging out in your millionaire boyfriend's hotel, having the time of my life, instead of spending the evening in Jessie's tiny apartment where I have to prepare food and put up decorations myself. No offence, Jessie."

"None taken, but why are you making out that you're the only one who's going to put any effort into the food and the decorations?"

"Because I know you two. You'll start on the wine and stand around chatting while you watch me do all the work."

"But you're so good at it," Irina said. "And you only get annoyed with us for doing everything wrong."

They exchanged smiles and Erin couldn't help but chuckle at the familiar banter.

"Go on," Jessie said. "Go and see Lewis and stop pretending you don't want to."

She did want to see him, and with the train ticket in her hand all she could think of was the look on his face when she walked into the hotel. That and the idea that she could end this year with him, and wake up to start the new year with him.

And if she was honest with herself, starting the year with him was exactly what she wanted to do.

Chapter Forty-One

It was surprising there was a train going to the Cotswolds on New Year's Eve at all, so Erin tried not to be too impatient when it was delayed. Once she was finally on the train and chugging towards Chipping Campden – and Lewis – her excitement levels rose until she felt like a tightly wound ball of energy which might explode at any moment. The thought of surprising him felt wonderful, and she was so grateful to her girls for pushing her into it.

She exchanged frenzied messages with them throughout her journey and was entertained by their banter and the photos Alicia sent of Jessie and Irina drinking wine and apparently being little help with the party preparations.

When she arrived at the station, she rushed outside and into a taxi, directing the driver to take her to the hotel.

Stepping out onto the quaint main street in Chipping Campden, it was hard to believe it was little more than a week since she'd arrived for the first time.

Music drifted from the hotel, and warmth flooded through her at being back there. It was exactly the place she wanted to be. Not that she wouldn't have enjoyed the party at Jessie's place, but deep down, she knew her heart wouldn't have been fully in it.

Pulling her phone from her pocket, she was surprised that she hadn't heard from Lewis. He'd messaged briefly the previous evening, but there'd been nothing since. Earlier, she'd been worried that he'd call her while she was on the way and she'd either have to lie or ruin the surprise. Now, it struck her as a little unnerving that she hadn't heard anything. Presumably, the party at the hotel was keeping him busy.

As she lugged her case to the door, the thought that he might not be happy to see her crept in, overshadowing her excitement slightly. Maybe a surprise was a bad approach.

She gave herself a mental shake and pushed the door open to find the lounge full of people. Music mingled with the hum of chatter and laughter.

Her eyes scanned the crowd, seeking Lewis, or another familiar face.

She only recognised one person. Warren. He wasn't in his chef's whites but the standard staff uniform as he wandered through the throng with a cheerful grin and a plate of pastries.

A moment passed before he caught her eye and smiled.

"Hi," he said, as he neared her. "Did you bring Lewis with you?"

"I just arrived," she told him, confused. "Is Lewis here?"

"No." His brow wrinkled. "I'm not entirely sure where he is. I sort of thought he was with you. Haven't seen him for a couple of days."

"He was in London with me for a day, but then he came back."

He shrugged. "He's been messaging on the staff group, but essentially told us to look after the place."

"I thought he'd be here for the party…" She trailed off at the sight of Ivy entering the lounge from the direction of the dining room. As soon as she spotted Erin, she made a beeline for her.

"Is Lewis with you?" she asked, concern clear in her eyes.

"No. I just arrived looking for him."

Warren wandered away again.

"Where is he?" Erin asked Ivy.

"At home, as far as I know."

"I assumed he'd be here."

Ivy tilted her head. "He came back from London and picked Molly up, but hasn't been back to the hotel since. I've been telling him for ages to take time off, but now that he has, I'm worried about him. This isn't like him. Especially not with the party and everything."

"Have you spoken to him?" Erin asked.

"I called him earlier. He said he was fine, and he just didn't feel like being at the hotel." She tipped her head towards the dining room. "Anna and Carla are here. Usually we all celebrate New Year's together. His sisters are worried about him, too. They said they went to see him earlier, and he was in a weird mood."

"I just assumed he'd be here," Erin said again. "I didn't even think to go to his house."

"So he doesn't know you're coming?"

"No. Now I wonder whether surprising him was a good idea."

"Go and see him," Ivy said. "I'm sure he'll be happy to see you. Maybe you can convince him to come to the party."

"I'll try." She nodded decisively and turned to the door.

Ivy called her back, then leaned in close and lowered her voice. "I just want you to know that you're not treading on any toes as far as I'm concerned. I love Lewis, but only as a friend."

Erin winced. "He told you what I said."

"Yes. And you have absolutely nothing to worry about. I know I was a little unfriendly, but only because I was concerned about Lewis. If you make him happy – and it appears you do –

then I'm happy too." She gave a shy smile. "I'd like it if we could be friends."

"I'd like that too."

"Good. Now find him and figure out what's going on with him."

She didn't need any more encouragement, and was out of the door and striding along the street, cursing her suitcase, which slowed her pace.

The quiet cottage came alive with the sound of barking the moment Erin rang the bell. She smiled to herself when she heard Lewis's voice through the door, talking to Molly and telling her to calm down.

Then the door opened, and he looked up at her from his hunched position, a hand on Molly's collar. When his gaze collided with Erin's, his fingers slackened and he released Molly, who bounded around Erin's legs.

"Hi," she said, eyes trailing over him as he straightened up. In the back of her mind, she'd expected him to look as worn out as the last time she'd seen him, but he looked fresh in his jeans and T-shirt. "Surprise!" she added weakly when he just stared at her.

His lips parted as though he were about to speak, but no words came. He shook his head and his face broke into a smile as he stepped outside. In an instant, he swept her into his arms and left her feet dangling above the ground as he swung her around.

"Happy to see me then?" she asked when he stopped spinning.

"So happy." His hands came to cup her face as he kissed her greedily. "This is the best surprise ever."

"From a guy who once won twenty-six million on the lottery, that's quite the compliment." She took his face in her hands and held his gaze. "I missed you," she sighed.

"I missed you too." His arms tightened around her back as he kissed her again.

"I thought you'd be at the hotel," she said, drawing back enough to register his bare feet. She ushered him inside. "I went there first."

"I didn't want to work today."

"Everyone is worried about you," she said, tilting her head as they moved into the hallway. "Ivy and your sisters."

"I know, but it's ridiculous. All I did was take some time off, which is what they've been nagging me to do for years."

"Are you okay?" she asked, resting a hand on his chest. "I was worried about you, too."

"I'm great." He slipped his arms around her waist and pulled her close. "Even better now you're here. How long are you staying?"

"A couple of days. Then I need to get back to work. I just realised I wanted to start the new year with you." She wrinkled her nose. "Actually, my friends kind of pushed me in the direction of the train station, but as soon as they suggested I should be here with you, I knew they were right."

"I like your friends already."

She stroked the fine hairs at his nape. "I'm sorry I seemed so hesitant about us."

"I'm just glad you're here now."

She felt a warm glow at his infectious grin. "Are you going to explain why you're not at the hotel for the party?"

His eyes flashed with mirth. "Because I'm a millionaire and I don't have to go to work if I don't want to."

"You just figured that out?" she asked, eyebrows rising.

"I just figured out a lot of stuff, thanks to you."

"How do you mean?"

"I mean, you inspired me and I've been making plans."

"That's still pretty cryptic."

He kissed her hard, then took her hand and led her towards the living room. "Come in and get comfy and I'll tell you everything."

Chapter Forty-Two

As they sat close together on the couch, Erin beamed in response to the twinkle in Lewis's eyes. When Molly sniffed around their feet, he patted the space between them and she jumped up into it, snuggling down and resting her face on Lewis's thigh.

"I'm keeping her," he said, running a hand from her head down her back.

"I thought you didn't have time for a dog?"

"I didn't, but I want a dog. I want Molly, so I'll make time." He took Erin's hand and entwined their fingers. "I still think my dad was nuts to buy me a dog without discussing it with me, but I think he was right. I'd never have got one myself because I'd got it into my head that I had to work crazy hours, but I don't. Since I won the money, I feel as though I've been in this wild spin. It shot my life in a different direction and I got dragged along doing whatever it was I thought I should be doing."

"Without stopping to think about what you actually wanted?" Erin guessed.

"Exactly. Throwing myself into running the hotel was my way of hiding from the world. Especially since I found it so awkward to be around people after I won the money. It was easier to spend all my time at the hotel. I knew what my role was there."

He sighed as he ran his thumb back and forth across her palm. "As soon as you mentioned me hiring a manager for the hotel, it made total sense. And it's not as though no one suggested it to me before, but I'd always brushed the idea aside."

"Are you going to do it?"

"Yes. When you asked if I'd take time off work to visit you, I hated that you doubted whether I'd do it. I want to make time for you. I want to start doing things I enjoy instead of hiding away in the hotel."

"I think it's a good idea to cut down on work," she said. "For your health as well."

"I already knew I should slow down. I just couldn't bring myself to make changes." He looked at her intently. "When I came back from London, I had a feeling of dread at going to the hotel. And I got thinking about what you said about creating the life you want. I'm in such a privileged position and I want to stop feeling so guilty about it."

"You feel guilty for being rich?"

"Yeah, I think I do. It seems unfair."

"You do a lot of good with the money," she pointed out.

He gave her a reluctant smile. "I've been thinking about that, too. I'm going to find a new financial advisor. I'll keep Mr Garrett on for the hotel accounts, but I really think philanthropic work shouldn't feel soul destroying."

"It really shouldn't," Erin agreed.

"I need to find someone who can rein me in if I get carried away, but with Mr Garrett everything felt like a battle. We aren't on the same page."

"That sounds like a good idea." She grinned at him. "What else are you going to do?"

"I want to spend more time at home. I have this beautiful

house which I hardly make use of." He looked thoughtful. "I'd like to spend a lot of time in London, as well."

Her smile spread wide. "Would you really?"

"I've never spent much time there," he said, mischief dancing in his eyes. "I think I'd like to play tourist."

"So you're just interested in sightseeing?" she asked, cocking her head playfully.

"There's one specific attraction for me." His silky-smooth tone sent a shiver through her as he leaned in to kiss her. It was only a soft brush of lips at first, but a moment later he nudged Molly off the couch and pulled Erin closer. "I'm so happy you're here," he said between kisses.

"You might not be so happy when I make you go back to the hotel."

He pulled back. "What are you talking about?"

"We should put in an appearance at the party."

"Now?" He blinked slowly. "Did you miss what I said about cutting down on work? I want to spend the evening here, with you. I'm not working on New Year's Eve."

"No, but we could join the party without you working. Your sisters and Ivy are there, and they're all worried about you."

"I'm not sure I can be in the hotel and not end up working."

"You don't need to worry about that. I won't let you work. I think it would be fun, though."

"Okay. Here's what I'll agree to. We can go for one drink and then come back here for our own party."

"You sound very demanding," she told him. "What happens if I want to stay for a second drink?"

He rolled his eyes. "Then we'll stay for another drink, of course, but can you at least let me feel like I'm making the rules?"

"Okay." Grinning, she hopped off the couch. "Let's go now, because I actually like the sound of ending the night with our own private party."

. . .

Despite only having been away from the place for two days, Lewis was greeted like the proverbial lost sheep when he walked back into the hotel. Ivy made a big fuss of him as soon as she spotted him, as did his sisters.

Watching the other staff work while he did nothing wasn't a comfortable feeling, but Erin had him pinned at her side as they propped up the bar with Anna and Carla.

"They are being paid," Erin said, squeezing his hand and drawing him from his trance.

His eyes darted to her. "What?"

"The staff who you're staring at as though they're slaves who need to be freed. They're being paid and they did have a choice in whether they worked this evening. You don't need to feel guilty."

Rationally, he knew she was right, but it was hard to get rid of the guilt that squeezed at his chest. At least he had a good distraction from it with Erin beside him.

"I still can't believe you're here," he said, easing his arm around her waist to pull her in for a kiss.

"You two are a little sickening." Carla's voice interrupted them after a moment. "Happy for you and everything," she added, when Anna gave her arm a shove. "Just not so keen on the public displays of affection."

Lewis pulled away reluctantly and was immediately distracted by Warren appearing beside them with a tray laden with glasses of sparkling wine.

"You all need to grab one of these and head into the lounge so you don't miss the countdown," he said. "While you're there you can protect me from the drunk old lady who keeps flirting with me."

Carla's eyes sparkled with mischief. "Would you like one of us to pretend to be your girlfriend?" she asked, linking her arm with Anna's while she plucked a glass from the tray. "Who would you prefer?"

"I think I'd prefer to take my chances with the old lady," Warren said without missing a beat. He raised an eyebrow at Lewis as he dished out the rest of the drinks and took the last one for himself. "Come on," he said, setting off for the lounge.

Lewis took Erin's hand and glanced back at Carla. "You really love winding him up, don't you?"

"I would love it," Carla replied with a frown. "Except he's not easy to wind up. I think he's immune to my brand of teasing."

"I wish *I* was," Anna muttered. "You're so embarrassing!"

"You wouldn't have found it at all embarrassing if you didn't have a crush on Warren."

"I don't have a crush on him," Anna hissed. Her cheeks had gone bright red but she was also prone to blushing at nothing so it didn't necessarily mean anything.

"Come on," Erin said, tugging on his arm and leaving the sound of his bickering sisters to fade as they moved out of the dining room.

"Do you think Anna does have a thing for Warren?" he asked, utterly confused by his sisters. A familiar feeling.

"Maybe," Erin said as they entered the lounge.

Lewis frowned. "I hope not."

"Really? You'd have a problem with that?"

He glanced around to check his sisters weren't within hearing range. "Only because she's not Warren's type. He'd never go out with her. Carla, maybe, but not Anna. Although, I don't think he'd go near either of them on the basis that they're my sisters. He has strong principles about that sort of thing."

"I guess things could be a little awkward if he dated one of your sisters."

Lewis shrugged. "Maybe." Glancing across the room, he caught Warren glaring at him while an elderly lady pawed at his arm. "Someone should probably save him." He looked around at his sisters who'd just wandered in. "Anna can you go and help Warren?"

Her eyes flashed with the kind of annoyance she usually reserved for Carla. "I do not have a crush on him!"

"I never said you did," he pointed out. "Just go and rescue him."

"Can you both leave me alone, please?" she snapped before taking a long swig of her drink.

"What did I do?" he asked Erin. "And why did you make me leave my house?"

She nestled against his side, grinning. At least his squabbling siblings seemed to amuse her.

"Thanks a lot for your help," Warren said mockingly as he and Ivy joined their little group. "If Ivy hadn't come and saved me that little old lady would have had her tongue down my throat on the stroke of midnight." He draped an arm around Ivy's shoulders and leaned his head close to hers. "I suppose that means you get the pleasure of kissing me at midnight!"

"Don't even think about it," Ivy said, wriggling out of his clutches. She turned her watch to him. "Someone loud needs to start the countdown."

"I'm not sure why you're looking at me." He turned her wrist, pointing the watch in Carla's direction. "She's the mouthy one."

Carla looked as though she might protest, then gave a resigned shrug and stood on her tiptoes to look over the room. "Ten," she shouted, making Lewis wince. "Nine, eight, seven..."

Everyone joined in, but Lewis was feeling impatient and didn't wait for the countdown to end. Instead, he turned to Erin and cupped her face with his hands. A glorious wave of contentment washed over him as their lips met. He only vaguely registered the remainder of the countdown and then the shouts of 'Happy New Year' which rang around the room. Distant pops of fireworks had him glancing down at Molly who seemed unperturbed by the excitement around her.

"Happy New Year!" Erin said, giving him another peck.

"Happy New Year," he muttered in reply as she moved away to hug his sisters and Ivy. His eyes were still fixed on her when Warren enveloped him in a bear hug.

"Look at that grin," he said, tugging on Lewis's cheek.

"Get off," Lewis said, swatting him playfully away.

His friend remained with an arm around his shoulders, turning to follow his gaze which he couldn't seem to drag away from Erin.

Warren sighed. "You really do have all the luck, don't you?"

It was something that Lewis had been told a lot over the last few years, but he'd never felt quite as lucky as he did in that moment.

Finally, he felt as though he'd got everything he'd always wanted.

Acknowledgments

While writing is generally a solitary business, there are lots of people who help and support me to make the books fit for publishing.

I am so grateful to Kathy Robinson and Sue Oxley. Your proofreading skills are excellent and you're also very good at reassuring me that the books aren't terrible! I feel so lucky to have you both in my corner.

Thanks also to my beta reading team: Sarah Painter, Clodagh Murphy, Dua Roberts, Sian Taylor and Anthea Kirk. I really appreciate your feedback and your cheerleading!

I would also like to thank the *Happy Writers* who I meet up with once or twice a week in a lovely cafe in Munich. We talk about books and publishing, and share our latest story ideas. We drink lots of coffee, sometimes eat cake and we get a lot of writing done too. I would probably be a recluse without this wonderful group.

I feel so incredibly lucky to have found such a brilliant cover designer in Diane Meacham. You absolutely nail it every time and are a joy to work with. Thank you.

A huge thank you to my wonderful husband, Mario. I couldn't do any of this without you.

Of course, I owe a huge thank you to my readers. I am so grateful that you choose to read my books. Thank you for all your lovely, uplifting messages.

I also want to give a quick mention to my reader group, Hannah's Happy Readers! You're such a great group and I really appreciate everyone's enthusiasm. It always gives me a boost.

Last but not least, thank you to the lovely ladies in The Friendly Book Community. I think it might be the nicest group on Facebook! If you want to talk books (and cake!) check them out.

Also by Hannah Ellis

Fireworks over the Loch (Book 3)

The Cafe at the Loch (Book 4)

Secrets at the Loch (Book 5)

Surprises at the Loch (Book 6)

Finding Hope at the Loch (Book 7)

Fragile Hearts by the Loch (Book 8)

New Arrivals at the Loch (Book 9)

The Lucy Mitchell Series

Beyond the Lens (Book 1)

Beneath These Stars (Book 2)

Always With You (Standalone novel)

The Friends Like These Series

Friends Like These (Book 1)

Christmas with Friends (Book 2)

My Kind of Perfect (Book 3)

A Friend in Need (Book 4)

All of Hannah's books can be found here:

http://Author.to/HannahEllis

Hannah has also written a series of children's books aimed at 5-9 year olds under the pen name, Hannah Sparks. You can find the first book in that series here: https://mybook.to/WhereDragonsFly

About the Author

When she's not writing, Hannah enjoys spending time with her husband and kids. She loves to read, do jigsaw puzzles and go for long walks. She also enjoys yoga and drinks a lot of tea!

Hannah can be found online at the following places:

Facebook: @authorhannahellis

Instagram: @authorhannahellis

Website: www.authorhannahellis.com

If you'd like to be kept up to date with news about Hannah's books you can sign up to receive emails from her through her website:

www.authorhannahellis.com/newsletter

Made in the USA
Las Vegas, NV
10 November 2024

11467950R00173

Can a kiss under the mistletoe lead to something more?

Erin Grant has worked hard to build a life she loves. With a wonderfully quirky flat in London, a supportive group of friends and a fulfilling job, she has everything she needs.

But a festive escape to the Cotswolds leaves her questioning what she's been missing.

Between enchanting Christmas markets, ice-skating beneath twinkling fairy lights, and cosy chats by the fire, sparks fly with Lewis, the charming hotel manager.

But Lewis has a secret, and as the festive season unfolds, it becomes harder for him to explain everything to Erin. Opening up might shatter their fairy-tale romance.

For their budding relationship to last beyond the Christmas season they're both going to have to decide what they really want. And what they're willing to risk to get it.

Cover Design by dmeacham design

ISBN 9783948922573
9 783948 922573
9000